Hunted Down

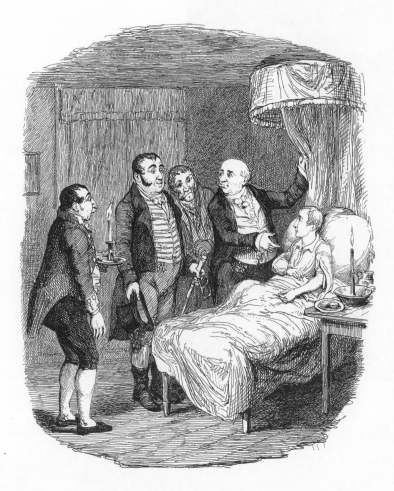

'Oliver waited on by the Bow Street Runners' – one of George
Cruikshank's famous illustrations for *Oliver Twist*

Hunted Down

The Detective Stories of
CHARLES DICKENS

Edited and with an Introduction by

PETER HAINING

PETER OWEN
London & Chester Springs

PETER OWEN PUBLISHERS
73 Kenway Road London SW5 0RE

Peter Owen books are distributed in the USA by
Dufour Editions Inc. Chester Springs PA 19425–0007

First published in Great Britain 1996
© Peter Haining 1996

A catalogue record for this book is available
from the British Library

ISBN 0–7206–0994–1

Printed and made in Great Britain by
Biddles of Guildford and King's Lynn

Contents

Dickens has as good a title as Edgar Allan Poe
to be called the father of the modern detective
story and 'Inspector Bucket of the Detective',
the human bloodhound of *Bleak House*, is probably
the most vividly presented fictional detective
before Sherlock Holmes.

Julian Symons: *Charles Dickens* (1951)

Introduction

In an age dominated by fictional detectives – Morse, Wexford, Dalgliesh and the others of their kind who are as frequently seen on television as on the printed page – all the crime novelists who have made their reputations with fictional sleuths owe a debt of gratitude to Charles Dickens, one of the great pioneers of the genre.

Dickens is, of course, already deservedly famous for such memorable characters as Mr Pickwick, Scrooge, Fagin, Micawber, Sydney Carton et al., yet less so for his detectives who have actually had a profound effect on the development of crime fiction. These officers of the law were born out of the young author's early experiences as a solicitor's clerk and reporter: he was a fascinated and intimate eyewitness of the birth of the police detective force in London in the middle years of the nineteenth century. As Professor Ian Ousby has written in his excellent study, *Bloodhounds of Heaven: The Detective in English Fiction from Godwin to Doyle* (1976): 'Dickens was the first major publicist for the police detective. In his work he seized on the Detective Department as on a personal discovery and treated it with a mixture of boyish awe and proprietary affection.'

It was with the character of Inspector Bucket, who appears in *Bleak House* (1852–3) to solve the murder of an unscrupulous lawyer, that Dickens created the first significant detective in English literature. Yet Bucket was far from being his only detective or even the only one to

7

break new ground in crime fiction. For in the emaciated, unprepossessing form of Mr Nadgett in *Martin Chuzzlewit* (1843–4) we have the first serious private detective in an English novel; while in an even earlier short story, 'The Drunkard's Death' (1836), an officer known simply as Tom, who operates with an anonymous colleague, amounts to the prototype of all undercover policemen who go to ground to mingle with the criminal underworld in order to bring villains to justice. And among Dickens's detective policemen can be encountered the hulking Inspector Charley Wield with his 'large, moist, knowing eye'; the shrewd, hard-headed Scottish-born officer with a name identical to one of this century's most famous real-life crime fighters, Inspector Stalker; and the resourceful Inspector Field who is no stranger to the meanest and most crime-ridden areas of London.

To the list of these senior officers' various Sergeants and Constables with such names as Witchem, Straw, Mith, Black, Green, Parker and Williams, must be added the River Policeman Pea; Mr Tatt, a former public servant and 'quite an amateur detective in his way'; and the energetic Actuary Mr Meltham, who doubles as a private detective to solve a murder and is endowed with the same single-minded dedica-tion as Sherlock Holmes – though he predates him in literary terms by almost thirty years.

Nor must we forget the clever wife of Inspector Bucket who, in my estimation, deserves the title of the first female amateur detective in fiction. For of her it is said that she is 'a lady of a natural detective genius which, if it had been improved by professional exercise, might have done great things, but which has paused at the level of a clever amateur'.

Together, these characters represent a formidable achievement in any writer's canon of work – all the more so considering that Dickens, unlike his modern counterparts, had virtually no literary models to draw upon. He had, though, created something timely, as the distinguished crime writer and historian Julian Symons has written: 'Dickens uses from the first tricks which resemble remarkably those of the modern detective-story writer. He presents characters whose relation to each other is apparently inexplicably strange; the reader's curiosity is roused by this strangeness, and he reads the books partly with the object of solving a problem.'

Charles Dickens, one of the pioneers of detective fiction, aged 47 –
engraving after the portrait by W. P. Frith, RA

Readers familiar with Dickens's work know only too well that quite a number of his stories contain elements of crime, mystery and detection that reflect his tireless interest in the society in which he lived, and about which he wrote so brilliantly. Indeed, some of his very earliest writings are about crime of one kind or another and he was actually working on a novel of suspected murder, *The Mystery of Edwin Drood*, when he died in 1870. The first twenty-three chapters which Dickens *did* complete are enough to indicate that the final work might well have been one of the greatest mystery novels of all time. As it is, the unfinished manuscript provides a mystery in itself that has challenged the minds of criminologists and crime writers for well over a hundred years.

Dickens was no armchair detective-story writer. He travelled the night streets of London in the company of detective officers to see their work at first hand. He frequently attended the London magistrates courts and was present at a number of important murder trials. He took a close interest, too, in several of the most notorious criminals of the day, including Henry Hocket, the Hampstead killer, and James Blomfield Rush, a Norfolk farmer who was convicted of murdering two of his neighbours. Dickens even visited the scene of Rush's crime in 1849, although he later confessed in a letter to a friend that he was 'very unimpressed' at the manner in which the search for the murder weapon was being conducted by the local police.

Dickens certainly had a strong stomach: he attended the public execution at Newgate in July 1840 of François Courvoisier, the Swiss valet who had robbed and killed Lord William Russell, and was also among the crowd of 50,000 who gathered on 13 November 1849 to watch the hanging of Frederick and Maria Manning, the murderers of the money-lender, Patrick O'Connor. The couple were put to death on top of Horsemonger Lane Jail – the first husband and wife team to drop together in England since 1700 – and Dickens hired a nearby roof for himself and his friends to get a better view of the couple as they swung, quivering, in the air. Later that same day he took up his pen to write a letter to *The Times* complaining about the 'indecent spectacle of public executions'. (It was this case, of course, that Dickens used to such good effect in the writing of *Bleak House*!)

Dickens actually turned detective himself on one occasion, when a pickpocket who might have stepped right out of the pages of *Oliver*

Twist tried to dip the author's pockets as he was walking along a busy London thoroughfare. Feeling a hand steal inside his coat – and without a second moment's thought – Dickens spun round, and when the guilty party took to his heels he ran after him. Following a lengthy chase through crowded streets, the pickpocket was apprehended, subdued and handed over by an understandably triumphant Dickens to his friends the police!

He also enjoyed creating and solving puzzles in the manner of the amateur detective. When *Adam Bede*, the first novel by 'George Eliot' (Mary Ann Evans), was published in 1859, Dickens guessed the sex of the anonymous author as soon as he read the book. Writing in a letter to a friend he said, 'If those two volumes, or a part of them, were not written by a woman – then I should begin to believe that I am a woman myself!'

Although Charles Dickens did mention the police on a few instances in his early newspaper reports, it was not until the summer of 1850 that he personally met some officers and began to seriously start on the various short stories and novels that would earn him such an important role in the development of detective fiction. It is these Tales and self-contained episodes from the relevant novels that I have gathered together in this first collection devoted specifically to Dickens's detective fiction. Some notes about these selections may be of added interest to the reader.

The earliest clear indication of Dickens's interest in the officers of the law is to be found in the pages of the comic serial story that made his name, *Pickwick Papers*, published in 1836–7. For here we meet the unfortunate Constable Daniel Grummer who brings Pickwick and Tracy Tupman before the Ipswich magistrate George Nupkins on a charge of assault. But thanks to his rambling and confused statement, Grummer totally fails in his case and is ignominiously ordered out of the court. His last plaintive address to Nupkins, 'but, your wash-up!', gives every indication that Dickens had nothing but a mild contempt for lawmen at that juncture of his life.

The same might be said of the two Bow Street Runners, Blathers and Duff, who appear for just a few brief pages in *Oliver Twist* (1837) to investigate Bill Sikes's burglary of the Maylies' house. They seem merely there to provide a comic interlude, with the detective work, such as it is, being carried out by the benevolent Mr Brownlow who took Oliver into his home.

Dickens's first serious detective is, in fact, Mr Nadgett, who appeared in 1844 in the later part of the serialisation of *Martin Chuzzlewit*. As the first of his kind he is a truly extraordinary figure. 'He was a short, dried-up, withered old man,' Dickens wrote. 'The secret manner of the man disarmed suspicion in this wise; suggesting, not that he was watching any one, but that he thought some other man was watching him. He went about so stealthily, and kept himself so wrapped up in himself, that the whole object of his life appeared to be to avoid notice and preserve his own mystery.'

Yet Nadgett is also a man of supreme patience and determination, as P. Claxton Williams wrote in *The Dickensian* magazine a few years back. 'Secretive, shabby and unassuming, he set himself his task with a terrible purposeful vigour, rising, at the crucial moment, like a dark spirit in the path of Jonas Chuzzlewit, to confound him with proofs of the dark deed that he hoped had passed unseen.'

Nadgett is certainly no dashing emissary of the law, but a man of mystery and a rather sinister one, too, who is employed by the Anglo-Bengalee Disinterested Loan and Life Insurance Company as a secret enquiry agent. Yet it is as a result of his investigations and observations that Jonas Chuzzlewit is finally brought to book. Although readers are never left in any doubt of Jonas's guilt, many of the stock-in-trade qualities of later fictional detectives were embodied by Dickens in his portrait of Nadgett on the hunt.

Nor did the author's inventiveness end there. For when Nadgett finally reveals all, he provides, as the critic John Woolford observed in an essay in the *Daily Telegraph* in October 1994 marking the 150th anniversary of the novel, 'The prototype of the detective's summing-up, perfected by whodunnit writers from Conan Doyle to Ruth Rendell.'

This ground-breaking summation, which opens this collection and which I have entitled 'Nemesis', brings into the spotlight the very first private eye in English literature.

'The Drunkard's Death', the second item in the collection, is something of a curiosity from Dickens's early years. It is effectively a story tinged with a heavy moral message about a confirmed and irredeemable drunkard who allows his rage for drink to destroy his relationship with his wife, family and friends. But at the heart of the story are two mysterious law officers who ply the old man with drink in order to discover the hiding-place of his son who has committed a revenge murder. The tale, written in 1836, paints a remorselessly grim picture of Victorian London – crime-ridden Whitefriars in particular – as well as depicting in Tom and his colleague two of the forerunners of today's celebrated undercover cops whose lineage can be traced through *The Professionals* and beyond.

Quite different in tone is 'The Automaton Police', an episode from one of Dickens's lesser-known humorous works, *The Mudfog Association*, which I have included for a little light relief after the harshness of the preceeding story and also because it illustrates the author's growing interest in the policing of London. The idea of a highway patrolled by robot policemen was certainly intended by Dickens to raise a smile on his readers' faces, as was the proposal in the same episode for a pocket-picking machine! Indeed, all the reports of the meetings of *The Mudfog Association* which he wrote for *Bentley's Miscellany* during the winter of 1837 were actually clever satires on the proceedings of the British Association for the Advancement of Science which had then just been established. But with today's writers of fiction contemplating a future where the law is upheld by officers like Judge Dredd and the part-man, part-machine Robocop, who is to say that even in his lighter moments Dickens was not extemporizing on future crime fighters?

It was in 1842, after two exceptionally brutal murders in London, that a Detective Branch of the police was formed at Scotland Yard. It consisted of two inspectors, six sergeants and the first chief, Nicholas Pearce, who was a former member of the Bow Street Runners. These men were detailed for exclusive plainclothes detective work and thereby created the embryo CID that would eventually be formalised in 1876. Dickens, not surprisingly in the light of his interest, was the first writer to recognise the importance of this revolutionary step in law enforcement and used it as his inspiration to create his first officer, 'Sergeant Witchem of the Detectives'.

Witchem made his début, albeit briefly, in 'The Modern Science of Thief-Taking', which was published in Number 16 of Dickens's newly-launched magazine, *Household Words* (13 July 1850). At first glance he seemed to be similar to Nadgett: a short, thickset man with features scarred by smallpox. But on closer examination the Sergeant proved to be a man of some intelligence and one who gave the impression of being reserved and deep in thought as if making secret calculations. It was also soon apparent that he was renowned in the force for his acquaintance with fashionable society – the 'swell mob' as they were known.

Sergeant Witchem was, in fact, based on a real officer of the new force whom Dickens had met. It was from this man and several of his colleagues that he learned all about the force and its activities. That first story not only gave an insight into the methods of the Detectives, but also poked a little fun at the ordinary beat policemen: in particular one slow-witted constable, X 49, who had proved no match for Witchem and his colleagues. (Shades here of BBC Radio's famous PC49 – with his favourite catch-phrase, 'Oh, my Sunday helmet!' – played by Brian Reece, who was the favourite of a whole generation of young listeners from 1947 to 1953.)

The resourceful Sergeant also deserves the credit for being the first serial story detective because he featured again in Dickens's two-part story 'A Detective Police Party', which appeared on the front pages of the 27 July and 10 August issues of his magazine, with its sequel 'Three Detective Anecdotes' on 14 September. Witchem had, however, now to give rank to the formidable Inspectors Wield and Stalker, although before the end of the story he had single-handedly arrested a notorious horse-thief in Northamptonshire and taken him to London. No mean achievement, as the thief was being accompanied at the time by 'two big and ugly-looking campanions'.

Inspector Wield, who I mentioned earlier with his 'knowing eye', was a portly, middle-aged man with a husky voice, famous among his men for his habit of 'emphasising his conversation by the aid of a corpulent fore-finger which is constantly in juxtaposition with his eyes and nose'. Stalker, on the other hand, was a phlegmatic Scot, 'in appearance not at all unlike a very acute, thoroughly-trained schoolmaster'.

The four other sergeants who also appeared in the story are equally memorable. First, Dornton: a ruddy-faced, middle-aged man already well known for his single-minded pursuit of the clues that help him get his man – notably a Doctor Dundey who had robbed a bank in Ireland and had to be tracked to America before he could be arrested. Second,

Sergeant Mith, a man with a fresh, bright complexion whose air of simplicity hides a rare ability to catch housebreakers. Third, Fendall, a deceptively quiet and well-spoken officer adept at tackling enquiries of a delicate nature. And finally Sergeant Straw, a wiry little man whose meek appearance and skill at asking apparently innocent questions enable him to trap many an unwary villain.

In the cases that make up 'Three Detective Anecdotes', Inspector Wield is again featured along with Sergeants Dornton, Mith and the intrepid Witchem. In the second of these episodes, 'The Artful Touch', Dickens also introduces us to Mr Tatt, 'the amateur detective' who is a friend of Sergeant Witchem and helps him in the recovery of a diamond pin stolen on Derby Day at Epsom.

The police series in *Household Words* was evidently a great success with readers, and the following spring Dickens proposed a sequel which he provisionally entitled 'A Night in a Station House'. Because of the pressure of work, he invited his co-editor, William Wills, a man who had turned to journalism after falling on hard times, to accompany him on a night-time visit to a police station. A copy of a letter from Dickens to Wills outlining this project still survives:

> If you would go down to our friend Mr Yardley at Scotland Yard and get a letter or order to the acting chief authority at that station-house in Bow Street, to enable us to hear the charges, observe the internal economy of the station all night, go round to the cells with the visiting policemen, etc., I would stay there, say from twelve at night to four in the morning. If you could conveniently borrow an hour or two from the night we could both go. If not, I would go alone. It would make a wonderfully good paper.

In fact Wills was as excited by the idea as Dickens, and the two men subsequently spent the night together at the station-house, combining their respective talents to write the story which Dickens finally edited before it appeared as 'The Metropolitan Protectives' in the issue of *Household Words* on 26 April 1851. What, however, made the tale especially intriguing was the light it threw on some of the less savoury aspects of London policing. Today we have become almost blasé about stories of corrupt policemen, drunkenness among officers and even dereliction of duty. But although the public in Dickens's time had good reason to believe such things *did* take place in the force, it was his eyewitness account that spotlighted the facts in print. Though disguised by fictional names, there is no doubt that PC John Jones, who was found drunk on duty and dismissed the force, or Sergeant Jenkins, who had failed to report a burglary and been suspended from duty, were both based upon policemen that Dickens and Wills had heard all about during their visit.

But having observed the police at work in the comparative safety of their station-house, Dickens now wanted to see what life was like after dark for the city's detectives out on London's mean streets. Another nocturnal outing was arranged that spring and from it came the story of Inspector Field, the shrewd, brave and knowledgeable officer immortalised in 'On Duty with Inspector Field'. Here was a man who knew the lowest haunts and worst villains in the metropolis and in whose company the reader found himself visiting places he would never have dared to enter: Rats' Castle, a thieves' paradise near St Giles' Church; the notorious house of ill-fame on Ratcliffe Highway; and the vile criminal haunts of Wentworth Street.

Inspector Field and his posse of constables – Black, Green, Parker, Rogers, White and Williams – are vividly drawn characters, highly evocative of their type; as, indeed, are the villains who cross their paths: Bully Bark, the receiver of stolen goods; the grandiloquent thief known as 'The Earl of Warwick'; and Blackey, the impostor sitting by London Bridge who has been begging for twenty-five years with his skin specially painted to resemble a terrible disease.

'Down with the Tide', which Dickens wrote two years later in February 1853, was a first excursion in print with the newly-formed river police whose task was to stem the flow of smuggled goods and the flight of escaped criminals on the River Thames. Here again River Policeman Pea had a real-life counterpart who had conducted Dickens around the dangerous reaches of the river and inspired him to write this chilling little tale.

There is no doubt that all of these stories in *Household Words* had a marked effect on the popular taste in literature, as the literary historian E. A. Osborne commented in *The Bookman* in February 1932. 'It is significant,' he wrote, 'that it is after this period (1845–1850) that a whole spate of detective reminiscences appeared.' (*The Recollections of a Policeman* by 'Waters' (William Russell), published in 1852, was one of the earliest and most celebrated of these works.)

But important though such autobiographies are as accounts of the criminal times, it is Dickens who once again led the way with his next novel, *Bleak House*, published in serial form through the winter of 1852–3, which introduced Inspector Bucket – 'the first detective of importance in English literature,' according to Chris Steinbrunner and Otto Penzler, the authors of the *Encyclopedia of Mystery and Detection* (1976).

Bucket, with his resounding cry, 'I am Inspector Bucket of the Detective, I am!', became at a stroke the prototype of the police detective as we know him: stolid and unexceptional, but honest, hard-working, fair, competent and most likely successful. A stout, middle-aged man dressed invariably in black with an affable manner and sharp eye, he also has the ability to think clearly and act patiently while all around him is panic and confusion. For as he says on one occasion with more than a little hint of self-satisfaction, 'I don't suppose there's a move on the board that would surprise *me*.'

One of Dickens's earliest descriptions of the Inspector reveals him to be a man who is simultaneously both very ordinary and very extraordinary: 'Studious in his observations of human nature, on the whole a benignant philosopher not disposed to be severe upon the follies of mankind, Mr Bucket pervades a vast number of houses and strolls about an infinity of streets, to outward appearances rather languishing for want of an object.'

Bucket has, in fact, that special ability of the outstanding detective to move effortlessly between the milieux of normal society and the criminal underworld, confronting the members of either group with his deceptively loaded question, 'Now you know *me*, don't you?' His reputation, we learn, has also been built on an uncanny ability – verging on the supernatural, some say – to impress as well as mystify people. He can spot clues in the most unlikely places and in the most casually uttered sentences.

In fact, the whole key to Bucket's success lies in his *intelligence*. He is, truly, the forerunner of a whole school of such fictional sleuths whose world is made complete by a clever and supportive wife and a devoted assistant, Constable Darby. Summarising the Inspector's importance, Bruce Cassiday has written in his *Roots of Detection: The Art of Deduction before Sherlock Holmes* (1983):

> Although Dickens goes at it all backwards, to the modern way of thinking, by letting Inspector Bucket solve the murder offstage and then *explain* it onstage . . . one of the most important elements of the detective-genre-to-come is the wrap-up explanation of the chain of deduction that leads to the solution. Dickens clearly understands the use of clues, hard evidence – even today's 'smoking gun' appears in an earlier incarnation – in his wrap-up. And note that some eighty years before Dashiell Hammett popularized Nick and Nora Charles as a husband-and-wife detective team, Dickens clearly established a similar team in Mr and Mrs Bucket!

(This unique figure, demonstrating his remarkable skills, will be found in the episode I have extracted from the book and entitled 'Inspector Bucket's Job'.)

Having drawn on the crime of Frederick and Maria Manning for *Bleak House*, Dickens found the inspiration for his next detective tale, 'Hunted Down', in the events surrounding another recent case – that of Thomas Griffiths Wainewright who in 1830 had poisoned his sister-in-law for her £18,000 insurance money. He wrote the drama especially for the *New York Ledger*, where it was published in issues 24–26 between 20 August and 3 September 1859.

The focus of this story of pure detection narrated by a Mr Sampson, the chief manager of the Inestimable Life Assurance Company, concerns one of his employees, Mr Meltham, who has fallen in love with a girl who recently took out a life insurance policy with the company. When she dies from the effects of a slow poison that has undoubtedly been secretly administered to her, Meltham turns detective to hunt down the man he knows has killed the girl. His methods are varied – disguise, deception as a supposed drunkard and even the hiring of rooms opposite those of the suspect in order to trap him. (Interestingly, these rooms are in the Middle Temple, where half a century later the English writer R. Austin Freeman would place his character Dr Thorndyke, a forensic scientist and lawyer, who has since been called the greatest medico-legal detective of all time.)

'Hunted Down' has many admirers among modern crime novelists, not least of them the doyen of American detective fiction, Ellery Queen, who wrote of the story some years ago, 'True, the character who plays the role of the detective cannot be claimed by any modern school: he is not a dilettante or scientist whose forte is deduction; nor is he the tough hombre of the hard-boiled species; yet in motives and actions, he is undeniably a realistic sleuth.'

Nevertheless, with Meltham and his predecessor Mr Nadgett, plus the cases of the detective police and the exploits of Inspectors Field and Bucket, Charles Dickens had now assured for all time his influence upon, and importance to, the development of the modern detective story.

In what was to prove the last decade of his life, Dickens again featured the London police in two of his novels, *Great Expectations* (1861) and *Our Mutual Friend* (1864–5), as well as in another short story which has a unique claim to fame, 'Poor Mercantile Jack'.

Great Expectations, with its unforgettable cast of characters – including the convicts Abel Magwitch and Compeyson, 'the worst of scoundrels'; Bentley Drummle, 'The Spider'; Mr Jaggers, the criminal lawyer of Little Britain; Miss Havisham, Uncle Pumblechook and the narrator/hero, Pip – is one of the pinnacles of Dickens's art as a storyteller. In it he masterfully uses the trick of concealment to induce the reader to believe that Pip's fortune comes from the benevolent Miss Havisham rather than from the unlikely source of Magwitch.

Our Mutual Friend, a story of attempted murder, robbery and deception, perhaps does not reach the same heights, although because of some of its well-aimed criticisms it has been described as among his very best works of satire. The book is, however, of interest to students of crime fiction because of the appearance of the aptly-named Mr Inspector, a police officer who investigates what becomes known as the 'Harmon Murder'. A verbose and rather slow-witted man, the Inspector only appears twice in the story: early on to take notes of the apparent crime and then towards the end of the narrative when he wrongly charges John Rokesmith, alias Julius Handford, alias John Harmon with his own murder!

'Poor Mercantile Jack', which appeared in 1860 as one of the tales in the *Uncommercial Traveller*, is far less well known than either of these novels, yet is of more interest to our study. The tales are all told by a compulsive traveller who lives in Covent Garden, London, but is always on the move about the country, often taking on new occupations to earn his keep and thereby falling into various adventures. What makes 'Poor Mercantile Jack' particularly interesting is the fact that the traveller has joined the police force in Liverpool in order to discover the whereabouts and activities of an unfortunate seaman recently returned from sea. He goes in search of Jack in the company of three officers with the apposite names of Quickear, Sharpeye and Trampfoot, and their investigations offer a vivid picture of the life of Liverpool seamen and their haunts in the middle of the Victorian era. 'Poor Mercantile Jack' is also the only detective story written by Dickens in which the narrator is a policeman.

Charles Dickens's final excursion into the genre which he had so brilliantly begun to develop was also to be his last work: the unfinished *Mystery of Edwin Drood* (1870). This, too, achieved another first – being the first detective story set in a church.

The tale of the disappearance of Edwin Drood one stormy night and the insistence of his uncle, John Jasper, the choirmaster of Cloisterham Cathedral, that he has been done away with, was left unfinished at that juncture by the author as a result of a massive stroke which killed him on the night of 8 June 1870. Ever since, the story has challenged all lovers of detective fiction. Indeed, dozens of solutions have been put forward in the intervening years – but notwithstanding this, the importance of the incomplete text should never be overlooked, as H. R. F. Keating, himself a major modern crime writer, has insisted:

> In *Drood*, Dickens embraced the crime novel proper in a story whose whole action and *raison d'être* was the mystery of the death of young Edwin Drood. The book was written at the height of his powers, despite the strain he was putting on himself with his reading tours that contributed to his comparatively early death. Even as the mere stump of what it might have been (and it is more than that) the book is enormously rewarding to read.

One of the most popular theories about the book concerns the shadowy figure of Dick Datchery, a white-haired man with black eyebrows who appears in Cloisterham shortly after Drood's disappearance and is plainly intent on watching Mr Jasper. He, it is said, is more than likely a criminal investigator or police detective through whom Dickens intended to reveal the solution to the mystery.

Of the many books and essays about *The Mystery of Edwin Drood* that I have read, one has always appealed to me more than any other: 'The Edwin Drood Syndicate' by M. R. James, the famous ghost story writer and self-professed admirer of Dickens. Strangely, though, his contribution to this continuing saga, which appeared in two parts in *The Cambridge Review* of 30 November and 7 December 1905, has never been reprinted in any volume of James's work – or anywhere else for that matter. I am therefore pleased to be able to include it in this book by way of a finale.

Together, the stories in this book represent Charles Dickens's contribution to detective fiction and the influence each has had on the genre is not difficult to see. Indeed, I wholeheartedly agree with what another of today's leading crime novelists, Peter Lovesey, wrote recently: 'The architects of the popular detective story like Dickens built citadels of suspense that still dominate the scene.'

In the pages that follow you are invited to visit again those citadels and judge for yourself the qualities of the men who were Charles Dickens's pioneer detectives.

Peter Haining

[ONE]

Nemesis

The night had now come, when the old clerk Chuffey was to be delivered over to his keepers. In the midst of his guilty distractions, Jonas had not forgotten it.

It was a part of his guilty state of mind to remember it; for on his persistence in the scheme depended one of his precautions for his own safety. A hint, a word, from the old man, uttered at such a moment in attentive ears, might fire the train of suspicion, and destroy him. His watchfulness of every avenue by which the discovery of his guilt might be approached, sharpened with his sense of the danger by which he was encompassed. With murder on his soul, and its innumerable alarms and terrors dragging at him night and day, he would have repeated the crime, if he had seen a path of safety stretching out beyond. It was in his punishment; it was in his guilty condition. The very deed which his fears rendered insupportable, his fears would have impelled him to commit again.

But keeping the old man close, according to his design, would serve his turn. His purpose was to escape, when the first alarm and wonder had subsided: and when he could make the attempt without awakening instant suspicion. In the meanwhile these women would keep him quiet; and if the talking humour came upon him, would not be easily startled. He knew their trade.

Nor had he spoken idly when he said the old man should be gagged.

23

He had resolved to ensure his silence; and he looked to the end, not the means. He had been rough and rude and cruel to the old man all his life; and violence was natural to his mind in connexion with him. 'He shall be gagged if he speaks, and pinioned if he writes,' said Jonas, looking at him; for they sat alone together. 'He is mad enough for that; I'll go through with it!'

Hush!

Still listening! To every sound. He had listened ever since, and it had not come yet. The exposure of the Assurance office; the flight of Crimple and Bullamy with the plunder, and among the rest, as he feared, with his own bill, which he had not found in the pocket-book of the murdered man, and which with Mr Pecksniff's money had probably been remitted to one of other of those trusty friends for safe deposit at the banker's; his immense losses, and peril of being still called to account as a partner in the broken firm; all these things rose in his mind at one time and always, but he could not contemplate them. He was aware of their presence, and of the rage, discomfiture, and despair, they brought along with them; but he thought – of his own controlling power and direction he thought – of the one dread question only. When they would find the body in the wood.

He tried – he had never left off trying – not to forget it was there, for that was impossible, but to forget to weary himself by drawing vivid pictures of it in his fancy: by going softly about it and about it among the leaves, approaching it nearer and nearer through a gap in the boughs, and startling the very flies that were thickly sprinkled all over it, like heaps of dried currants. His mind was fixed and fastened on the discovery, for intelligence of which he listened intently to every cry and shout; listened when any one came in or went out; watched from the window the people who passed up and down the street; mistrusted his own looks and words. And the more his thoughts were set upon the discovery, the stronger was the fascination which attracted them to the thing itself: lying alone in the wood. He was for ever showing and presenting it, as it were, to every creature whom he saw. 'Look here! Do you know of this? Is it found? Do you suspect *me*?' If he had been condemned to bear the body in his arms, and lay it down for recognition at the feet of every one he met, it could not have been more constantly with him, or a cause of more monotonous and dismal occupation than it was in this state of his mind.

Still he was not sorry. It was no contrition or remorse for what he had done that moved him; it was nothing but alarm for his own security. The vague consciousness he possessed of having wrecked his fortune in the murderous venture, intensified his hatred and revenge, and made him set the greater store by what he had gained. The man was dead; nothing could undo that. He felt a triumph yet, in the reflection.

He had kept a jealous watch on Chuffey ever since the deed; seldom leaving him but on compulsion, and then for as short intervals as possible. They were alone together now. It was twilight, and the appointed time drew near at hand. Jonas walked up and down the room. The old man sat in his accustomed corner.

The slightest circumstance was matter of disquiet to the murderer, and he was made uneasy at this time by the absence of his wife, who had left home early in the afternoon, and had not returned yet. No tenderness for her was at the bottom of this; but he had a misgiving that she might have been waylaid, and tempted into saying something that would criminate him when the news came. For anything he knew, she might have knocked at the door of his room, while he was away, and discovered his plot. Confound her, it was like her pale face to be wandering up and down the house! Where was she now?

'She went to her good friend, Mrs Todgers,' said the old man, when he asked the question with an angry oath.

Aye! To be sure! Always stealing away into the company of that woman. She was no friend of his. Who could tell what devil's mischief they might hatch together! Let her be fetched home directly.

The old man, muttering some words softly, rose as if he would have gone himself, but Jonas thrust him back into his chair with an impatient imprecation, and sent a servant-girl to fetch her. When he had charged her with her errand he walked to and fro again, and never stopped till she came back, which she did pretty soon: the way being short, and the woman having made good haste.

Well! Where was she? Had she come?

No. She had left there, full three hours.

'Left there! Alone?'

The messenger had not asked; taking that for granted.

'Curse you for a fool. Bring candles!'

She had scarcely left the room when the old clerk, who had been unusually observant of him ever since he had asked about his wife, came suddenly upon him.

'Give her up!' cried the old man. 'Come! Give her up to me! Tell me what you have done with her. Quick! I have made no promises on that score. Tell me what you have done with her.'

He laid his hands upon his collar as he spoke, and grasped it: tightly too.

'You shall not leave me!' cried the old man. 'I am strong enough to cry out to the neighbours, and I will, unless you give her up. Give her up to me!'

Jonas was so dismayed and conscience-stricken, that he had not even hardihood enough to unclench the old man's hands with his own; but stood looking at him as well as he could in the darkness, without moving a finger. It was as much as he could do to ask him what he meant.

'I will know what you have done with her!' retorted Chuffey. 'If you hurt a hair of her head, you shall answer it. Poor thing! Poor thing! Where is she?'

'Why, you old madman!' said Jonas, in a low voice, and with trembling lips. 'What Bedlam fit has come upon you now?'

'It is enough to make me mad, seeing what I have seen in this house!' cried Chuffey. 'Where is my dear old master! Where is his only son that I have nursed upon my knee, a child! Where is she, she who was the last; she that I've seen pining day by day, and heard weeping in the dead of night! She was the last, the last of all my friends! Heaven help me, she was the very last!'

Seeing that the tears were stealing down his face, Jonas mustered courage to unclench his hands, and push him off before he answered:

'Did you hear me ask for her? Did you hear me send for her? How can I give you up what I haven't got, idiot! Ecod, I'd give her up to you and welcome, if I could; and a precious pair you'd be!'

'If she has come to any harm,' cried Chuffey, 'mind! I'm old and silly; but I have my memory sometimes; and if she has come to any harm –'

'Devil take you,' interrupted Jonas, but in a suppressed voice still; 'what harm do you suppose she has come to? I know no more where she is than you do; I wish I did. Wait till she comes home, and see; she can't be long. Will that content you?'

'Mind!' exclaimed the old man. 'Not a hair of her head! not a hair of her head ill-used! I won't bear it. I – I – have borne it too long, Jonas. I am silent, but I – I – I can speak. I – I – I can speak –' he stammered, as he crept back to his chair, and turned a threatening, though a feeble, look upon him.

'You can speak, can you!' thought Jonas. 'So, so, we'll stop your speaking. It's well I knew of this in good time. Prevention is better than cure.'

He had made a poor show of playing the bully and evincing a desire to conciliate at the same time, but was so afraid of the old man that great drops had started out upon his brown; and they stood there yet. His unusual tone of voice and agitated manner had sufficiently expressed his fear; but his face would have done so now, without that aid, as he again walked to and fro, glancing at him by the candle-light.

He stopped at the window to think. An opposite shop was lighted up; and the tradesman and a customer were reading some printed bill together across the counter. The sight brought him back, instantly, to the occupation he had forgotten. 'Look here! Do you know of this? Is it found? Do you suspect *me*?'

A hand upon the door. 'What's that!'

'A pleasant evenin',' said the voice of Mrs Gamp, 'though warm, which, bless you, Mr Chuzzlewit, we must expect when cowcumbers is three for twopence. How does Mr Chuffey find his self to-night, sir?'

Mrs Gamp kept particularly close to the door in saying this, and curtseyed more than usual. She did not appear to be quite so much at her ease as she generally was.

'Get him to his room,' said Jonas, walking up to her, and speaking in her ear. 'He has been raving to-night – stark mad. Don't talk while he's here, but come down again.'

'Poor sweet dear!' cried Mrs Gamp, with uncommon tenderness. 'He's all of a tremble.'

'Well he may be,' said Jonas, 'after the mad fit he has had. Get him up-stairs.'

She was by this time assisting him to rise.

'There's my blessed old chick!' cried Mrs Gamp, in a tone that was at once soothing and encouraging. 'There's my darlin' Mr Chuffey! Now come up to your own room, sir, and lay down on your bed a bit; for you're a-shakin' all over, as if your precious jints was hung upon wires. That's a good creetur! Come with Sairey!'

'Is she come home?' inquired the old man.

'She'll be here directly minnit,' returned Mrs Gamp. 'Come with Sairey, Mr Chuffey. Come with your own Sairey!'

The good woman had no reference to any female in the world in promising this speedy advent of the person for whom Mr Chuffey inquired, but merely threw it out as a means of pacifying the old man. It had its effect, for he permitted her to lead him away: and they quitted the room together.

Jonas looked out of the window again. They were still reading the printed paper in the shop opposite, and a third man had joined in the perusal. What could it be, to interest them so?

A dispute or discussion seemed to arise among them, for they all looked up from their reading together, and one of the three, who had been glancing over the shoulder of another, stepped back to explain or illustrate some action by his gestures.

Horror! How like the blow he had struck in the wood!

It beat him from the window as if it had lighted on himself. As he staggered into a chair he thought of the change in Mrs Gamp, exhibited in her new-born tenderness to her charge. Was that because it was found? – because she knew of it? – because she suspected him?

'Mr Chuffey is a-lyin' down,' said Mrs Gamp, returning, 'and much good may it do him, Mr Chuzzlewit, which harm it can't and good it may, be joyful!'

'Sit down,' said Jonas, hoarsely, 'and let us get this business done. Where is the other woman?'

'The other person's with him now,' she answered.

'That's right,' said Jonas. 'He is not fit to be left to himself. Why, he fastened on me to-night; here, upon my coat; like a savage dog. Old as he is, and feeble as he is usually, I had some trouble to shake him off. You – Hush! – It's nothing. You told me the other woman's name. I forget it.'

'I mentioned Betsey Prig,' said Mrs Gamp.

'She is to be trusted, is she?'

'That she ain't!' said Mrs Gamp; 'nor have I brought her, Mr Chuzzlewit. I've brought another, which engages to give every satigefaction.'

'What is her name?' asked Jonas.

Mrs Gamp looked at him in an odd way without returning any answer, but appeared to understand the question too.

'What is her name?' repeated Jonas.

'Her name,' said Mrs Gamp, 'is Harris.'

It was extraordinary how much effort it cost Mrs Gamp to pronounce the name she was commonly so ready with. She made some three or four gasps before she could get it out; and, when she had uttered it, pressed her hand upon her side, and turned up her eyes, as if she were going to faint away. But, knowing her to labour under a complication of internal disorders, which rendered a few drops of spirits indispensable at certain times to her existence, and which came on very strong when that remedy was not at hand, Jonas merely supposed her to be the victim of one of these attacks.

'Well!' he said, hastily, for he felt how incapable he was of confining his wandering attention to the subject. 'You and she have arranged to take care of him, have you?'

Mrs Gamp replied in the affirmative, and softly discharged herself of her familiar phrase, 'Turn and turn about; one off, one on.' But she spoke so tremulously that she felt called upon to add, 'which fiddle-strings is weakness to expredge my nerves this night!'

Jonas stopped to listen. Then said, hurriedly:

'We shall not quarrel about terms. Let them be the same as they were before. Keep him close, and keep him quiet. He must be restrained. He has got it in his head to-night that my wife's dead, and has been attacking me as if I had killed her. It's – it's common with mad people to take the worst fancies of those they like best. Isn't it?'

Mrs Gamp assented with a short groan.

'Keep him close, then, or in one of his fits he'll be doing me a mischief. And don't trust him at any time; for when he seems most rational, he's wildest in his talk. But that you know already. Let me see the other.'

'The t'other person, sir?' said Mrs Gamp.

'Aye! Go you to him and send the other. Quick! I'm busy.'

Mrs Gamp took two or three backward steps towards the door, and stopped there.

'It is your wishes, Mr Chuzzlewit,' she said, in a sort of quavering croak, 'to see the t'other person. Is it?'

But the ghastly change in Jonas told her that the other person was already seen. Before she could look round towards the door, she was put aside by old Martin's hand; and Chuffey and John Westlock entered with him.

'Let no one leave the house,' said Martin. 'This man is my brother's son. Ill-met, ill-trained, ill-begotten. If he moves from the spot on which he stands, or speaks a word above his breath to any person here, open the window, and call for help!'

'What right have you to give such directions in this house?' asked Jonas faintly.

'The right of your wrong-doing. Come in there!'

An irrepressible exclamation burst from the lips of Jonas, as Lewsome entered at the door. It was not a groan, or a shriek, or a word, but was wholly unlike any sound that had ever fallen on the ears of those who heard it, while at the same time it was the most sharp and terrible expression of what was working in his guilty breast, that nature could have invented.

He had done murder for this! He had girdled himself about with perils, agonies of mind, innumerable fears, for this! He had hidden his secret in the wood; pressed and stamped it down into the bloody ground; and here it started up when least expected, miles upon miles away; known to many; proclaiming itself from the lips of an old man who had renewed his strength and vigour as by a miracle, to give it voice against him!

He leaned his hand on the back of a chair, and looked at them. It was in vain to try to do so scornfully, or with his usual insolence. He required the chair for his support. But he made a struggle for it.

'I know that fellow,' he said, fetching his breath at every word, and pointing his trembling finger towards Lewsome. 'He's the greatest liar alive. What's his last tale? Ha, ha! You're rare fellows, too! Why, that uncle of mine is childish; he's even a greater child than his brother, my father, was, in his old age; or than Chuffey is. What the devil do you mean,' he added, looking fiercely at John Westlock and Mark Tapley (the latter had entered with Lewsome), 'by coming here, and bringing two idiots and a knave with you to take my house by storm? Hallo, there! Open the door! Turn these strangers out!'

'I tell you what,' cried Mr Tapley, coming forward, 'if it wasn't for your name, I'd drag you through the streets of my own accord, and single-handed, I would! Ah, I would! Don't try and look bold at me. You can't do it! Now go on, sir,' this was to old Martin. 'Bring the murderin' wagabond upon his knees! If he wants noise, he shall have enough of it; for as sure as he's a shiverin' from head to foot, I'll raise a uproar at this winder that shall bring half London in. Go on, sir! Let him try me once, and see whether I'm a man of my word or not.'

With that, Mark folded his arms, and took his seat upon the window-ledge, with an air of general preparation for anything, which seemed to imply that he was equally ready to jump out himself, or to throw Jonas out, upon receiving the slightest hint that it would be agreeable to the company.

Old Martin turned to Lewsome:

'This is the man,' he said, extending his hand towards Jonas. 'Is it?'

'You need do no more than look at him to be sure of that, or of the truth of what I have said,' was the reply. 'He is my witness.'

'Oh, brother!' cried old Martin, clasping his hands and lifting up his eyes. 'Oh, brother, brother! Were we strangers half our lives that you might breed a wretch like this, and I make life a desert by withering every flower that grew about me! Is it the natural end of your precepts and mine, that this should be the creature of your rearing, training, teaching, hoarding, striving for: and I the means of bringing him to punishment, when nothing can repair the wasted past!'

He sat down upon a chair as he spoke, and turning away his face, was silent for a few moments. Then with recovered energy he proceeded:

'But the accursed harvest of our mistaken lives shall be trodden down. It is not too late for that. You are confronted with this man, yon monster there; not to be spared, but to be dealt with justly. Hear what he says! Reply, be silent, contradict, repeat, defy, do what you please. My course will be the same. Go on! And you,' he said to Chuffey, 'for the love of your old friend, speak out, good fellow!'

'I have been silent for his love!' cried the old man. 'He urged me to it. He made me promise it upon his dying bed. I never would have spoken, but for your finding out so much. I have thought about it ever since: I couldn't help that: and sometimes I have had it all before me in a dream: but in the daytime, not in sleep. Is there such a kind of dream?' said Chuffey, looking anxiously in old Martin's face.

As Martin made him an encouraging reply, he listened attentively to his voice, and smiled.

'Ah, aye!' he cried. 'He often spoke to me like that. We were at school together, he and I. I couldn't turn against his son, you know – his only son, Mr Chuzzlewit!'

'I would to Heaven you had been his son!' said Martin.

'You speak so like my dear old master,' cried the old man with a childish delight, 'that I almost think I hear him. I can hear you quite as well as I used to hear him. It makes me young again. He never spoke unkindly to me, and I always understood him. I could always see him too, though my sight was dim. Well, well! He's dead, he's dead. He was very good to me, my dear old master!'

He shook his head mournfully over the brother's hand. At this moment Mark, who had been glancing out of the window, left the room.

'I couldn't turn against his only son, you know,' said Chuffey. 'He has nearly driven me to do it sometimes; he very nearly did to-night. Ah!' cried the old man, with a sudden recollection of the cause. 'Where is she? She's not come home!'

'Do you mean his wife?' said Mr Chuzzlewit.

'Yes.'

'I have removed her. She is in my care, and will be spared the present knowledge of what is passing here. She has known misery enough, without that addition.'

Jonas heard this with a sinking heart. He knew that they were on his heels, and felt that they were resolute to run him to destruction. Inch by inch the ground beneath him was sliding from his feet; faster and faster the encircling ruin contracted and contracted towards himself, its wicked centre, until it should close in and crush him.

And now he heard the voice of his accomplice stating to his face, with every circumstance of time and place and incident; and openly proclaiming, with no reserve, suppression, passion, or concealment; all the truth. The truth, which nothing would keep down; which blood would not smother, and earth would not hide; the truth, whose terrible inspiration seemed to change dotards into strong men; and on whose avenging wings, one whom he had supposed to be at the extremest corner of the earth came swooping down upon him.

He tried to deny it, but his tongue would not move. He conceived some desperate thought of rushing away, and tearing through the streets; but his limbs would as little answer to his will as his stark, stiff, staring face. All this time the voice went slowly on, denouncing him. It was as if every drop of blood in the wood had found a voice to jeer him with.

When it ceased, another voice took up the tale, but strangely: for the old clerk, who had watched, and listened to the whole, and had wrung his hands from time to time, as if he knew its truth and could confirm it, broke in with these words:

'No, no, no! you're wrong; you're wrong – all wrong together! Have patience, for the truth is only known to me!'

'How can that be,' said his old master's brother, 'after what you have heard? Besides, you said just now, above-stairs, when I told you of the accusation against him, that you knew he was his father's murderer.'

'Aye, yes! and so he was!' cried Chuffey, wildly. 'But not as you suppose – not as you suppose. Stay! Give me a moment's time. I have it all here – all here! It was foul, foul, cruel, bad; but not as you suppose. Stay, stay!'

He put his hands up to his head, as if it throbbed or pained him. After looking about him in a wandering and vacant manner for some moments, his eyes rested upon Jonas, when they kindled up with sudden recollection and intelligence.

'Yes!' cried old Chuffey, 'yes! That's how it was. It's all upon me now. He – he got up from his bed before he died, to be sure, to say that he forgave him; and he came down with me into this room; and when he saw him – his only son, the son he loved – his speech forsook him: he had no speech for what he knew – and no one understood him except me. But I did – I did!'

Old Martin regarded him in amazement; so did his companions. Mrs Gamp, who had said nothing yet; but had kept two-thirds of herself behind the door, ready for escape, and one-third in the room, ready for siding with the strongest party; came a little further in and remarked, with a sob, that Mr Chuffey was 'the sweetest old creetur goin'.'

'He bought the stuff,' said Chuffey, stretching out his arm towards Jonas, while an unwonted fire shone in his eye, and lightened up his face; 'he bought the stuff, no doubt, as you have heard, and brought it home. He mixed the stuff – look at him! – with some sweetmeat in a jar, exactly as the medicine for his father's cough was mixed, and put it in a drawer; in that drawer yonder in the desk; he knows which drawer I mean! He kept it there locked up. But his courage failed him, or his heart was touched – my God! I hope it was his heart! He was his only son! – and he did not put it in the usual place, where my old master would have taken it twenty times a day.'

The trembling figure of the old man shook with the strong emotions that possessed him. But, with the same light in his eye, and with his arm outstretched, and with his grey hair stirring on his head, he seemed to grow in size, and was like a man inspired. Jonas shrunk from looking at him, and cowered down into the chair by which he had held. It seemed as if this tremendous Truth could make the dumb speak.

'I know it every word now!' cried Chuffey. 'Every word! He put it in that drawer, as I have said. He went so often there, and was so secret, that his father took notice of it; and when he was out, had it opened. We were there together, and we found the mixture – Mr Chuzzlewit and I. He took it into his possession, and made light of it at the time; but in the night he came to my bedside, weeping, and told me that his own son had it in his mind to poison him. "Oh, Chuff," he said, "oh, dear old Chuff! a voice came into my room to-night, and told me that this crime began with me. It began when I taught him to be too covetous of what I have to leave, and made the expectation of it his great business!" Those were his words; aye, they are his very words! If he was a hard man now and then, it was for his only son. He loved his only son, and he was always good to me!'

Jonas listened with increased attention. Hope was breaking in upon him.

' "He shall not weary for my death, Chuff:" that was what he said next,' pursued the old clerk, as he wiped his eyes; 'that was what he said next, crying like a little child: "He shall not weary for my death, Chuff. He shall have it now; he shall marry where he has a fancy, Chuff, although it don't please me; and you and I will go away and live upon a little. I always loved him; perhaps he'll love *me* then. It's a dreadful thing to have my own child thirsting for my death. But I might have known it. I have sown, and I must reap. He shall believe that I am taking this; and when I see that he is sorry, and has all he wants, I'll tell him that I found it out, and I'll forgive him. He'll make a better man of his own son, and be a better man himself, perhaps, Chuff!'' '

Poor Chuffey paused to dry his eyes again. Old Martin's face was hidden in his hands. Jonas listened still more keenly, and his breast heaved like a swollen water, but with hope. With growing hope.

'My dear old master made believe next day,' said Chuffey, 'that he had opened the drawer by mistake with a key from the bunch, which happened to fit it (we had one made and hung upon it); and that he had been surprised to find his fresh supply of cough medicine in such a place, but supposed it had been put there in a hurry when the drawer stood open. We burnt it; but his son believed that he was taking it – he knows he did. Once Mr Chuzzlewit to try him took heart to say it had a strange taste; and he got up directly, and went out.'

Jonas gave a short, dry cough; and, changing his position for an easier one, folded his arms without looking at them, though they could now see his face.

'Mr Chuzzlewit wrote to her father; I mean the father of the poor thing who's his wife;' said Chuffey; 'and got him to come up: intending to hasten on the marriage. But his mind, like mine, went a little wrong through grief, and then his heart broke. He sank and altered from the time when he came to me in the night; and never held up his head again. It was only a few days, but he had never changed so much in twice the years. "Spare him, Chuff!" he said, before he died. They were the only words he could speak. "Spare him, Chuff!" I promised him I would. I've tried to do it. He's his only son.'

In his recollection of the last scene in his old friend's life, poor Chuffey's voice, which had grown weaker and weaker, quite deserted him. Making a motion with his hand, as if he would have said that Anthony had taken it, and had died with it in his, he retreated to the corner where he usually concealed his sorrows; and was silent.

Jonas could look at his company now, and vauntingly too. 'Well!' he said, after a pause. 'Are you satisfied? Or have you any more of your plots to broach? Why that fellow, Lewsome, can invent 'em for you by the score. Is this all? Have you nothing else?'

Old Martin looked at him steadily.

'Whether you are what you seemed to be at Pecksniff's, or are some-thing else and a mountebank, I don't know and I don't care,' said Jonas, looking downward with a smile, 'but I don't want you here. You were here so often when your brother was alive, and were always so fond of him (your dear, dear brother, and you would have been cuffing one another before this, ecod!), that I am not surprised at your being attached to the place; but the place is not attached to you, and you can't leave it too soon, though you may leave it too late. And for my wife, old man, send her home straight, or it will be the worse for her. Ha, ha! You carry it with a high hand too! But it isn't hanging yet for a man to keep a penn'orth of poison for his own purposes, and have it taken from him by two old crazy jolter-heads who go and act a play about it. Ha, ha! Do you see the door?'

His base triumph, struggling with his cowardice, and shame, and guilt, was so detestable, that they turned away from him, as if he were some obscene and filthy animal, repugnant to the sight. And here that last black crime was busy with him too; working within him to his perdition. But for that, the old clerk's story might have touched him, though never so lightly; but for that, the sudden removal of so great a load might have brought about some wholesome change even in him. With that deed done, however; with that unnecessary wasteful danger haunting him; despair was in his very triumph and relief; wild, ungovern-able, raging despair, for the uselessness of the peril into which he had plunged; despair that hardened him and maddened him, and set his teeth a-grinding in a moment of his exultation.

'My good friend!' said old Martin, laying his hand on Chuffey's sleeve. 'This is no place for you to remain in. Come with me.'

'Just his old way!' cried Chuffey, looking up into his face. 'I almost believe it's Mr Chuzzlewit alive again. Yes! Take me with you! Stay, though, stay.'

'For what?' asked old Martin.

'I can't leave her, poor thing!' said Chuffey. 'She has been very good to me. I can't leave her, Mr Chuzzlewit. Thank you kindly. I'll remain here. I hav'n't long to remain; it's no great matter.'

As he meekly shook his poor, grey head, and thanked old Martin in these words, Mrs Gamp, now entirely in the room, was affected to tears.

'The mercy as it is!' she said, 'as sech a dear, good, reverend creetur never got into the clutches of Betsey Prig, which but for me he would have done, undoubted, facts bein' stubborn and not easy drove!'

'You heard me speak to you just now, old man,' said Jonas to his uncle. 'I'll have no more tampering with my people, man or woman. Do you see the door?'

'Do *you* see the door?' returned the voice of Mark, coming from that direction. 'Look at it!'

He looked, and his gaze was nailed there. Fatal, ill-omened, blighted threshold, cursed by his father's footsteps in his dying hour, cursed by his young wife's sorrowing tread, cursed by the daily shadow of the old clerk's figure, cursed by the crossing of his murderer's feet – what men were standing in the doorway!

Nadgett foremost.

Hark! It came on, roaring like a sea! Hawkers burst into the street, crying it up and down; windows were thrown open that the inhabitants might hear it; people stopped to listen in the road and on the pavement; the bells, the same bells, began to ring: tumbling over one another in a dance of boisterous joy at the discovery (that was the sound they had in his distempered thoughts), and making their airy playground rock.

'That is the man,' said Nadgett. 'By the window!'

Three others came in, laid hands upon him, and secured him. It was so quickly done, that he had not lost sight of the informer's face for an instant when his wrists were manacled together.

'Murder,' said Nadgett, looking round on the astonished group. 'Let no one interfere.'

The sounding street repeated Murder; barbarous and dreadful Murder; Murder, Murder, Murder. Rolling on from house to house, and echoing from stone to stone, until the voices died away into the distant hum, which seemed to mutter the same word!

They all stood silent; listening, and gazing in each other's faces, as the noise passed on.

Old Martin was the first to speak, 'What terrible history is this?' he demanded.

'Ask *him*,' said Nadgett. 'You're his friend, sir. He can tell you, if he will. He knows more of it than I do, though I know much.'

'How do you know much?'

'I have not been watching him so long for nothing,' returned Nadgett. 'I never watched a man so close as I have watched him.'

Another of the phantom forms of this terrific Truth! Another of the many shapes in which it started up about him, out of vacancy. This man, of all men in the world, a spy upon him; this man, changing his identity: casting off his shrinking, purblind, unobservant character, and springing up into a watchful enemy! The dead man might have come out of the grave, and not confounded and appalled him more.

The game was up. The race was at an end; the rope was woven for his neck. If, by a miracle, he could escape from this strait, he had but to turn his face another way, no matter where, and there would rise some new avenger front to front with him; some infant in an hour grown old, or old man in an hour grown young, or blind man with his sight restored, or deaf man with his hearing given him. There was no chance. He sank down in a heap against the wall, and never hoped again from that moment.

'I am not his friend, although I have the dishonour to be his relative,' said Mr Chuzzlewit. 'You may speak to me. Where have you watched, and what have you seen?'

'I have watched in many places,' returned Nadgett, 'night and day. I have watched him lately, almost without rest or relief;' his anxious face and bloodshot eyes confirmed it. 'I little thought to what my watching was to lead. As little as he did when he slipped out in the night, dressed in those clothes which he afterwards sunk in a bundle at London Bridge!'

Jonas moved upon the ground like a man in bodily torture. He uttered a suppressed groan, as if he had been wounded by some cruel weapon; and plucked at the iron band upon his wrists, as though (his hands being free) he would have torn himself.

'Steady, kinsman!' said the chief officer of the party. 'Don't be violent.'

'Whom do you call kinsman?' asked old Martin sternly.

'You,' said the man, 'among others.'

Martin turned his scrutinising gaze upon him. He was sitting lazily across a chair with his arms resting on the back; eating nuts, and throwing the shells out of window as he cracked them; which he still continued to do while speaking.

'Aye,' he said, with a sulky nod. 'You may deny your nephews till you die, but Chevy Slyme is Chevy Slyme still, all the world over. Perhaps even you may feel it some disgrace to your own blood to be employed in this way. I'm to be bought off.'

'At every turn!' cried Martin, 'Self, self, self. Every one among them for himself!'

'You had better save one or two among them the trouble then, and be for them as well as *your*self,' replied his nephew. 'Look here at me! Can you see the man of your family who has more talent in his little finger than all the rest in their united brains, dressed as a police officer without being ashamed? I took up with this trade on purpose to shame you. I didn't think I should have to make a capture in the family, though.'

'If your debauchery, and that of your chosen friends, has really brought you to this level,' returned the old man, 'keep it. You are living honesty, I hope, and that's something.'

'Don't be hard upon my chosen friends,' returned Slyme, 'for they were sometimes your chosen friends too. Don't say you never employed my friend Tigg, for I know better. We quarrelled upon it.'

'I hired the fellow,' retorted Mr Chuzzlewit, 'and I paid him.'

'It's well you paid him,' said his nephew, 'for it would be too late to do so now. He has given his receipt in full – or had it forced from him rather.'

The old man looked at him as if he were curious to know what he meant, but scorned to prolong the conversation.

'I have always expected that he and I would be brought together again in the course of business,' said Slyme, taking a fresh handful of nuts from his pocket; 'but I thought he would be wanted for some swindling job; it never entered my head that I should hold a warrant for the apprehension of his murderer.'

'*His* murderer!' cried Mr Chuzzlewit, looking from one to another.

'His or Mr Montague's,' said Nadgett. 'They are the same, I am told. I accuse him yonder of the murder of Mr Montague, who was found last night, killed, in a wood. You will ask me why I accuse him, as you have already asked me how I know so much. I'll tell you. It can't remain a secret long.'

The ruling passion of the man expressed itself even then, in the tone of regret in which he deplored the approaching publicity of what he knew.

'I told you I had watched him,' he proceeded. 'I was instructed to do so by Mr Montague, in whose employment I have been for some time. We had our suspicions of him; and you know what they pointed at, for you have been discussing it since we have been waiting here, outside the room. If you care to hear now it's all over, in what our suspicions began, I'll tell you plainly: in a quarrel (it first came to our ears through a hint of his own) between him and another office in which his father's life was insured, and which had so much doubt and distrust upon the subject, that he compounded with them, and took half the money; and was glad to do it. Bit by bit, I ferreted out more circumstances against him, and not a few. It required a little patience, but it's my calling. I found the nurse – here she is to confirm me; I found the doctor, I found the undertaker, I found the undertaker's man. I found out how the old gentleman there, Mr Chuffey, had behaved at the funeral; and I found out what this man,' touching Lewsome on the arm, 'had talked about in his fever. I found out how he conducted himself before his father's death, and how since, and how at the time; and writing it all down, and putting it carefully together, made case enough for Mr Montague to tax him with the crime, which (as he himself believed until to-night) he had committed. I was by when this was done. You see him now. He is only worse than he was then.'

Oh, miserable, miserable fool! oh, insupportable, excruciating torture! To find alive and active – a party to it all – the brain and right-hand of the secret he had thought to crush! In whom, though he had walled the murdered man up, by enchantment in a rock, the story would have lived and walked abroad ! He tried to stop his ears with his fettered arms, that he might shut out the rest.

As he crouched upon the floor, they drew away from him as if a pestilence were in his breath. They fell off, one by one, from that part of the room, leaving him alone upon the ground. Even those who had him in their keeping shunned him, and (with the exception of Slyme, who was still occupied with his nuts) kept apart.

'From that garret-window opposite,' said Nadgett, pointing across the narrow street, 'I have watched this house and him for days and nights. From that garret-window opposite I saw him return home, alone, from a journey on which he had set out with Mr Montague. That was my token that Mr Montague's end was gained; and I might rest easy

Mr Nadgett (at the rear) 'the first serious private detective in an
English novel'. An illustration by Phiz for *Martin Chuzzlewit*

on my watch, though I was not to leave it until he dismissed me. But, standing at the door opposite, after dark, that same night, I saw a countryman steal out of this house, by a side-door in the court, who had never entered it. I knew his walk, and that it was himself, disguised. I followed him immediately. I lost him on the western road, still travelling westward.'

Jonas looked up at him for an instant, and muttered an oath.

'I could not comprehend what this meant,' said Nadgett: 'but, having seen so much, I resolved to see it out, and through. And I did. Learning, on inquiry at his house from his wife, that he was supposed to be sleeping in the room from which I had seen him go out, and that he had given strict orders not to be disturbed, I knew that he was coming back; and for his coming back I watched. I kept my watch in the street – in doorways, and such places – all that night; at the same window, all next day; and when night came on again, in the street once more. For I knew he would come back, as he had gone out, when this part of the town was empty. He did. Early in the morning, the same countryman came creeping, creeping, creeping home.'

'Look sharp!' interposed Slyme, who had now finished his nuts. 'This is quite irregular, Mr Nadgett.'

'I kept at the window all day,' said Nadgett, without heeding him. 'I think I never closed my eyes. At night, I saw him come out with a bundle. I followed him again. He went down the steps at London Bridge, and sunk it in the river. I now began to entertain some serious fears, and made a communication to the Police, which caused that bundle to be –'

'To be fished up,' interrupted Slyme. 'Be alive, Mr Nadgett.'

'It contained the dress I had seen him wear,' said Nadgett; 'stained with clay, and spotted with blood. Information of the murder was received in town last night. The wearer of that dress is already known to have been seen near the place; to have been lurking in that neighbourhood; and to have alighted from a coach coming from that part of the country, at a time exactly tallying with the very minute when I saw him returning home. The warrant has been out, and these officers have been with me, some hours. We chose our time; and seeing you come in, and seeing this person at the window –'

'Beckoned to him,' said Mark, taking up the thread of the narrative, on hearing this allusion to himself, 'to open the door; which he did with a deal of pleasure.'

'That's all at present,' said Nadgett, putting up his great pocketbook, which from mere habit he had produced when he began his revelation, and had kept in his hand all the time; 'but there is plenty more to come. You asked me for the facts, so far I have related them, and need not detain these gentlemen any longer. Are you ready, Mr Slyme?'

'And something more,' replied that worthy, rising. 'If you walk round to the office, we shall be there as soon as you. Tom! Get a coach!'

[TWO]

The Drunkard's Death

We will be bold to say, that there is scarcely a man in the constant habit of walking, day after day, through any of the crowded thoroughfares of London, who cannot recollect among the people whom he 'knows by sight,' to use a familiar phrase, some being of abject and wretched appearance whom he remembers to have seen in a very different condition, whom he has observed sinking lower and lower, by almost imperceptible degrees, and the shabbiness and utter destitution of whose appearance, at last, strike forcibly and painfully upon him, as he passes by. Is there any man who has mixed much with society, or whose avocations have caused him to mingle, at one time or other, with a great number of people, who cannot call to mind the time when some shabby, miserable wretch, in rags and filth, who shuffles past him now in all the squalor of disease and poverty, was a respectable tradesman, or clerk, or a man following some thriving pursuit, with good prospects, and decent means? – or cannot any of our readers call to mind from among the list of their *quondam* acquaintance, some fallen and degraded man, who lingers about the pavement in hungry misery – from whom every one turns coldly away, and who preserves himself from sheer starvation, nobody knows how? Alas! such cases are of too frequent occurrence to be rare items in any man's experience; and but too often arise from one cause – drunkenness – that fierce rage for the slow, sure poison, that oversteps every other consideration; that casts

'A Pickpocket in Custody' – a George Cruikshank illustration for
Sketches by Boz

aside wife, children, friends, happiness, and station; and hurries its victims madly on to degradation and death.

Some of these men have been impelled, by misfortune and misery, to the vice that has degraded them. The ruin of worldly expectations, the death of those they loved, the sorrow that slowly consumes, but will not break the heart, has driven them wild; and they present the hideous spectacle of madmen, slowly dying by their own hands. But by far the greater part have wilfully, and with open eyes, plunged into the gulf from which the man who once enters it never rises more, but into which he sinks deeper and deeper down, until recovery is hopeless.

Such a man as this once stood by the bedside of his dying wife, while his children knelt around, and mingled low bursts of grief with their innocent prayers. The room was scantily and meanly furnished; and it needed but a glance at the pale form from which the light of life was fast passing away, to know that grief, and want, and anxious care, had been busy at the heart for many a weary year. An elderly woman, with her face bathed in tears, was supporting the head of the dying woman – her daughter – on her arm. But it was not towards her that the wan face turned; it was not her hand that the cold and trembling fingers clasped; they pressed the husband's arm; the eyes so soon to be closed in death rested on his face, and the man shook beneath their gaze. His dress was slovenly and disordered, his face inflamed, his eyes bloodshot and heavy. He had been summoned from some wild debauch to the bed of sorrow and death.

A shaded lamp by the beside cast a dim light on the figures around, and left the remainder of the room in thick, deep shadow. The silence of night prevailed without the house, and the stillness of death was in the chamber. A watch hung over the mantel-shelf; its low ticking was the only sound that broke the profound quiet, but it was a solemn one, for well they knew, who heard it, that before it had recorded the passing of another hour, it would beat the knell of a departed spirit.

It is a dreadful thing to wait and watch for the approach of death; to know that hope is gone, and recovery impossible; and to sit and count the dreary hours through long, long nights – such nights as only watchers by the bed of sickness know. It chills the blood to hear the dearest secrets of the heart – the pent-up, hidden secrets of many years – poured forth by the unconscious helpless being before you; and to think how little the reserve and cunning of a whole life will avail, when fever and delirium tear off the mask at last. Strange tales have been told in the wanderings of dying men; tales so full of guilt and crime, that those who stood by the sick person's couch have fled in horror and affright, lest they should be scared to madness by what they heard and saw; and many a wretch has died alone, raving of deeds the very name of which has driven the boldest man away.

But no such ravings were to be heard at the bedside by which the children knelt. Their half-stifled sobs and moanings alone broke the silence of the lonely chamber. And when at last the mother's grasp relaxed, and, turning one look from the children to the father, she vainly strove to speak, and fell backward on the pillow, all was so calm and tranquil that she seemed to sink to sleep. They leant over her; they called upon her name, softly at first, and then in the loud and piercing tones of desperation. But there was no reply. They listened for her breath, but no sound came. They felt for the palpitation of the heart, but no faint throb responded to the touch. That heart was broken, and she was dead!

The husband sunk into a chair by the bedside, and clasped his hands upon his burning forehead. He gazed from child to child, but when a weeping eye met his, he quailed beneath its look. No word of comfort was whispered in his ear, no look of kindness lighted on his face. All shrunk from and avoided him; and when at last he staggered from the room, no one sought to follow or console the widower.

The time had been when many a friend would have crowded round him in his affliction, and many a heartfelt condolence would have met him in his grief. Where were they now? One by one, friends, relations, the commonest acquaintance even, had fallen off from and deserted the drunkard. His wife alone had clung to him in good and evil, in sickness and poverty, and how had he rewarded her? He had reeled from the tavern to her bedside in time to see her die.

He rushed from the house, and walked swiftly through the streets. Remorse, fear, shame, all crowded on his mind. Stupefied with drink, and bewildered with the scene he had just witnessed, he re-entered the tavern he had quitted shortly before. Glass succeeded glass. His blood mounted, and his brain whirled round. Death! Every one must die, and why not *she*? She was too good for him; her relations had often told him so. Curses on them! Had they not deserted her, and left her to whine away the time at home? Well – she was dead, and happy perhaps. It was better as it was. Another glass – one more! Hurrah! It was a merry life while it lasted; and he would make the most of it.

Time went on; the three children who were left to him, grew up, and were children no longer. The father remained the same – poorer, shabbier, and more dissolute-looking, but the same confirmed and irreclaimable drunkard. The boys had, long ago, run wild in the streets, and left him; the girl alone remained, but she worked hard, and words or blows could always procure him something for the tavern. So he went on in the old course, and a merry life he led.

One night, as early as ten o'clock – for the girl had been sick for many days, and there was, consequently, little to spend at the public-house – he bent his steps homeward, bethinking himself that if he would have her able to earn money, it would be as well to apply to the parish surgeon, or, at all events, to take the trouble of inquiring what ailed her, which he had not yet thought it worth while to do. It was a wet December night; the wind blew piercing cold, and the rain poured heavily down. He begged a few halfpence from a passer-by, and having bought a small loaf (for it was his interest to keep the girl alive, if he could), he shuffled onwards as fast as the wind and rain would let him.

At the back of Fleet Street, and lying between it and the water-side, are several mean and narrow courts, which form a portion of Whitefriars: it was to one of these that he directed his steps.

The alley into which he turned might, for filth and misery, have competed with the darkest corner of this ancient sanctuary in its dirtiest and most lawless time. The houses, varying from two stories in height to four, were stained with every indescribable hue that long exposure to the weather, damp, and rottenness can impart to tenements composed originally of the roughest and coarsest materials. The windows were patched with paper, and stuffed with the foulest rags; the doors were falling from their hinges; poles with lines on which to dry clothes, projected from every casement, and sounds of quarrelling or drunkenness issued from every room.

The solitary oil lamp in the centre of the court had been blown out, either by the violence of the wind or the act of some inhabitant who had excellent reasons for objecting to his residence being rendered too conspicuous; and the only light which fell upon the broken and uneven pavement, was derived from the miserable candles that here and there twinkled in the rooms of such of the more fortunate residents as could afford to indulge in so expensive a luxury. A gutter ran down the centre of the alley – all the sluggish odours of which had been called forth by the rain; and as the wind whistled through the old houses, the doors and shutters creaked upon their hinges, and the windows shook in their frames, with a violence which every moment seemed to threaten the destruction of the whole place.

The man whom we have followed into this den, walked on in the darkness, sometimes stumbling into the main gutter, and at others into some branch repositories of garbage which had been formed by the rain, until he reached the last house in the court. The door, or rather what was left of it, stood ajar, for the convenience of the numerous lodgers; and he proceeded to grope his way up the old and broken stair, to the attic story.

He was within a step or two of his room-door, when it opened, and a girl, whose miserable and emaciated appearance was only to be equalled by that of the candle which she shaded with her hand, peeped anxiously out.

'Is that you, father?' said the girl.

'Who else should it be?' replied the man gruffly. 'What are you trembling at? It's little enough that I've had to drink to-day, for there's no drink without money, and no money without work. What the devil's the matter with the girl?'

'I am not well, father – not at all well,' said the girl, bursting into tears.

'Ah!' replied the man, in the tone of a person who is compelled to admit a very unpleasant fact, to which he would rather remain blind, if he could. 'You must get better somehow, for we must have money. You must go to the parish doctor, and make him give you some medicine. They're paid for it, damn 'em. What are you standing before the door for? Let me come in, can't you?'

'Father,' whispered the girl, shutting the door behind her, and placing herself before it, 'William has come back.'

'Who?' said the man, with a start.

'Hush!' replied the girl, 'William; brother William.'

'And what does he want?' said the man, with an effort at composure
– 'money? meat? drink? He's come to the wrong shop for that, if he does.
Give me the candle – give me the candle, fool – I ain't going to hurt
him.' He snatched the candle from her hand, and walked into the room.

Sitting on an old box, with his head resting on his hand, and his
eyes fixed on a wretched cinder fire that was smouldering on the hearth,
was a young man of about two-and-twenty, miserably clad in an old
coarse jacket and trousers. He started up when his father entered.

'Fasten the door, Mary,' said the young man hastily – 'Fasten the
door. You look as if you didn't know me, father. It's long enough
since you drove me from home; you may well forget me.'

'And what do you want here, now?' said the father, seating himself
on a stool, on the other side of the fireplace. 'What do you want here,
now?'

'Shelter,' replied the son. 'I'm in trouble: that's enough. If I'm caught
I shall swing; that's certain. Caught I shall be, unless I stop here; that's
as certain. And there's an end of it.'

'You mean to say, you've been robbing, or murdering, then?' said
the father.

'Yes, I do,' replied the son. 'Does it surprise you, father?' He looked
steadily in the man's face, but he withdrew his eyes, and bent them on
the ground.

'Where's your brothers?' he said, after a long pause.

'Where they'll never trouble you,' replied his son: 'John's gone to
America, and Henry's dead.'

'Dead!' said the father, with a shudder, which even he could not
repress.

'Dead,' replied the young man. 'He died in my arms – shot like a
dog, by a gamekeeper. He staggered back, I caught him, and his blood
trickled down my hands. It poured out from his side like water. He
was weak, and it blinded him, but he threw himself down on his knees,
on the grass, and prayed to God, that if his mother was in heaven, He
would hear her prayers for pardon for her youngest son. "I was her
favourite boy, Will," he said, "and I am glad to think, now, that when
she was dying, though I was a very young child then, and my little
heart was almost bursting, I knelt down at the foot of the bed, and thanked
God for having made me so fond of her as to have never once done

anything to bring the tears into her eyes. O Will, why was she taken away, and father left?" There's his dying words, father,' said the young man; 'make the best you can of 'em. You struck him across the face, in a drunken fit, the morning we ran away; and here's the end of it.'

The girl wept aloud; and the father, sinking his head upon his knees, rocked himself to and fro.

'If I am taken,' said the young man, 'I shall be carried back into the country, and hung for that man's murder. They cannot trace me here, without your assistance, father. For aught I know, you may give me up to justice; but unless you do, here I stop, until I can venture to escape abroad.'

For two whole days, all three remained in the wretched room, without stirring out. On the third evening, however, the girl was worse than she had been yet, the few scraps of food they had were gone. It was indispensably necessary that somebody should go out; and as the girl was too weak and ill, the father went, just at nightfall.

He got some medicine for the girl, and a trifle in the way of pecuniary assistance. On his way back, he earned sixpence by holding a horse; and he turned homewards with enough money to supply their most pressing wants for two or three days to come. He had to pass the public-house. He lingered for an instant, walked past it, turned back again, lingered once more, and finally slunk in. Two men whom he had not observed, were on the watch. They were on the point of giving up their search in despair, when his loitering attracted their attention; and when he entered the public-house, they followed him.

'You'll drink with me, master,' said one of them, proffering him a glass of liquor.

'And me too,' said the other, replenishing the glass as soon as it was drained of its contents.

The man thought of his hungry children, and his son's danger. But they were nothing to the drunkard. He *did* drink; and his reason left him.

'A wet night, Warden,' whispered one of the men in his ear, as he at length turned to go away, after spending in liquor one-half of the money on which, perhaps, his daughter's life depended.

'The right sort of night for our friends in hiding, Master Warden,' whispered the other.

'Sit down here,' said the one who had spoken first, drawing him

into a corner. 'We have been looking arter the young un. We came to
tell him it's all right now, but we couldn't find him 'cause we hadn't
got the precise direction. But that ain't strange, for I don't think he
know'd it himself, when he come to London, did he?'

'No, he didn't,' replied the father.

The two men exchanged glances.

'There's a vessel down at the docks, to sail at midnight, when it's
high water,' resumed the first speaker, 'and we'll put him on board.
His passage is taken in another name, and what's better than that, it's
paid for. It's lucky we met you.'

'Very,' said the second.

'Capital luck,' said the first, with a wink to his companion.

'Great,' replied the second, with a slight nod of intelligence.

'Another glass here; quick' – said the first speaker. And in five
minutes more, the father had unconsciously yielded up his own son
into the hangman's hands.

Slowly and heavily the time dragged along, as the brother and sister,
in their miserable hiding-place, listened in anxious suspense to the slightest
sound. At length, a heavy footstep was heard upon the stair; it approached
nearer; it reached the landing; and the father staggered into the room.

The girl saw that he was intoxicated, and advanced with the candle
in her hand to meet him; she stopped short, gave a loud scream, and
fell senseless on the ground. She had caught sight of the shadow of a
man reflected on the floor. They both rushed in, and in another instant
the young man was a prisoner, and handcuffed.

'Very quietly done,' said one of the men to his companion, 'thanks
to the old man. Lift up the girl, Tom – come, come, it's no use crying,
young woman. It's all over now, and can't be helped.'

The young man stooped for an instant over the girl, and then turned
fiercely round upon his father, who had reeled against the wall, and
was gazing on the group with drunken stupidity.

'Listen to me, father,' he said, in a tone that made the drunkard's
flesh creep. 'My brother's blood, and mine, is on your head: I never
had kind look, or word, or care, from you, and alive or dead, I never
will forgive you. Die when you will, or how, I will be with you. I
speak as a dead man now, and I warn you, father, that as surely as you
must one day stand before your Maker, so surely shall your children be

there, hand in hand, to cry for judgment against you.' He raised his manacled hands in a threatening attitude, fixed his eyes on his shrinking parent, and slowly left the room; and neither father nor sister ever beheld him more, on this side of the grave.

When the dim and misty light of a winter's morning penetrated into the narrow court, and struggled through the begrimed window of the wretched room, Warden awoke from his heavy sleep, and found himself alone. He rose, and looked round him; the old flock mattress on the floor was undisturbed; everything was just as he remembered to have seen it last: and there were no signs of any one, save himself, having occupied the room during the night. He inquired of the other lodgers, and of the neighbours; but his daughter had not been seen or heard of. He rambled through the streets, and scrutinised each wretched face among the crowds that thronged them, with anxious eyes. But his search was fruitless, and he returned to his garret when night came on, desolate and weary.

For many days he occupied himself in the same manner, but no trace of his daughter did he meet with, and no word of her reached his ears. At length he gave up the pursuit as hopeless. He had long thought of the probability of her leaving him, and endeavouring to gain her bread in quiet, elsewhere. She had left him at last to starve alone. He ground his teeth, and cursed her!

He begged his bread from door to door. Every halfpenny he could wring from the pity or credulity of those to whom he addressed himself, was spent in the old way. A year passed over his head; the roof of a jail was the only one that had sheltered him for many months. He slept under archways, and in brickfields – anywhere, where there was some warmth or shelter from the cold and rain. But in the last stage of poverty, disease, and houseless want, he was a drunkard still.

At last, one bitter night, he sunk down on a door-step faint and ill. The premature decay of vice and profligacy had worn him to the bone. His cheeks were hollow and livid; his eyes were sunken, and their sight was dim. His legs trembled beneath his weight, and a cold shiver ran through every limb.

And now the long-forgotten scenes of a misspent life crowded thick and fast upon him. He thought of the time when he had a home – a happy, cheerful home – and of those who peopled it, and flocked about him then, until the forms of his elder children seemed to rise from the grave, and stand about him – so plain, so clear, and so distinct they were that he could touch and feel them. Looks that he had long forgotten were fixed upon him once more; voices long since hushed in death sounded in his ears like the music of village bells. But it was only for an instant. The rain beat heavily upon him; and cold and hunger were gnawing at his heart again.

He rose, and dragged his feeble limbs a few paces further. The street was silent and empty; the few passengers who passed by, at that late hour, hurried quickly on, and his tremulous voice was lost in the violence of the storm. Again that heavy chill struck through his frame, and his blood seemed to stagnate beneath it. He coiled himself up in a projecting doorway, and tried to sleep.

But sleep had fled from his dull and glazed eyes. His mind wandered strangely, but he was awake, and conscious. The well-known shout of drunken mirth sounded in his ear, the glass was at his lips, the board was covered with choice rich food – they were before him: he could see them all, he had but to reach out his hand, and take them – and, though the illusion was reality itself, he knew that he was sitting alone in the deserted street, watching the rain-drops as they pattered on the stones; that death was coming upon him by inches – and that there were none to care for or help him.

Suddenly he started up, in the extremity of terror. He had heard his own voice shouting in the night air, he knew not what, or why. Hark! A groan! – another! His senses were leaving him: half-formed and incoherent words burst from his lips; and his hands sought to tear and lacerate his flesh. He was going mad, and he shrieked for help till his voice failed him.

He raised his head, and looked up the long dismal street. He recollected that outcasts like himself, condemned to wander day and night in those dreadful streets, had sometimes gone distracted with their own loneliness. He remembered to have heard many years before that a homeless wretch had once been found in a solitary corner, sharpening a rusty knife to plunge into his own heart, preferring death to that endless, weary, wandering to and fro. In an instant his resolve was taken, his limbs received new life; he ran quickly from the spot, and paused not for breath until he reached the river-side.

He crept softly down the steep stone stairs that lead from the commencement of Waterloo Bridge, down to the water's level. He crouched into a corner, and held his breath, as the patrol passed. Never did prisoner's heart throb with the hope of liberty and life half so eagerly as did that of the wretched man at the prospect of death. The watch passed close to him, but he remained unobserved; and after waiting till the sound of footsteps had died away in the distance, he cautiously descended, and stood beneath the gloomy arch that forms the landing-place from the river.

The tide was in, and the water flowed at his feet. The rain had ceased, the wind was lulled, and all was, for the moment, still and quiet – so quiet, that the slightest sound on the opposite bank, even the rippling of the water against the barges that were moored there, was distinctly audible to his ear. The stream stole languidly and sluggishly on. Strange and fantastic forms rose to the surface, and beckoned him to approach; dark gleaming eyes peered from the water, and seemed to mock his hesitation, while hollow murmurs from behind urged him onwards. He retreated a few paces, took a short run, desperate leap, and plunged into the river.

Not five seconds had passed when he rose to the water's surface – but what a change had taken place in that short time, in all his thoughts and feelings! Life – life in any form, poverty, misery, starvation – anything but death. He fought and struggled with the water that closed over his head, and screamed in agonies of terror. The curse of his own son rang in his ears. The shore – but one foot of dry ground – he could almost touch the step. One hand's breadth nearer, and he was saved – but the tide bore him onward, under the dark arches of the bridge, and he sank to the bottom.

Again he rose, and struggled for life. For one instant – for one brief instant – the buildings on the river's banks, the lights on the bridge through which the current had borne him, the black water, and the fast-flying clouds, were distinctly visible – once more he sunk, and once again he rose. Bright flames of fire shot up from earth to heaven, and reeled before his eyes, while the water thundered in his ears, and stunned him with its furious roar.

A week afterwards the body was washed ashore, some miles down the river, a swollen and disfigured mass. Unrecognised and unpitied, it was borne to the grave; and there it has long since mouldered away!

[THREE]

The Automaton Police

MR CRINKLES exhibited a most beautiful and delicate machine, of little larger size than an ordinary snuff-box, manufactured entirely by himself, and composed exclusively of steel, by the aid of which more pockets could be picked in one hour than by the present slow and tedious process in four-and-twenty. The inventor remarked that it had been put into active operation in Fleet Street, the Strand, and other thoroughfares, and had never been once known to fail.

After some slight delay, occasioned by the various members of the section buttoning their pockets,

THE PRESIDENT narrowly inspected the invention, and declared that he had never seen a machine of more beautiful or exquisite construction. Would the inventor be good enough to inform the section whether he had taken any and what means for bringing it into general operation?

MR CRINKLES stated that, after encountering some preliminary difficulties, he had succeeded in putting himself in communication with Mr Fogle Hunter, and other gentlemen connected with the swell mob, who had awarded the invention the very highest and most unqualified approbation. He regretted to say, however, that these distinguished practitioners, in common with a gentleman of the name of Gimlet-eyed Tommy, and other members of a secondary grade of the profession whom he was understood to represent, entertained an insuperable objection to its being brought into general use, on the ground that it would have the inevitable effect of almost entirely superseding manual labour, and throwing a great number of highly-deserving persons out of employment.

THE PRESIDENT hoped that no such fanciful objections would be allowed to stand in the way of such a great public improvement.

MR CRINKLES hoped so too; but he feared that if the gentlemen of the swell mob persevered in their objection, nothing could be done.

PROFESSOR GRIME suggested, that surely, in that case, Her Majesty's Government might be prevailed upon to take it up.

MR CRINKLES said, that if the objection were found to be insuperable he should apply to Parliament, which he thought could not fail to recognise the utility of the invention.

THE PRESIDENT observed that, up to this time Parliament had certainly got on very well without it; but, as they did their business on a very large scale, he had no doubt they would gladly adopt the improvement. His only fear was that the machine might be worn out by constant working.

MR COPPERNOSE called the attention of the section to a proposition of great magnitude and interest, illustrated by a vast number of models, and stated with much clearness and perspicuity in a treatise entitled 'Practical Suggestions on the necessity of providing some harmless and wholesome relaxation for the young noblemen of England.' His proposition was, that a space of ground of not less than ten miles in length and four in breadth should be purchased by a new company, to be incorporated by Act of Parliament, and inclosed by a brick wall of not less than twelve feet in height. He proposed that it should be laid out with highway roads, turnpikes, bridges, miniature villages, and every object that could conduce to the comfort and glory of Four-in-hand Clubs, so that they might be fairly presumed to require no drive beyond it. This delightful retreat would be fitted up with most commodious and extensive stables, for the convenience of such of the nobility and gentry as had a taste for ostlering, and with houses of entertainment furnished in the most expensive and handsome style. It would be further provided with whole streets of door-knockers and bell-handles of extra size, so constructed that they could be easily wrenched off at night, and regularly screwed on again, by attendants provided for the purpose, every day. There would also be gas lamps of real glass, which

'The Automaton Police Office, and Real Offenders' by George Cruikshank

could be broken at a comparatively small expense per dozen, and a broad and handsome foot pavement for gentlemen to drive their cabriolets upon when they were humorously disposed – for the full enjoyment of which feat live pedestrians would be procured from the workhouse at a very small charge per head. The place being inclosed, and carefully screened from the intrusion of the public, there would be no objection to gentlemen laying aside any article of their costume that was considered to interfere with a pleasant frolic, or, indeed, to their walking about without any costume at all, if they liked that better. In short, every facility of enjoyment would be afforded that the most gentlemanly person could possibly desire. But as even these advantages would be incomplete unless there were some means provided of enabling the nobility and gentry to display their prowess when they sallied forth after dinner, and as some inconvenience might be experienced in the event of their being reduced to the necessity of pummelling each other, the inventor had turned his attention to the construction of an entirely new police force, composed exclusively of automaton figures, which, with the assistance of the ingenious Signor Gagliardi, of Windmill-street, in the Haymarket, he had succeeded in making with such nicety, that a policeman, cab-driver, or old woman, made upon the principle of the models exhibited, would walk about until knocked down like any real man; nay, more, if set upon and beaten by six or eight noblemen or gentlemen, after it was down, the figure would utter divers groans, mingled with entreaties for mercy, thus rendering the illusion complete, and the enjoyment perfect. But the invention did not stop even here; for station-houses would be built, containing good beds for noblemen and gentlemen during the night, and in the morning they would repair to a commodious police office, where a pantomimic investigation would take place before the automaton magistrates, – quite equal to life, – who would fine them in so many counters, with which they would be previously provided for the purpose. This office would be furnished with an inclined plane, for the convenience of any nobleman or gentleman who might wish to bring in his horse as a witness; and the prisoners would be at perfect liberty, as they were now, to interrupt the complainants as much as they pleased, and to make any remarks that they thought proper. The charge for these amusements would amount to very little more than they already cost, and the inventor submitted that the public would be much benefited and comforted by the proposed arrangement.

PROFESSOR NOGO wished to be informed what amount of automaton police force it was proposed to raise in the first instance.

MR COPPERNOSE replied, that it was proposed to begin with seven divisions of police of a score each, lettered from A to G inclusive. It was proposed that not more than half this number should be placed on active duty, and that the remainder should be kept on shelves in the police office ready to be called out at a moment's notice.

THE PRESIDENT, awarding the utmost merit to the ingenious gentleman who had originated the idea, doubted whether the automaton police would quite answer the purpose. He feared that noblemen and gentlemen would perhaps require the excitement of threshing living subjects.

MR COPPERNOSE submitted, that as the usual odds in such cases were ten noblemen or gentlemen to one policeman or cab-driver, it could make very little difference in point of excitement whether the policeman or cab-driver were a man or a block. The great advantage would be, that a policeman's limbs might be all knocked off, and yet he would be in a condition to do duty next day. He might even give his evidence next morning with his head in his hand, and give it equally well.

PROFESSOR MUFF. – Will you allow me to ask you, sir, of what materials it is intended that the magistrates' heads shall be composed?

MR COPPERNOSE. – The magistrates will have wooden heads of course, and they will be made of the toughest and thickest materials that can possibly be obtained.

PROFESSOR MUFF. – I am quite satisfied. This is a great invention.

PROFESSOR NOGO. – I see but one objection to it. It appears to me that the magistrates ought to talk.

MR COPPERNOSE no sooner heard this suggestion than he touched a small spring in each of the two models of magistrates which were placed upon the table; one of the figures immediately began to exclaim with great volubility that he was sorry to see gentlemen in such a situation, and the other to express a fear that the policeman was intoxicated.

The section, as with one accord, declared with a shout of applause that the invention was complete; and the President, much excited, retired with Mr Coppernose to lay it before the council.

FOUR

The Modern Science of Thief-Taking

If thieving be an Art (and who denies that its more subtle and delicate branches deserve to be ranked as one of the Fine Arts?), thief-taking is a Science. All the thief's ingenuity; all his knowledge of human nature; all his courage; all his coolness; all his imperturbable powers of face; all his nice discrimination in reading the countenances of other people; all his manual and digital dexterity; all his fertility in expedients, and promptitude in acting upon them; all his Protean cleverness of disguise and capability of counterfeiting every sort and condition of distress; together with a great deal more patience, and the additional qualification, integrity, are demanded for the higher branches of thief-taking.

If an urchin picks your pocket, or a bungling 'artist' steals your watch so that you find it out in an instant, it is easy enough for any private in any of the seventeen divisions of London Police to obey your panting demand to 'Stop thief!' But the tricks and contrivances of those who wheedle money out of your pocket rather than steal it; who cheat you with your eyes open; who clear every vestige of plate out of your pantry while your servant is on the stairs; who set up imposing warehouses, and ease respectable firms of large parcels of goods; who steal the acceptances of needy or dissipated young men; – for the detection and punishment of such impostors a superior order of police is requisite.

To each division of the Force is attached two officers, who are de-nominated 'detectives.' The staff, or head-quarters, consists of six sergeants and two inspectors. Thus the Detective Police, of which we hear so much, consists of only forty-two individuals, whose duty it is to wear no uniform, and to perform the most difficult operations of their craft. They have not only to counteract the machinations of every sort of rascal whose only means of existence is avowed rascality, but to clear up family mysteries, the investigation of which demands the utmost delicacy and tact.

One instance will show the difference between a regular and a detective policeman. Your wife discovers on retiring for the night, that her toilette has been plundered; her drawers are void; except the ornaments she now wears, her beauty is as unadorned as that of a quakeress: not a thing is left; all the fond tokens you gave her when her pre-nuptial lover, are gone; your own miniature, with its setting of gold and brilliants; her late mother's diamonds; the bracelets 'dear papa' presented on her last birth-day; the top of every bottle in the dressing-case brought from Paris by Uncle John, at the risk of his life, in February 1848, are off – but the glasses remain. Every valuable is swept away with the most discriminating villainy; for no other thing in the chamber has been touched; not a chair has been moved; the costly pendule on the chimney-piece still ticks; the entire apartment is as neat and trim as when it had received the last finishing sweep of the housemaid's duster. The entire establishment runs frantically up stairs and down stairs; and finally congregates in my Lady's Chamber. Nobody knows anything whatever about it; yet everybody offers a suggestion, although they have not an idea 'who ever did it.' The housemaid bursts into tears; the cook declares she thinks she is going into hysterics; and at last you suggest sending for the Police; which is taken as a suspicion of, and insult on the whole assembled household, and they descend into the lower regions of the house in the sulks.

X 49 arrives. His face betrays sheepishness, combined with mystery. He turns his bull's-eye into every corner, and upon every countenance (including that of the cat), on the premises. He examines all the locks, bolts, and bars, bestowing extra diligence on those which enclosed the stolen treasures. These he declares have been 'Wiolated;' by which he means that there has been more than one 'Rape of the Lock.' He then mentions about the non-disturbance of other valuables; takes you solemnly aside, darkens his lantern, and asks if you suspect any of your

London police officers almost overwhelmed by crime and
criminals – an illustration by Phiz

servants, in a mysterious whisper, which implies that *he* does. He then
examines the upper bedrooms, and in that of the female servants he
discovers the least valuable of the rings, and a cast-off silver tooth-pick
between the mattresses. You have every confidence in your maids; but
what *can* you think? You suggest their safe custody; but your wife
intercedes, and the policeman would prefer speaking to his inspector
before he locks anybody up.

Had the whole matter remained in the hands of X 49, it is possible
that your troubles would have lasted you till now. A train of legal proceedings – actions for defamation of character and suits for damages –
would have followed, which would have cost more than the value of
the jewels, and the entire execration of all your neighbours and every
private friend of your domestics. But, happily, the Inspector promptly
sends a plain, earnest-looking man, who announces himself as one of
the two Detectives of the X division. He settles the whole matter in ten
minutes. His examination is ended in five. As a connoisseur can determine the painter of a picture at the first glance, or a wine-taster the
precise vintage of a sherry by the merest sip; so the Detective at once
pounces upon the authors of the work of art under consideration, by

the style of performance; if not upon the precise executant, upon the 'school' to which he belongs. Having finished the toilette branch of the inquiry, he takes a short view of the parapet of your house, and makes an equally cursory investigation of the attic window fastenings. His mind is made up, and most likely he will address you in these words: –

'All right, Sir. This is done by one of "The Dancing School!"'

'Good Heavens!' exclaims your plundered partner. 'Impossible, why *our* children go to Monsieur Pettitoes, of No. 81, and I assure you he is a highly respectable professor. As to his pupils, I –'

The Detective smiles and interrupts. 'Dancers,' he tells her, 'is a name given to the sort of burglar by whom she had been robbed; and every branch of the thieving profession is divided into gangs, which are termed "Schools."' From No. 82 to the end of the street the houses are unfinished. The thief made his way to the top of one of these, and crawled to your garret –'

'But we are forty houses distant, and why did he not favour one of my neighbours with his visit?' you ask.

'Either their uppermost stories are not so practicable, or the ladies have not such valuable jewels.'

'But how do they know that?'

'By watching and inquiry. This affair may have been in action for more than a month. Your house has been watched; your habits ascertained; they have found out when you dine – how long you remain in the dining-room. A day is selected; while you are busy dining, and your servants busy waiting on you, the thing is done. Previously, many journeys have been made over the roofs, to find out the best means of entering your house. The attic is chosen; the robber gets in, and creeps noiselessly, or "dances" into the place to be robbed.'

'Is there *any* chance of recovering our property?' you ask anxiously, seeing the whole matter at a glance.

'I hope so. I have sent some brother officers to watch the Fences' houses.'

'Fences?'

'Fences,' explains the Detective, in reply to your innocent wife's inquiry, 'are purchasers of stolen goods. Your jewels will be forced out of their settings, and the gold melted.'

The lady tries, ineffectually, to suppress a slight scream.

'We shall see, if, at this unusual hour of the night, there is any bustle in or near any of these places; if any smoke is coming out of any one of their furnaces, where the melting takes place. *I* shall go and seek out the precise "garretter" – that's another name these plunderers give themselves – whom I suspect. By his trying to "sell" your domestics by placing the ring and tooth-pick in their bed, I think I know the man. It is just in his style.'

The next morning, you find all these suppositions verified. The Detective calls, and obliges you at breakfast – after a sleepless night – with a complete list of the stolen articles, and produces some of them for identification. In three months, your wife gets nearly every article back; her damsels' innocence is fully established; and the thief is taken from his 'school' to spend a long holiday in a penal colony.

This is a mere common-place transaction, compared with the achievements of the staff of the little army of Detective policemen at headquarters. Sometimes they are called upon to investigate robberies; so executed, that no human ingenuity appears to ordinary observers capable of finding the thief. He leaves not a trail or a trace. Every clue seems cut off; but the experience of a Detective guides him into tracks quite invisible to other eyes. Not long since, a trunk was rifled at a fashionable hotel. The theft was so managed, that no suspicion could rest on any one. The Detective sergeant who had been sent for, fairly owned, after making a minute examination of the case, that he could afford no hope of elucidating the mystery. As he was leaving the bed-room, however, in which the plundered portmanteau stood, he picked up an ordinary shirt-button from the carpet. He silently compared it with those on the shirts in the trunk. It did not match them. He said nothing, but hung about the hotel for the rest of the day. Had he been narrowly watched, he would have been set down for an eccentric critic of linen. He was looking out for a shirt-front or wristband without a button. His search was long and patient; but at length it was rewarded. One of the inmates of the house showed a deficiency in his dress, which no one but a Detective would have noticed. He looked as narrowly as he dared at the pattern of the remaining fasteners. It corresponded with that of the little tell-tale he had picked up. He went deeper into the subject, got a trace of some of the stolen property, ascertained a connexion between it and the suspected person, confronted him with the owner of the trunk, and finally succeeded in convicting him of the theft. – At another hotel-robbery, the blade of a knife, broken in the lock of a portmanteau, formed the clue. The Detective employed in that case was for some time indefatigable in seeking out knives with broken blades. At length he found one belonging to an under-waiter, who proved to have been the thief.

The swell mob – the London branch of which is said to consist of from one hundred and fifty to two hundred members – demand the greatest amount of vigilance to detect. They hold the first place in the 'profession.'

Their cleverness consists in evading the law; the most expert are seldom taken. One 'swell,' named Mo. Clark, had an iniquitous career of a quarter of a century, and never was captured during that time. He died a 'prosperous gentleman' at Boulogne, whither he had retired to live on his 'savings,' which he had invested in house property. An old hand named White lived unharmed to the age of eighty; but he had not been prudent, and existed on the contributions of the 'mob,' till his old acquaintances were taken away, either by transportation or death, and the new race did not recognise his claims to their bounty. Hence he died in a workhouse. The average run of liberty which one of this class counts upon is four years.

The gains of some of the swell mob are great. They can always command capital to execute any especial scheme. Their travelling expenses are large; for their harvests are great public occasions, whether in town or country. As an example of their profits, the exploits of four of them at the Liverpool Cattle Show some seven years ago, may be mentioned. The London Detective Police did not attend, but one of them waylaid the rogues at the Euston Station. After an attendance of four days, the gentlemen he was looking for appeared, handsomely attired, the occupants of first-class carriages. The Detective, in the quietest manner possible, stopped their luggage; they entreated him to treat them like 'gentlemen.' He did so, and took them into a private room, where they were so good as to offer him fifty pounds to let them go. He declined, and over-hauled their booty; it consisted of several gold pins, watches, (some of great value,) chains and rings, silver snuff-boxes, and bank-notes of the value of one hundred pounds! Eventually, however, as owners could not be found for some of the property, and some others would not prosecute, they escaped with a light punishment.

In order to counteract the plans of the swell mob, two of the sergeants of the Detective Police make it their business to know every one of them personally. The consequence is, that the appearance of either of these officers upon any scene of operations is a bar to anything or anybody being 'done.' This is an excellent characteristic of the Detectives, for they thus become as well a Preventive Police. We will give an illustration: –

You are at the Oxford commemoration. As you descend the broad stairs of the Roebuck to dine, you overtake on the landing a gentleman of foreign aspect and elegant attire. The variegated pattern of his vest, the jetty gloss of his boots, and the exceeding whiteness of his gloves – one of which he crushes in his somewhat delicate hand – convince you that he is going to the grand ball, to be given that evening at Merton. The glance he gives you while passing, is sharp, but comprehensive; and if his eye does rest upon any one part of your person and its accessories more than another, it is upon the gold watch which you have just taken out to see if dinner be 'due.' As you step aside to make room for him, he acknowledges the courtesy with 'Par-r-r-don,' in the richest Parisian *gros parle*, and a smile so full of intelligence and courtesy, that you hope he speaks English, for you set him down as an agreeable fellow, and mentally determine that if he dines in the Coffeeroom, you will make his acquaintance.

On the mat at the stair-foot there stands a man. A plain, honest-looking fellow, with nothing formidable in his appearance, or dreadful in his countenance; but the effect his apparition takes on your friend in perspective, is remarkable. The poor little fellow raises himself on his toes, as if he had been suddenly overbalanced by a bullet; his cheek pales, and his lip quivers, as he endeavours ineffectually to suppress the word '*coquin!*' He knows it is too late to turn back (he evidently would, if he could), for the man's eye is upon him. There is no help for it, and he speaks first; but in a whisper. He takes the new comer aside, and all you can overhear is spoken by the latter, who says he insists on Monsieur withdrawing his 'School' by the seven o'clock train.

You imagine him to be some poor wretch of a schoolmaster in difficulties; captured, alas, by a bailiff. They leave the inn together, perhaps for a sponging house. So acute is your pity, that you think of rushing after them, and offering bail. You are, however very hungry, and, at this moment, the waiter announces that dinner is on table.

In the opposite box there are covers for four, but only three convives. They seem quiet men – not gentlemen, decidedly, but well enough behaved.

'What has become of Monsieur?' asks one. None of them can divine.

'Shall we wait any longer for him?'

'Oh, no – Waiter – Dinner!'

By their manner, you imagine that the style of the Roebuck is a 'cut above them.' They have not been much used to plate. The silver forks are so curiously heavy, that one of the guests, in a dallying sort of way, balances a prong across his fingers, while the chasing of the castors engages the attention of a second. This is all done while they talk. When the fish is brought, the third casts a careless glance or two at the dish cover, and when the waiter has gone for the sauce, he taps it with his nails, and says enquiringly to his friend across the table, 'Silver?'

The other shakes his head, and intimates a hint that it is *only* plated. The waiter brings the cold punch, and the party begin to enjoy themselves. They do not drink much, but they mix their drinks rather injudiciously. They take sherry upon cold punch, and champagne upon that, dashing in a little port and bottled stout between. They are getting merry, not to say jolly, but not at all inebriated. The amateur of silver dish-covers has told a capital story, and his friends are revelling in the heartiest of laughs, when an apparition appears at the end of the table. You never saw such a change as his presence causes, when he places his knuckles on the edge of the table and looks at the diners *seriatim*; the courtiers of the sleeping beauty suddenly struck somniferous were nothing to this change. As if by magic, the loud laugh is turned to silent consternation. You now, most impressively, understand the meaning of the term 'dumbfoundered.' The mysterious stranger makes some enquiry about 'any cash?'

The answer is 'Plenty.'

'All square with the landlord, then?' asks the same inflexible voice as – to my astonishment – that which put the Frenchman to the torture.

'To a penny,' the reply.

'*Quite* square?' continues the querist, taking with his busy eye a rapid inventory of the plate.

'S' help me – '

'Hush!' interrupts the dinner spoiler, holding up his hand in a cautionary manner. 'Have you done anything to-day?'

'Not a thing.'

Then there is some more in a low tone; but you again distinguish the word 'school,' and 'seven o'clock train.' They are too old to be the Frenchman's pupils; perhaps they are his assistants. Surely they are not all the victims of the same *capias* and the same officer!

By this time the landlord, looking very nervous, arrives with his bill: then comes the head waiter, who clears the table; carefully counting the forks. The reckoning is paid, and the trio steal out of the room with the man of mystery behind them, – like sheep driven to the shambles.

You follow to the Railway station, and there you see the Frenchman, who complains bitterly of being 'sold for nothing' by his enemy. The other three utter a confirmative groan. In spite of the evident omnipotence of their persevering follower, your curiosity impels you to address him. You take a turn on the platform together, and he explains the whole mystery. 'The fact is,' he begins, 'I am Sergeant Witchem, of the Detective police.'

'And your four victims are?' –

'Members of a crack school of swell-mobsmen.'

'What do you mean by "school"?'

'Gang. There is a variety of gangs – that is to say, of men who 'work' together, who play into one another's hands. These gentlemen hold the first rank, both for skill and enterprise, and had they been allowed to remain would have brought back a considerable booty. Their chief is the Frenchman.'

'Why do they obey your orders so passively?'

'Because they are sure that if I were to take them into custody, which I could do, knowing what they are, and present them before a magistrate, they would all be committed to prison for a month, as rogues and vagabonds.'

'They prefer then to have lost no inconsiderable capital in dress and dinner, to being laid up in jail.'

'Exactly so.'

The bell rings, and all five go off into the same carriage to London.

This is a circumstance that actually occurred; and a similar one happened when the Queen went to Dublin. The mere appearance of one of the Detective officers before a 'school' which had transported itself in the Royal train, spoilt their speculation; for they all found it more advantageous to return to England in the same steamer with the officer, than to remain with the certainty of being put in prison for fourteen or twenty-eight days as rogues and vagabonds.

So thoroughly well acquainted with these men are the Detective officers we speak of, that they frequently tell what they have been about by the expression of their eyes and their general manner. This process is aptly termed 'reckoning them up.' Some days ago, two skilful officers, whose personal acquaintance with the swell mob is complete, were walking along the Strand on other business, when they saw two of the best dressed and best mannered of the gang enter a jeweller's shop. They waited till they came out, and, on scrutinising them, were convinced, by a certain conscious look which they betrayed, that they had stolen something. They followed them, and in a few minutes something was passed from one to the other. The officers were convinced, challenged them with the theft, and succeeded in eventually convicting them of stealing two gold eye-glasses, and several jewelled rings. 'The eye,' said our informant, 'is the great detector. We can tell in a crowd what a swell-mobsman is about by the expression of his eye.'

It is supposed that the number of persons who make a trade of thieving in London is not more than six thousand; of these, nearly two hundred are first-class thieves or swell-mobsmen; six hundred 'macemen,' and trade swindlers, bill-swindlers, dog-stealers, &c.; About forty burglars, 'dancers,' 'garretteers,' and other adepts with the skeleton-keys. The rest are pickpockets, 'gonophs' – mostly young thieves who sneak into areas, and rob tills – and other pilferers.

To detect and circumvent this fraternity, is the science of thief-taking. Here, it is, however, impossible to give even an imperfect notion of the high amount of skill, intelligence, and knowledge, concentrated in the character of a clever Detective Policeman. We shall therefore furnish the sketch in another paper.

FIVE

A Detective Police Party

I

In pursuance of the intention mentioned at the close of a former paper on 'The Modern Science of Thief-taking,' we now proceed to endeavour to convey to our readers some faint idea of the extraordinary dexterity, patience, and ingenuity, exercised by the Detective Police. That our description may be as graphic as we can render it, and may be perfectly reliable, we will make it, so far as in us lies, a piece of plain truth. And first, we have to inform the reader how the anecdotes we are about to communicate, came to our knowledge.

We are not by any means devout believers in the Old Bow-Street Police. To say the truth, we think there was a vast amount of humbug about those worthies. Apart from many of them being men of very indifferent character, and far too much in the habit of consorting with thieves and the like, they never lost a public occasion of jobbing and trading in mystery and making the most of themselves. Continually puffed besides by incompetent magistrates anxious to conceal their own deficiencies, and hand-in-glove with the penny-a-liners of that time, they became a sort of superstition. Although as a Preventive Police they were utterly ineffective, and as a Detective Police were very loose and uncertain in their operations, they remain with some people, a superstition to the present day.

Police officers making an arrest in a London lodging house. Anonymous sketch

On the other hand, the Detective Force organised since the establishment of the existing Police, is so well chosen and trained, proceeds so systematically and quietly, does its business in such a workman-like manner, and is always so calmly and steadily engaged in the service of the public, that the public really do not know enough of it, to know a tithe of its usefulness. Impressed with this conviction, and interested in the men themselves, we represented to the authorities at Scotland Yard, that we should be glad, if there were no official objection, to have some talk with the Detectives. A most obliging and ready permission being given, a certain evening was appointed with a certain Inspector for a social conference between ourselves and the Detectives, at our Office in Wellington Street, Strand, London. In consequence of which appointment the party 'came off,' which we are about to describe. And we beg to repeat that, avoiding such topics as it might for obvious reasons be injurious to the public, or disagreeable to respectable individuals, to touch upon in print, our description is as exact as we can make it.

The reader will have the goodness to imagine the Sanctum Sanctorum of Household Words. Anything that best suits the reader's fancy, will best represent that magnificent chamber. We merely stipulate for a round table in the middle, with some glasses and cigars arranged upon it; and the editorial sofa elegantly hemmed in between that stately piece of furniture and the wall.

It is a sultry evening at dusk. The stones of Wellington Street are hot and gritty, and the watermen and hackney-coachmen at the Theatre opposite, are much flushed and aggravated. Carriages are constantly setting down the people who have come to Fairy-Land; and there is a mighty shouting and bellowing every now and then, deafening us for the moment, through the open windows.

Just at dusk, Inspectors Wield and Stalker are announced; but we do not undertake to warrant the orthography of any of the names here mentioned. Inspector Wield presents Inspector Stalker. Inspector Wield is a middle-aged man of a portly presence, with a large, moist, knowing eye, a husky voice, and a habit of emphasising his conversation by the aid of a corpulent fore-finger, which is constantly in juxta-position with his eyes or nose. Inspector Stalker is a shrewd, hard-headed Scotchman – in appearance not at all unlike a very acute, thoroughly-trained schoolmaster, from the Normal Establishment at Glasgow. Inspector Wield one might have known, perhaps, for what he is – Inspector Stalker, never.

The ceremonies of reception over, Inspectors Wield and Stalker observe that they have brought some sergeants with them. The sergeants are presented – five in number, Sergeant Dornton, Sergeant Witchem, Sergeant Mith, Sergeant Fendall, and Sergeant Straw. We have the whole Detective Force from Scotland Yard with one exception. They sit down in a semi-circle (the two Inspectors at the two ends) at a little distance from the round table, facing the editorial sofa. Every man of them, in a glance, immediately takes an inventory of the furniture and an accurate sketch of the editorial presence. The Editor feels that any gentleman in company could take him up, if need should be, without the smallest hesitation, twenty years hence.

The whole party are in plain clothes. Sergeant Dornton, about fifty years of age, with a ruddy face and a high sun-burnt forehead, has the air of one who has been a Sergeant in the army – he might have sat to Wilkie for the Soldier in the Reading of the Will. He is famous for steadily pursuing the inductive process, and, from small beginnings, working on from clue to clue until he bags his man. Sergeant Witchem, shorter and thicker-set, and marked with the small pox, has something of a reserved and thoughtful air, as if he were engaged in deep arithmetical calculations. He is renowned for his acquaintance with the swell mob. Sergeant Mith, a smooth-faced man with a fresh bright complexion, and a strange air of simplicity, is a dab at housebreakers. Sergeant Fendall, a light-haired, well-spoken, polite person, is a prodigious hand at pursuing private inquiries of a delicate nature. Straw, a little wiry Sergeant of meek demeanour and strong sense, would knock at a door and ask a series of questions in any mild character you chose to prescribe to him, from a charity-boy upwards, and seem as innocent as an infant. They are, one and all, respectable-looking men; of perfectly good deportment and unusual intelligence; with nothing lounging or slinking in their manners; with an air of keen observation, and quick perception when addressed; and generally presenting in their faces, traces more or less marked of habitually leading lives of strong mental excitement. They have all good eyes; and they all can, and they all do, look full at whomsoever they speak to.

We light the cigars, and hand round the glasses (which are very temperately used indeed), and the conversation begins by a modest amateur reference on the Editorial part to the swell mob. Inspector Wield immediately removes his cigar from his lips, waves his right hand, and says, 'Regarding the Swell Mob, Sir, I can't do better than call upon Sergeant Witchem. Because the reason why? I'll tell you. Sergeant Witchem is better acquainted with the Swell mob than any officer in London.'

Our heart leaping up when we beheld this rainbow in the sky, we turn to Sergeant Witchem, who very concisely, and in well-chosen language, goes into the subject forthwith. Meantime, the whole of his brother officers are closely interested in attending to what he says, and observing its effect. Presently they begin to strike in, one or two together, when an opportunity offers, and the conversation becomes general. But these brother officers only come in to the assistance of each other – not to the contradiction – and a more amicable brotherhood there could not be. From the swell mob, we diverge to the kindred topics of cracksmen, fences, public-house dancers, area-sneaks, designing young people who go out 'gonophing,' and other 'schools,' to which our readers have already been introduced. It is observable throughout these revelations, that Inspector Stalker, the Scotchman, is always exact and statistical, and that when any question of figures arises, everybody as by one consent pauses, and looks to him.

When we have exhausted the various schools of Art – during which discussion the whole body have remained profoundly attentive, except when some unusual noise at the Theatre over the way has induced some gentleman to glance inquiringly towards the window in that direction, behind his next neighbour's back – we burrow for information on such points as the following. Whether there really are any highway robberies in London, or whether some circumstances not convenient to be mentioned by the aggrieved party, usually precede the robberies complained of, under that head, which quite change their character? Certainly the latter, almost always. Whether in the case of robberies in houses, where servants are necessarily exposed to doubt, innocence under suspicion ever becomes so like guilt in appearance, that a good officer need be cautious how he judges it? Undoubtedly. Nothing is so common or deceptive as such appearances at first. Whether in a place of public amusement, a thief knows an officer, and an officer knows a thief, – supposing them, beforehand, strangers to each other – because each recognises in the other, under all disguise, an inattention to what is going on, and a purpose that is not the purpose of being entertained? Yes. That's the way exactly. Whether it is reasonable or ridiculous to trust to the alleged experiences of thieves as narrated by themselves, in prisons, or penitentiaries, or anywhere? In general, nothing more absurd. Lying is their habit and their trade; and they would rather lie – even if they hadn't an interest in it, and didn't want to make themselves agreeable – than tell the truth.

From these topics, we glide into a review of the most celebrated and horrible of the great crimes that have been committed within the last fifteen or twenty years. The men engaged in the discovery of almost all of them, and in the pursuit or apprehension of the murderers, are here, down to the very last instance. One of our guests gave chase to and boarded the Emigrant Ship, in which the murderess last hanged in London was supposed to have embarked. We learn from him that his errand was not announced to the passengers, who may have no idea of it to this hour. That he went below, with the captain, lamp in hand – it being dark, and the whole steerage abed and seasick – and engaged the Mrs Manning who *was* on board, in a conversation about her luggage, until she was, with no small pains, induced to raise her head, and turn her face towards the light. Satisfied that she was not the object of his search, he quietly re-embarked in the Government steamer alongside, and steamed home again with the intelligence.

When we have exhausted these subjects, too, which occupy a considerable time in the discussion, two or three leave their chairs, whisper Sergeant Witchem, and resume their seats. Sergeant Witchem, leaning forward a little, and placing a hand on each of his legs, then modestly speaks as follows:

'My brother-officers wish me to relate a little account of my taking Tally-ho Thompson. A man oughtn't to tell what he has done himself; but still, as nobody was with me, and, consequently, as nobody but myself can tell it, I'll do it in the best way I can, if it should meet your approval.'

We assure Sergeant Witchem that he will oblige us very much, and we all compose ourselves to listen with great interest and attention.

'Tally-ho Thompson,' says Sergeant Witchem, after merely wetting his lips with his brandy-and-water, 'Tally-ho Thompson was a famous horse-stealer, couper, and magsman. Thompson, in conjunction with a pal that occasionally worked with him, gammoned a countryman out of a good round sum of money, under pretence of getting him a situation – the regular old dodge – and was afterwards in the "Hue and Cry" for a horse – a horse that he stole, down in Hertfordshire. I had to look after Thompson, and I applied myself, of course, in the first instance, to discovering where he was. Now, Thompson's wife lived, along with a little daughter, at Chelsea. Knowing that Thompson was somewhere in the country, I watched the house – especially at post-time in the morning – thinking Thompson was pretty likely to write to her. Sure enough, one morning the postman comes up, and delivers a letter at Mrs Thompson's door. Little girl opens the door, and takes it in. We're not always sure of postmen, though the people at the post-offices are always very obliging. A postman may help us, or he may not, – just as it happens. However, I go across the road, and I say to the postman, after he has left the letter, "Good morning! how are you?" "How are *you*?" says he. "You've just delivered a letter for Mrs Thompson." "Yes, I have." "You didn't happen to remark what the post-mark was, perhaps?" "No," says he, "I didn't." "Come," says I, "I'll be plain with you. I'm in a small way of business, and I have given Thompson credit, and I can't afford to lose what he owes me. I know he's got money, and I know he's in the country, and if you could tell me what the post-mark was, I should be very much obliged to you, and you'd do a service to a tradesman in a small way of business that can't afford a loss." "Well," he said, "I do assure you that I did not observe what the post-mark was; all I know is, that there was money in the letter – I should say a sovereign." This was enough for me, because of course I knew that Thompson having sent his wife money, it was probable she'd write to Thompson, by return of post, to acknowledge the receipt. So I said "Thankee" to the postman, and I kept on the watch. In the afternoon I saw the little girl come out. Of course I followed her. She went into a stationer's shop, and I needn't say to you that I looked in at the window. She bought some writing-paper and envelopes, and a pen. I think to myself, "That'll do!" – watch her home again – and don't go away, you may be sure, knowing that Mrs Thompson was writing her

letter to Tally-ho, and that the letter would be posted presently. In about
an hour or so, out came the little girl again, with the letter in her hand.
I went up, and said something to the child, whatever it might have
been; but I couldn't see the direction of the letter, because she held it
with the seal upwards. However, I observed that on the back of the
letter there was what we call a kiss – a drop of wax by the side of the
seal – and again, you understand, that was enough for me. I saw her
post the letter, waited till she was gone, then went into the shop, and
asked to see the Master. When he came out, I told him, "Now, I'm an
Officer in the Detective Force; there's a letter with a kiss been posted
here just now, for a man that I'm in search of; and what I have to ask
of you, is, that you will let me look at the direction of that letter." He
was very civil – took a lot of letters from the box in the window –
shook 'em out on the counter with the faces downwards – and there
among 'em was the identical letter with the kiss. It was directed,
Mr Thomas Pigeon, Post-Office, B———, to be left 'till called for.
Down I went to B——— (a hundred and twenty miles or so) that
night. Early next morning I went to the Post-Office; saw the gentleman
in charge of that department; told him who I was; and that my object
was to see, and track, the party that should come for the letter for
Mr Thomas Pigeon. He was very polite, and said, "You shall have
every assistance we can give you; you can wait inside the office; and
we'll take care to let you know when anybody comes for the letter."
Well, I waited there, three days, and began to think that nobody ever
would come. At last the clerk whispered to me, "Here! Detective! Somebody's come for the letter!" "Keep him a minute," said I, and I ran
round to the outside of the office. There I saw a young chap with the
appearance of an Ostler, holding a horse by the bridle – stretching the
bridle across the pavement, while he waited at the Post-Office Window
for the letter. I began to pat the horse, and that; and I said to the boy,
"Why, this is Mr Jones's Mare!" "No. It an't." "No?" said I. "She's
very like Mr Jones's Mare!" "She an't Mr Jones's Mare, anyhow,"
says he. "It's Mr So-and-So's, of the Warwick Arms." And up he jumped,
and off he went – letter and all. I got a cab, followed on the box, and
was so quick after him that I came into the stable-yard of the Warwick
Arms, by one gate, just as he came in by another. I went into the bar,
where there was a young woman serving, and called for a glass of

brandy-and-water. He came in directly, and handed her the letter. She casually looked at it, without saying anything, and stuck it up behind the glass over the chimney-piece. What was to be done next?

'I turned it over in my mind while I drank my brandy-and-water (looking pretty sharp at the letter the while), but I couldn't see my way out of it at all. I tried to get lodgings in the house, but there had been a horse-fair, or something of that sort, and it was full. I was obliged to put up somewhere else, but I came backwards and forwards to the bar for a couple of days, and there was the letter, always behind the glass. At last I thought I'd write a letter to Mr Pigeon myself, and see what that would do. So I wrote one, and posted it, but I purposely addressed it, Mr John Pigeon, instead of Mr Thomas Pigeon, to see what *that* would do. In the morning (a very wet morning it was) I watched the postman down the street, and cut into the bar, just before he reached the Warwick Arms. In he came presently with my letter. "Is there a Mr John Pigeon staying here?" "No! – stop a bit though," says the barmaid; and she took down the letter behind the glass. "No," says she, "it's Thomas, and *he* is not staying here. Would you do me a favor, and post this for me, as it is so wet?" The postman said Yes; she folded it in another envelope, directed it, and gave it him. He put it in his hat, and away he went.

'I had no difficulty in finding out the direction of that letter. It was addressed, Mr Thomas Pigeon, Post-Office, R———, Northampton-shire, to be left till called for. Off I started directly for R———; I said the same at the Post-Office there, as I had said at B———; and again I waited three days before anybody came. At last another chap on horse-back came. "Any letters for Mr Thomas Pigeon?" "Where do you come from?" "New Inn, near R———." He got the letter, and away *he* went – at a canter.

'I made my enquiries about the New Inn, near R———, and hear-ing it was a solitary sort of house, a little in the horse line, about a couple of miles from the station, I thought I'd go and have a look at it. I found it what it had been described, and sauntered in, to look about me. The landlady was in the bar, and I was trying to get into conver-sation with her; asked her how business was, and spoke about the wet weather, and so on; when I saw, through an open door, three men sitting by the fire in a sort of parlor, or kitchen; and one of those men, according to the description I had of him, was Tally-ho Thompson!

'I went and sat down among 'em, and tried to make things agreeable; but they were very shy – wouldn't talk at all – looked at me, and at one another, in a way quite the reverse of sociable. I reckoned 'em up, and finding that they were all three bigger men than me, and considering that their looks were ugly – that it was a lonely place – railroad station two miles off – and night coming on – thought I couldn't do better than have a drop of brandy-and-water to keep my courage up. So I called for my brandy-and-water; and as I was sitting drinking it by the fire, Thompson got up and went out.

'Now the difficulty of it was, that I wasn't sure it *was* Thompson, because I had never set eyes on him before; and what I had wanted was to be quite certain of him. However, there was nothing for it now, but to follow, and put a bold face upon it. I found him talking, outside in the yard, with the landlady. It turned out afterwards, that he was wanted by a Northampton officer for something else, and that, knowing that officer to be pock-marked (as I am myself), he mistook me for him. As I have observed, I found him talking to the landlady, outside. I put my hand upon his shoulder – this way – and said, "Tally-ho Thompson, it's no use. I know you. I'm an officer from London, and I take you into custody for felony!" "That be d——d!" says Tally-ho Thompson.

'We went back into the house, and the two friends began to cut up rough, and their looks didn't please me at all, I assure you. "Let the man go. What are you going to do with him?" "I'll tell you what I'm going to do with him. I'm going to take him to London to-night, as sure as I'm alive. I'm not alone here, whatever you may think. You mind your own business, and keep yourselves to yourselves. It'll be better for you, for I know you both very well." *I*'d never seen or heard of 'em in all my life, but my bouncing cowed 'em a bit, and they kept off, while Thompson was making ready to go. I thought to myself, however, that they might be coming after me on the dark road, to rescue Thompson; so I said to the landlady, "What men have you got in the house, Missis?" "We haven't got no men here," she says, sulkily. "You have got an ostler, I suppose?" "Yes, we've got an ostler." "Let me see him." Presently he came, and a shaggy-headed young fellow he was. "Now attend to me, young man," says I; "I'm a Detective Officer

from London. This man's name is Thompson. I have taken him into
custody for felony. I'm going to take him to the railroad station. I call
upon you in the Queen's name to assist me; and mind you, my friend,
you'll get yourself into more trouble than you know of, if you don't!"
You never saw a person open his eyes so wide. "Now, Thompson,
come along!" says I. But when I took out the handcuffs, Thompson
cries, "No! None of that! I won't stand *them*! I'll go along with you
quiet, but I won't bear none of that!" "Tally-ho Thompson," I said,
"I'm willing to behave as a man to you, if you are willing to behave as
a man to me. Give me your word that you'll come peaceably along,
and I don't want to handcuff you." "I will," says Thompson, "but I'll
have a glass of brandy first." "I don't care if I've another," said I.
"We'll have two more, Missis," said the friends, "and con-found you,
Constable, you'll give your man a drop, won't you?" I was agreeable
to that, so we had it all round, and then my man and I took Tally-ho
Thompson safe to the railroad, and I carried him to London that night.
He was afterwards acquitted, on account of a defect in the evidence;
and I understand he always praises me up to the skies, and says I'm
one of the best of men.'

This story coming to a termination amidst general applause, Inspector Wield, after a little grave smoking, fixes his eye on his host, and
thus delivers himself:

'It wasn't a bad plant that of mine, on Fikey, the man accused of
forging the Sou' Western Railway debentures – it was only t'other day
– because the reason why? I'll tell you.

'I had information that Fikey and his brother kept a factory over
yonder there,' indicating any region on the Surrey side of the river,
'where he bought second-hand carriages; so after I'd tried in vain to
get hold of him by other means, I wrote him a letter in an assumed
name, saying that I'd got a horse and shay to dispose of, and would
drive down next day, that he might view the lot, and make an offer –
very reasonable it was, I said – a reg'lar bargain. Straw and me then
went off to a friend of mine that's in the livery and job business, and
hired a turn-out for the day, a precious smart turn-out, it was – quite a
slap-up thing! Down we drove, accordingly, with a friend (who's not
in the Force himself); and leaving my friend in the shay near a public-
house, to take care of the horse, we went to the factory, which was

some little way off. In the factory, there was a number of strong fellows
at work, and after reckoning 'em up, it was clear to me that it wouldn't
do to try it on there. They were too many for us. We must get our man
out of doors. "Mr Fikey at home?" "No, he ain't." "Expected home
soon?" "Why, no, not soon." "Ah! is his brother here?" "*I*'m his brother."
"Oh! well, this is an ill-conwenience, this is. I wrote him a letter yesterday, saying I'd got a little turn-out to dispose of, and I've took the
trouble to bring the turn-out down, a' purpose, and now he ain't in the
way." "No, he an't in the way. You couldn't make it convenient to call
again, could you?" "Why, no, I couldn't. I want to sell; that's the fact;
and I can't put it off. Could you find him anywheres?" At first he said
No, he couldn't, and then he wasn't sure about it, and then he'd go
and try. So, at last he went up-stairs, where there was a sort of loft,
and presently down comes my man himself, in his shirt sleeves.

' "Well," he says, "this seems to be rayther a pressing matter of
yours." "Yes," I says, "it *is* rayther a pressing matter, and you'll find it
a bargain – dirt-cheap." "I ain't in partickler want of a bargain just
now," he says, "but where is it?" "Why," I says, "the turn-out's just
outside. Come and look at it." He hasn't any suspicions, and away we
go. And the first thing that happens is, that the horse runs away with
my friend (who knows no more of driving than a child) when he takes
a little trot along the road to show his paces. You never saw such a
game in your life!

'When the bolt is over, and the turn-out has come to a stand-still
again, Fikey walks round and round it, as grave as a judge – me too.
"There, Sir!" I says. "There's a neat thing!" "It an't a bad style of
thing," he says. "I believe you," says I. "And there's a horse!" – for I
saw him looking at it. "Rising eight!" I says, rubbing his fore-legs.
(Bless you, there an't a man in the world knows less of horses than I
do, but I'd heard my friend at the Livery Stables say he was eight year
old, so I says, as knowing as possible, "Rising Eight.") "Rising eight,
is he?" says he. "Rising eight," says I. "Well," he says, "what do you
want for it?" "Why, the first and last figure for the whole concern is
five-and-twenty pound!" "That's very cheap!" he says, looking at me.
"An't it?" I says. "I told you it was a bargain! Now, without any higgling
and haggling about it, what I want is to sell and that's my price. Further,
I'll make it easy to you, and take half the money down, and you can

do a bit of stiff* for the balance." "Well," he says again, "that's very cheap." "I believe you," says I; "get in and try it, and you'll buy it. Come! take a trial!"

'Ecod, he gets in, and we get in, and we drive along the road, to show him to one of the railway clerks that was hid in the public-house window to identify him. But the clerk was bothered, and didn't know whether it was him, or wasn't – because the reason why? I'll tell you, – on account of his having shaved his whiskers. "It's a clever little horse," he says, "and trots well; and the shay runs light." "Not a doubt about it," I says. "And now, Mr Fikey, I may as well make it all right, without wasting any more of your time. The fact is, I'm Inspector Wield, and you're my prisoner." "You don't mean that?" he says. "I do, indeed." "Then burn my body," says Fikey, "if this ain't *too* bad!"

'Perhaps you never saw a man so knocked over with surprise. "I hope you'll let me have my coat?" he says. "By all means." "Well, then, let's drive to the factory." "Why, not exactly that, I think," said I; "I've been there, once before, to-day. Suppose we send for it." He saw it was no go, so he sent for it, and put it on, and we drove him up to London, comfortable.'

This reminiscence is in the height of its success, when a general proposal is made to the fresh-complexioned, smooth-faced officer, with the strange air of simplicity, to tell the 'Butcher's story.' But we must reserve the Butcher's story, together with another not less curious in its way, for a concluding paper.

II

The fresh-complexioned, smooth-faced officer, with the strange air of simplicity, began, with a rustic smile, and in a soft, wheedling tone of voice, to relate the Butcher's Story, thus:

'It's just about six years ago, now, since information was given at Scotland Yard of there being extensive robberies of lawns and silks going on, at some wholesale houses in the City. Directions were given for the business being looked into; and Straw, and Fendall, and me, we were all in it.'

*Give a bill.

'When you received your instructions,' said we, 'you went away, and held a sort of Cabinet Council together?'

The smooth-faced officer coaxingly replied, 'Ye-es. Just so. We turned it over among ourselves a good deal. It appeared, when we went into it, that the goods were sold by the receivers extraordinarily cheap – much cheaper than they could have been if they had been honestly come by. The receivers were in the trade, and kept capital shops – establishments of the first respectability – one of 'em at the West End, one down in Westminster. After a lot of watching and inquiry, and this and that among ourselves, we found that the job was managed, and the purchases of the stolen goods made, at a little public-house near Smithfield, down by Saint Bartholomew's; where the Warehouse Porters, who were the thieves, took 'em for that purpose, don't you see? and made appointments to meet the people that went between themselves and the receivers. This public-house was principally used by journeymen butchers from the country, out of place, and in want of situations; so, what did we do, but – ha, ha, ha! – we agreed that I should be dressed up like a butcher myself, and go and live there!'

Never, surely, was a faculty of observation better brought to bear upon a purpose, than that which picked out this officer for the part. Nothing in all creation, could have suited him better. Even while he spoke, he became a greasy, sleepy, shy, good-natured, chuckle-headed, unsuspicious, and confiding young butcher. His very hair seemed to have suet in it, as he made it smooth upon his head, and his fresh complexion to be lubricated by large quantities of animal food.

—— 'So I – ha, ha, ha!' (always with the confiding snigger of the foolish young butcher) 'so I dressed myself in the regular way, made up a little bundle of clothes, and went to the public-house, and asked if I could have a lodging there? They says, "yes, you can have a lodging here," and I got a bedroom, and settled myself down in the tap. There was a number of people about the place, and coming backwards and forwards to the house; and first one says, and then another says, "Are you from the country, young man?" "Yes," I says, "I am. I'm come out of Northamptonshire, and I'm quite lonely here, for I don't know London at all, and it's such a mighty big town?" "It *is* a big town," they says. "Oh, it's a *very* big town!" I says. "Really and truly I never was in such a town. It quite confuses of me!" – and all that, you know.

'When some of the Journeymen Butchers that used the house, found that I wanted a place, they says, "Oh, we'll get you a place!" And they actually took me to a sight of places, in Newgate Market, Newport Market, Clare, Carnaby – I don't know where all. But the wages was – ha, ha, ha! – was not sufficient, and I never could suit myself, don't you see? Some of the queer frequenters of the house, were a little suspicious of me at first, and I was obliged to be very cautious indeed, how I communicated with Straw or Fendall. Sometimes, when I went out, pretending to stop and look into the shop-windows, and just casting my eye round, I used to see some of 'em following me; but, being perhaps better accustomed than they thought for, to that sort of thing, I used to lead 'em on as far as I thought necessary or convenient – sometimes a long way – and then turn sharp round, and meet 'em, and say, "Oh, dear, how glad I am to come upon you so fortunate! This London's such a place, I'm blowed if I an't lost again!" And then we'd go back all together, to the public-house, and – ha, ha, ha! and smoke our pipes, don't you see?

'They were very attentive to me, I am sure. It was a common thing, while I was living there, for some of 'em to take me out, and show me London. They showed me the Prisons – showed me Newgate – and when they showed me Newgate, I stops at the place where the Porters pitch their loads, and says, "Oh dear, is this where they hang the men! Oh Lor!" "That!" they says, "what a simple cove he is! *That* an't it!" And then, they pointed out which *was* it, and I says "Lor!" and they says, "Now you'll know it agen, won't you?" And I said I thought I should if I tried hard – and I assure you I kept a sharp look out for the City Police when we were out in this way, for if any of 'em had happened to know me, and had spoke to me, it would have been all up in a minute. However, by good luck such a thing never happened, and all went on quiet: though the difficulties I had in communicating with my brother officers were quite extraordinary.

'The stolen goods that were brought to the public-house, by the Warehouse Porters, were always disposed of in a back parlor. For a long time, I never could get into into this parlor, or see what was done there. As I sat smoking my pipe, like an innocent young chap, by the tap-room fire, I'd hear some of the parties to the robbery, as they came in and out, say softly to the landlord, "Who's that? What does *he* do

here?" "Bless your soul," says the landlord, "He's only a" – ha, ha, ha!
– "he's only a green young fellow from the country, as is looking for
a butcher's sitiwation. Don't mind *him*!" So, in course of time, they
were so convinced of my being green, and got to be so accustomed to
me, that I was as free of the parlor as any of 'em, and I have seen as
much as Seventy Pounds worth of fine lawn sold there, in one night,
that was stolen from a warehouse in Friday Street. After the sale, the
buyers always stood treat – hot supper, or dinner, or what not – and
they'd say on those occasions "Come on, Butcher! Put your best leg
foremost, young 'un, and walk into it!" Which I used to do – and hear,
at table, all manner of particulars that it was very important for us
Detectives to know.

'This went on for ten weeks. I lived in the public-house all the time
and never was out of Butcher's dress – except in bed. At last, when I
had followed seven of the thieves, and set 'em to rights – that's an
expression of ours, don't you see, by which I mean to say that I traced
'em, and found out where the robberies were done, and all about 'em
– Straw, and Fendall, and I, gave one another the office, and at a time
agreed upon, a descent was made upon the public-house, and the apprehension effected. One of the first things the officers did, was to
collar me – for the parties to the robbery weren't to suppose yet, that I
was anything but a Butcher – on which the landlord cries out, "Don't
take *him*," he says, "whatever you do! He's only a poor young chap
from the country, and butter wouldn't melt in his mouth!" However,
they – ha, ha, ha! – they took me, and pretended to search my bedroom, where nothing was found but an old fiddle belonging to the
landlord, that had got there somehow or another. But, it entirely changed
the landlord's opinion, for when it was produced, he says "My fiddle!
The Butcher's a pur-loiner! I give him into custody for the robbery of
a musical instrument!"

'The man that had stolen the goods in Friday Street was not taken
yet. He had told me, in confidence, that he had his suspicions there
was something wrong (on account of the City Police having captured
one of the party), and that he was going to make himself scarce. I
asked him, "Where do you mean to go, Mr Shepherdson?" "Why,
Butcher," says he, "the Setting Moon, in the Commercial Road, is a
snug house, and I shall hang out there for a time. I shall call myself

Simpson, which appears to me to be a modest sort of a name. Perhaps you'll give us a look in, Butcher?" "Well," says I, "I think I *will* give you a call" – which I fully intended, don't you see, because, of course, he was to be taken! I went over to the Setting Moon next day, with a brother officer, and asked at the bar for Simpson. They pointed out his room, upstairs. As we were going up, he looks down over the bannisters, and calls out, "Halloa, Butcher! is that you?" "Yes, it's me. How do you find yourself?" "Bobbish," he says; "but who's that with you?" "It's only a young man, that's a friend of mine," I says. "Come along, then," says he; "any friend of the Butcher's is as welcome as the Butcher!" So, I made my friend acquainted with him, and we took him into custody.

'You have no idea, Sir, what a sight it was, in Court, when they first knew that I wasn't a Butcher, after all! I wasn't produced at the first examination, when there was a remand; but I was, at the second. And when I stepped into the box, in full police uniform, and the whole party saw how they had been done, actually a groan of horror and dismay proceeded from 'em in the dock!

'At the Old Bailey, when their trials came on, Mr Clarkson was engaged for the defence, and he *couldn't* make out how it was, about the Butcher. He thought, all along, it was a real Butcher. When the counsel for the prosecution said, "I will now call before you, gentlemen, the Police-officer," meaning myself, Mr Clarkson says, "Why Police-officer? Why more Police-officers? I don't want Police. We have had a great deal too much of the Police. I want the Butcher!" However, Sir, he had the Butcher and the Police-officer, both in one. Out of seven prisoners committed for trial, five were found guilty, and some of 'em were transported. The respectable firm at the West End got a term of imprisonment; and that's the Butcher's Story!'

The story done, the chuckle-headed Butcher again resolved himself into the smooth-faced Detective. But, he was so extremely tickled by their having taken him about, when he was that Dragon in disguise, to show him London, that he could not help reverting to that point in his narrative; and gently repeating, with the Butcher snigger, '"Oh, dear!" I says, "is that where they hang the men? Oh, Lor!" "*That!*" says they. "What a simple cove he is!"'

It being now late, and the party very modest in their fear of being too diffuse, there were some tokens of separation; when Sergeant Dornton, the soldierly-looking man, said, looking round him with a smile:

'Before we break up, Sir, perhaps you might have some amusement in hearing of the Adventures of a Carpet Bag. They are very short; and, I think, curious.'

We welcomed the Carpet Bag, as cordially as Mr Shepherdson welcomed the false Butcher at the Setting Moon. Sergeant Dornton proceeded:

'In 1847, I was dispatched to Chatham, in search of one Mesheck, a Jew. He had been carrying on, pretty heavily, in the bill-stealing way, getting acceptances from young men of good connexions (in the army chiefly), on pretence of discount, and bolting with the same.

'Mesheck was off, before I got to Chatham. All I could learn about him was, that he had gone, probably to London, and had with him – a Carpet Bag.

'I came back to town, by the last train from Blackwall, and made inquiries concerning a Jew passenger with – a Carpet Bag.

'The office was shut up, it being the last train. There were only two or three porters left. Looking after a Jew with a Carpet Bag, on the Blackwall Railway, which was then the high road to a great Military Depôt, was worse than looking after a needle in a hayrick. But it happened that one of these porters had carried, for a certain Jew, to a certain public-house, a certain – Carpet Bag.

'I went to the public-house, but the Jew had only left his luggage there for a few hours, and had called for it in a cab, and taken it away. I put such questions there, and to the porter, as I thought prudent, and got at this description of – the Carpet Bag.

'It was a bag which had, on one side of it, worked in worsted, a green parrot on a stand. A green parrot on a stand was the means by which to identify that – Carpet Bag.

'I traced Mesheck, by means of this green parrot on a stand, to Cheltenham, to Birmingham, to Liverpool, to the Atlantic Ocean. At Liverpool he was too many for me. He had gone to the United States, and I gave up all thoughts of Mesheck, and likewise of his – Carpet Bag.

'Many months afterwards – near a year afterwards – there was a Bank in Ireland robbed of seven thousand pounds, by a person of the name of Doctor Dundey, who escaped to America; from which country some of the stolen notes came home. He was supposed to have bought a farm in New Jersey. Under proper management, that estate could be seized and sold, for the benefit of the parties he had defrauded. I was sent off to America for this purpose.

'I landed at Boston. I went on to New York. I found that he had lately changed New York paper-money for New Jersey paper-money, and had banked cash in New Brunswick. To take this Doctor Dundey, it was necessary to entrap him into the State of New York, which required a deal of artifice and trouble. At one time, he couldn't be drawn into an appointment. At another time, he appointed to come to meet me, and a New York officer, on a pretext I made; and then his children had the measles. At last, he came, per steamboat, and I took him, and lodged him in a New York Prison called the Tombs; which I dare say you know, Sir?'

Editorial acknowledgment to that effect.

'I went to the Tombs, on the morning after his capture, to attend the examination before the magistrate. I was passing through the magistrate's private room, when, happening to look round me to take notice of the place, as we generally have a habit of doing, I clapped my eyes, in one corner, on a – Carpet Bag.

'What did I see upon that Carpet Bag, it you'll believe me, but a green parrot on a stand, as large as life!

' "That Carpet Bag, with the representation of a green parrot on a stand," said I, "belongs to an English Jew, named Aaron Mesheck, and to no other man, alive or dead!"

'I give you my word the New York Police officers were doubled up with surprise.

' "How do you ever come to know that?" said they.

' "I think I ought to know that green parrot by this time," said I; "for I have had as pretty a dance after that bird, at home, as ever I had, in all my life!" '

'And *was* it Mesheck's?' we submissively inquired.

'Was it, Sir? Of course it was! He was in custody for another offence, in that very identical Tombs, at that very identical time. And, more than that! Some memoranda, relating to the fraud for which I had vainly endeavoured to take him, were found to be, at that moment, lying in that very same individual – Carpet Bag!'

*

Such are the curious coincidences and such is the peculiar ability, always sharpening and being improved by practice, and always adapting itself to every variety of circumstances, and opposing itself to every new device that perverted ingenuity can invent, for which this important social branch of the public service is remarkable! For ever on the watch, with their wits stretched to the utmost, these officers have, from day to day and year to year, to set themselves against every novelty of trickery and dexterity that the combined imaginations of all the lawless rascals in England can devise, and to keep pace with every such invention that comes out. In the Courts of Justice, the materials of thousands of such stories as we have narrated – often elevated into the marvellous and romantic, by the circumstances of the case – are dryly compressed into the set phrase, 'in consequence of information I received, I did so and so.' Suspicion was to be directed, by careful inference and deduction, upon the right person; the right person was to be taken, wherever he had gone, or whatever he was doing to avoid detection: he is taken; there he is at the bar; that is enough. From information I, the officer, received, I did it; and, according to the custom in these cases, I say no more.

These games of chess, played with live pieces, are played before small audiences, and are chronicled nowhere. The interest of the game supports the player. Its results are enough for Justice. To compare great things with small, suppose LEVERRIER or ADAMS informing the public that from information he had received he had discovered a new planet; or COLUMBUS informing the public of his day that from information he had received, he had discovered a new continent; so the Detectives inform it that they have discovered a new fraud or an old offender, and the process is unknown.

Thus, at midnight, closed the proceedings of our curious and interesting party. But one other circumstance finally wound up the evening, after our Detective guests had left us. One of the sharpest among them, and the officer best acquainted with the swell mob, had his pocket picked, going home!

[SIX]

Three 'Detective' Anecdotes

I. The Pair of Gloves

'It's a singler story, Sir,' said Inspector Wield, of the Detective Police, who, in company with Sergeants Dornton and Mith, paid us another twilight visit, one July evening; 'and I've been thinking you might like to know it.

'It's concerning the murder of the young woman, Eliza Grimwood, some years ago, over in the Waterloo Road. She was commonly called The Countess, because of her handsome appearance and her proud way of carrying of herself; and when I saw the poor Countess (I had known her well to speak to), lying dead, with her throat cut, on the floor of her bedroom, you'll believe me that a variety of reflections calculated to make a man rather low in his spirits, came into my dead.

'That's neither here nor there. I went to the house the morning after the murder, and examined the body, and made a general observation of the bedroom where it was. Turning down the pillow of the bed with my hand, I found, underneath it, a pair of gloves. A pair of gentleman's dress gloves, very dirty; and inside the lining, the letters TR, and a cross.

'Well, Sir, I took them gloves away, and I showed 'em to the magistrate, over at Union Hall, before whom the case was. He says, "Wield," he says, "there's no doubt this is a discovery that may lead to something very important; and what you have got to do, Wield, is, to find out the owner of these gloves."

'I was of the same opinion, of course, and I went at it immediately. I looked at the gloves pretty narrowly, and it was my opinion that they had been cleaned. There was a smell of sulphur and rosin about 'em, you know, which cleaned gloves usually have, more or less. I took 'em over to a friend of mine at Kennington, who was in that line, and I put it to him. "What do you say now? Have these gloves been cleaned?" "These gloves have been cleaned," says he. "Have you any idea who cleaned them?" says I. "Not at all," says he; "I've a very distinct idea who *didn't* clean 'em, and that's myself. But I'll tell you what, Wield, there ain't above eight or nine reg'lar glove cleaners in London," – there were not, at that time, it seems – "and I think I can give you their addresses, and you may find out, by that means, who did clean 'em." Accordingly, he gave me the directions, and I went here, and I went there, and I looked up this man, and I looked up that man; but, though they all agreed that the gloves had been cleaned, I couldn't find the man, woman, or child, that had cleaned that aforesaid pair of gloves.

'What with this person not being at home, and that person being expected home in the afternoon, and so forth, the inquiry took me three days. On the evening of the third day, coming over Waterloo Bridge from the Surrey side of the river, quite beat, and very much vexed and disappointed, I thought I'd have a shilling's worth of entertainment at the Lyceum Theatre to freshen myself up. So I went into the Pit, at half-price, and I sat myself down next to a very quiet, modest sort of young man. Seeing I was a stranger (which I thought it just as well to appear to be) he told me the names of the actors on the stage, and we got into conversation. When the play was over, we came out together, and I said, "We've been very companionable and agreeable, and perhaps you wouldn't object to a drain?" "Well, you're very good," says he; "I *shouldn't* object to a drain." Accordingly, we went to a public house, near the Theatre, sat ourselves down in a quiet room upstairs on the first floor, and called for a pint of half-and-half, a-piece, and a pipe.

'Well, Sir, we put our pipes aboard and we drank our half-and-half, and sat a talking, very sociably, when the young man says, "You must excuse me stopping very long," he says, "because I'm forced to go home in good time. I must be at work all night." "At work all night?"

says I. "You ain't a Baker?" "No," he says, laughing, "I ain't a baker."
"I thought not," says I, "you haven't the looks of a baker." "No," says
he, "I'm a glove cleaner."

'I never was more astonished in my life, than when I heard them
words come out of his lips. "You're a glove cleaner, are you?" says I.
"Yes," he says, "I am." "Then, perhaps," says I, taking the gloves out
of my pocket, "you can tell me who cleaned this pair of gloves? It's a
rum story," I says. "I was dining over at Lambeth, the other day, at a
free-and-easy – quite promiscuous – with a public company – when
some gentleman, he left these gloves behind him! Another gentleman
and me, you see, we laid a wager of a sovereign, that I wouldn't find
out who they belonged to. I've spent as much as seven shillings already, in trying to discover; but, if you could help me, I'd stand another seven and welcome. You see there's TR and a cross, inside." "*I*
see," he says. "Bless you, *I* know these gloves very well! I've seen
dozens of pairs belonging to the same party." "No?" says I. "Yes,"
says he. "Then you know who cleaned 'em?" says I. "Rather so," says
he. "My father cleaned 'em."

' "Where does your father live?" says I. "Just round the corner,"
says the young man, "near Exeter Street, here. He'll tell you who they
belong to, directly." "Would you come round with me now?" says I.
"Certainly," says he, "but you needn't tell my father that you found me
at the play, you know, because he mightn't like it." "All right!" We
went round to the place, and there we found an old man in a white
apron, with two or three daughters, all rubbing and cleaning away at
lots of gloves, in a front parlour. "Oh, Father!" says the young man,
"here's a person been and made a bet about the ownership of a pair of
gloves, and I've told him you can settle it." "Good evening, Sir," says
I to the old gentleman. "Here's the gloves your son speaks of. Letters
TR, you see, and a cross." "Oh yes," he says, "I know these gloves
very well; I've cleaned dozens of pairs of 'em. They belong to Mr
Trinkle, the great upholsterer in Cheapside." "Did you get 'em from
Mr Trinkle, direct," says I, "if you'll excuse my asking the question?"
"No," says he; "Mr Trinkle always sends 'em to Mr Phibbs's, the haber-
dasher's, opposite his shop, and the haberdasher sends 'em to me."
"Perhaps *you* wouldn't object to a drain?" says I. "Not in the least!"
says he. So I took the old gentleman out, and had a little more talk

with him and his son, over a glass, and we parted ex-cellent friends.

'This was late on a Saturday night. First thing on the Monday morning, I went to the haberdasher's shop, opposite Mr Trinkle's, the great upholsterer's in Cheapside. "Mr Phibbs in the way?" "My name is Phibbs." "Oh! I believe you sent this pair of gloves to be cleaned?" "Yes, I did, for young Mr Trinkle over the way. There he is, in the shop!" "Oh! that's him in the shop, is it? Him in the green coat?" "The same individual." "Well, Mr Phibbs, this is an unpleasant affair; but the fact is, I am Inspector Wield of the Detective Police, and I found these gloves under the pillow of the young woman that was murdered the other day, over in the Waterloo Road?" "Good Heaven!" says he. "He's a most respectable young man, and if his father was to hear of it, it would be the ruin of him!" "I'm very sorry for it," says I, "but I must take him into custody." "Good Heaven!" says Mr Phibbs, again; "can nothing be done?" "Nothing," says I. "Will you allow me to call him over here," says he, "that his father may not see it done?" "I don't object to that," says I; "but unfortunately, Mr Phibbs, I can't allow of any communication between you. If any was attempted, I should have to interfere directly. Perhaps you'll beckon him over here?" Mr Phibbs went to the door and beckoned, and the young fellow came across the street directly; a smart, brisk young fellow.

' "Good morning, Sir," says I. "Good morning, Sir," says he. "Would you allow me to inquire, Sir," says I, "if you ever had any acquaintance with a party of the name of Grimwood?" "Grimwood! Grimwood!" says he, "No!" "You know the Waterloo Road?" "Oh! of course I know the Waterloo Road!" "Happen to have heard of a young woman being murdered there?" "Yes, I read it in the paper, and very sorry I was to read it." "Here's a pair of gloves belonging to you, that I found under her pillow the morning afterwards!"

'He was in a dreadful state, Sir; a dreadful state! "Mr Wield," he says, "upon my solemn oath I never was there. I never so much as saw her, to my knowledge, in my life!" "I am very sorry," says I. "To tell you the truth; I don't think you *are* the murderer, but I must take you to Union Hall in a cab. However, I think it's a case of that sort, that, at present, at all events, the magistrate will hear it in private."

A private examination took place, and then it came out that this young man was acquainted with a cousin of the unfortunate Eliza

Grimwood's, and that, calling to see this cousin a day or two before the murder, he left these gloves upon the table. Who should come in, shortly afterwards, but Eliza Grimwood! "Whose gloves are these?" she says, taking 'em up. "Those are Mr Trinkle's gloves," says her cousin. "Oh!" says she, "they are very dirty, and of no use to him, I am sure. I shall take 'em away for my girl to clean the stoves with." And she put 'em in her pocket. The girl had used 'em to clean the stoves, and, I have no doubt, had left 'em lying on the bedroom mantel-piece, or on the drawers, or somewhere; and her mistress, looking round to see that the room was tidy, had caught 'em up and put 'em under the pillow where I found 'em.

'That's the story, Sir.'

II. The Artful Touch

'One of the most *beautiful* things that ever was done, perhaps,' said Inspector Wield, emphasising the adjective, as preparing us to expect dexterity or ingenuity rather than strong interest, 'was a move of Sergeant Witchem's. It was a lovely idea!

'Witchem and me were down at Epsom one Derby Day, waiting at the station for the swell mob. As I mentioned, when we were talking about these things before, we are ready at the station when there's races, or an Agricultural Show, or a Chancellor sworn in for an university, or Jenny Lind, or any thing of that sort; and as the swell mob come down, we send 'em back again by the next train. But some of the swell mob, on the occasion of this Derby that I refer to, so far kiddied us as to hire a horse and shay; start away from London by Whitechapel, and miles round; come into Epsom from the opposite direction; and go to work, right and left, on the course, while we were waiting for 'em at the Rail. That, however, ain't the point of what I'm going to tell you.

'While Witchem and me were waiting at the station, there comes up one Mr Tatt; a gentleman formerly in the public line, quite an amateur Detective in his way, and very much respected. "Halloa, Charley Wield," he says. "What are you doing here? On the look out for some of your old friends?" "Yes, the old move, Mr Tatt." "Come along," he says, "you and Witchem, and have a glass of sherry." "We can't stir from

the place," says I, "till the next train comes in; but after that, we will
with pleasure." Mr Tatt waits, and the train comes in, and then Witchem
and me go off with him to the Hotel. Mr Tatt he's got up quite regardless of expense, for the occasion; and in his shirt-front there's a beautiful diamond prop, cost him fifteen or twenty pound – a very handsome
pin indeed. We drink our sherry at the bar, and have had our three or
four glasses, when Witchem cries, suddenly, "Look out, Mr Wield!
stand fast!" and a dash is made into the place by the swell mob – four
of 'em – that have come down as I tell you, and in a moment Mr
Tatt's prop is gone! Witchem, he cuts 'em off at the door, I lay about
me as hard as I can, Mr Tatt shows fight like a good 'un, and there we
are, all down together, heads and heels, knocking about on the floor of
the bar – perhaps you never see such a scene of confusion! However,
we stick to our men (Mr Tatt being as good as any officer), and we
take 'em all, and carry 'em off to the station. The station's full of
people, who have been took on the course; and it's a precious piece of
work to get 'em secured. However, we do it at last, and we search
'em; but nothing's found upon 'em, and they're locked up; and a pretty
state of heat we are in by that time, I assure you!

'I was very blank over it, myself, to think that the prop had been
passed away; and I said to Witchem, when we had set 'em to rights,
and were cooling ourselves along with Mr Tatt, "we don't take much
by *this* move, anyway, for nothing's found upon 'em, and it's only the
braggadocia* after all." "What do you mean, Mr Wield?" says Witchem.
"Here's the diamond pin!" and in the palm of his hand there it was,
safe and sound! "Why, in the name of wonder," says me and Mr Tatt,
in astonishment, how did you come by that?" "I'll tell you how I come
by it," says he. "I saw which of 'em took it; and when we were all
down on the floor together, knocking about, I just gave him a little
touch on the back of his hand, as I knew his pal would; and he thought
it was his pal; and gave it me!" It was beautiful, beau-ti-ful!

'Even that was hardly the best of the case, for that chap was tried at
the Quarter Sessions at Guildford. You know what Quarter Sessions
are, Sir. Well, if you'll believe me, while them slow justices were looking
over the Acts of Parliament, to see what they could do to him, I'm

*Three months' imprisonment as reputed thieves.

blowed if he didn't cut out of the dock before their faces! He cut out of the dock, Sir, then and there; swam across a river; and got up into a tree to dry himself. In the tree he was took – an old woman having seen him climb up – and Witchem's artful touch transported him!'

III. The Sofa

'What young men will do, sometimes, to ruin themselves and break their friends' hearts,' said Sergeant Dornton, 'it's surprising! I had a case at Saint Blank's Hospital which was of this sort. A bad case, indeed, with a bad end!

'The Secretary, and the House-Surgeon, and the Treasurer of Saint Blank's Hospital, came to Scotland Yard to give information of numerous robberies having been committed on the students. The students could leave nothing in the pockets of their great-coats, while the great-coats were hanging at the Hospital, but it was almost certain to be stolen. Property of various descriptions was constantly being lost; and the gentlemen were naturally uneasy about it, and anxious, for the credit of the Institution, that the thief or thieves should be discovered. The case was entrusted to me, and I went to the Hospital.

' "Now, gentlemen," said I, after we had talked it over, "I understand this property is usually lost from one room."

'Yes, they said. It was.

' "I should wish, if you please," said I, "to see that room."

'It was a good-sized bare room downstairs, with a few tables and forms in it, and a row of pegs, all round, for hats and coats.

' "Next, gentlemen," said I, "do you suspect anybody?"

'Yes, they said. They did suspect somebody. They were sorry to say, they suspected one of the porters.

' "I should like," said I, "to have that man pointed out to me, and to have a little time to look after him."

'He was pointed out, and I looked after him, and then I went back to the Hospital, and said, "Now, gentlemen, it's not the porter. He's, unfortunately for himself, a little too fond of drink, but he's nothing worse. My suspicion is, that these robberies are committed by one of the students; and if you'll put me a sofa into that room where the pegs are – as there's no closet – I think I shall be able to detect the thief. I wish the sofa, if you please, to be covered with chintz, or something of that sort, so that I may lie on my chest, underneath it, without being seen."

'The sofa was provided, and next day at eleven o'clock, before any of the students came, I went there, with those gentlemen, to get underneath it. It turned out to be one of those old-fashioned sofas with a great cross beam at the bottom, that would have broken my back in no time if I could ever have got below it. We had quite a job to break all this away in the time; however, I fell to work, and they fell to work, and we broke it out, and made a clear place for me. I got under the sofa, lay down on my chest, took out my knife, and made a convenient hole in the chintz to look through. It was then settled between me and the gentlemen that when the students were all up in the wards, one of the gentlemen should come in, and hang up a great-coat on one of the pegs. And that that great-coat should have, in one of the pockets, a pocket-book containing marked money.

'After I had been there some time, the students began to drop into the room, by ones, and twos, and threes, and to talk about all sorts of things, little thinking there was anybody under the sofa – and then to go upstairs. At last there came in one who remained until he was alone in the room by himself. A tallish, good-looking young man of one or two and twenty, with a light whisker. He went to a particular hat-peg, took off a good hat that was hanging there, tried it on, hung his own hat in its place, and hung that hat on another peg, nearly opposite to me. I then felt quite certain that he was the thief, and would come back by-and-bye.

'When they were all upstairs, the gentleman came in with the great-coat. I showed him where to hang it, so that I might have a good view of it; and he went away; and I lay under the sofa on my chest, for a couple of hours or so, waiting.

'At last, the same young man came down. He walked across the room, whistling – stopped and listened – took another walk and whistled – stopped again, and listened – then began to go regularly round the pegs, feeling in the pockets of all the coats. When he came to THE great-coat, and felt the pocket-book, he was so eager and so hurried that he broke the strap in tearing it open. As he began to put the money in his pocket, I crawled out from under the sofa, and his eyes met mine.

A dramatic moment from 'The Sofa', illustrated by E. G. Dalziel

'My face, as you may perceive, is brown now, but it was pale at that time, my health not being good; and looked as long as a horse's. Besides which, there was a great draught of air from the door, underneath the sofa, and I had tied a handkerchief round my head; so what I looked like, altogether, I don't know. He turned blue – literally blue – when he saw me crawling out, and I couldn't feel surprised at it.

' "I am an officer of the Detective Police," said I, "and have been lying here, since you first came in this morning. I regret, for the sake of yourself and your friends, that you should have done what you have; but this case is complete. You have the pocket-book in your hand and the money upon you; and I must take you into custody!"

'It was impossible to make out any case in his behalf, and on his trial he pleaded guilty. How or when he got the means I don't know; but while he was awaiting his sentence, he poisoned himself in Newgate.'

We inquired of this officer, on the conclusion of the foregoing anecdote, whether the time appeared long, or short, when he lay in that constrained position under the sofa?

'Why, you see, Sir,' he replied, 'if he hadn't come in, the first time, and I had not been quite sure he was the thief, and would return, the time would have seemed long. But, as it was, I being dead-certain of my man, the time seemed pretty short.'

[SEVEN]

The Metropolitan Protectives

Nervous old ladies, dyspeptic half-pay officers, suspicious quidnuncs, plot-dreading diplomatists, and grudging rate-payers, all having the fear of the forthcoming Industrial Invasion before their eyes, are becoming very anxious respecting the adequate efficiency of the London Police. Horrible rumours are finding their way into most of the clubs: reports are permeating into the tea-parties of suburban dowagers which darkly shadow forth dire mischief and confusion, the most insignificant result whereof is to be (of course) the overthrow of the British Constitution. Conspiracies of a comprehensive character are being hatched in certain back parlours, in certain back streets behind Mr Cantelo's Chicken Establishment in Leicester Square. A complicated web of machination is being spun – we have it on the authority of a noble peer – against the integrity of the Austrian Empire, at a small coffee-shop in Soho. Prussia is being menaced by twenty-four determined Poles and Honveds in the attics of a cheap *restaurateur* in the Haymarket. Lots are being cast for the assassination of Louis Napoleon, in the inner parlours of various cigar shops. America, as we learn from that mighty lever of the civilised world, the 'New York Weekly Herald' – at whose nod, it is well known, kings tremble on their thrones, and the earth shakes – is of opinion that the time bids fair for a descent of Red Republicans on Manchester. The English policemen have been tampered with, and are suborned. The great Mr Justice Maule can't find one anywhere. In

101

short, the peace of the entire continent of Europe may be considered as
already gone. When the various conspiracies now on foot are ripe, the
armies of the disaffected of all nations which are to land at the various
British ports under pretence of 'assisting' at the Great Glass show, are
to be privately and confidentially drilled in secret *Champs de Mars*,
and armed with weapons, stealthily abstracted from the Tower of London: while the Metropolitan Police and the Guards, both horse and
foot, will fraternise, and (to a man) pretend to be fast asleep.

Neither have our prudent prophets omitted to foretell minor disas-
ters. Gangs of burglars from the counties of Surrey, Sussex, and Lan-
cashire, are also to fraternise in London, and to 'rifle, rob, and plunder,'
as uninterruptedly as if every man's house were a mere Castle of An-
dalusia. Pickpockets – not in single spies but in whole battalions – are
to arrive from Paris and Vienna, and are to fall into compact organisation (through the medium of interpreters) with the united swell-mobs
of London, Liverpool, and Manchester!

In short, it would appear that no words can express our fearful condition, so well, as Mr Croaker's in 'The Good Natured Man.' 'I am so
frightened,' says he, 'that I scarce know whether I sit, stand, or go.
Perhaps at this moment I am treading on lighted matches, blazing brim-
stone, and barrels of gunpowder. They are preparing to blow me up
into the clouds. Murder! We shall be all burnt in our beds!'

Now, to the end that the prophets and their disciples may rest quietly
in *their* beds, we have benevolently abandoned our own bed for some
three nights or so, in order to report the results of personal inquiry into
the condition and system of the Protective Police of the Metropolis: the
Detective Police has been already described in the first volume of 'Household Words.' If, after our details of the patience, promptitude, order,
vigilance, zeal, and judgment, which watch over the peace of the huge
Babylon when she sleeps, the fears of the most apprehensive be not
dispelled, we shall have quitted our pillow, and plied our pen in vain!
But we have no such distrust.

Although the Metropolitan Police Force consists of nineteen super-
intendents, one hundred and twenty-four inspectors, five hundred and
eighty-five serjeants, and four thousand seven hundred and ninety-seven
constables, doing duty at twenty-five stations; yet, so uniform is the
order of proceeding in all, and so fairly can the description of what is

done at one station be taken as a specimen of what is done at the others, that, without farther preface, we shall take the reader into custody, and convey him at once to the Police Station, in Bow Street, Covent Garden.

A policeman keeping watch and ward at the wicket gives us admission, and we proceed down a long passage into an outer room, where there is a barrack bedstead, on which we observe Police-constable Clark, newly relieved, asleep, and snoring most portentously – a little exhausted, perhaps, by nine hours' constant walking on his beat. In the right-hand corner of this room – which is a bare room like a guardhouse without the drums and muskets – is a dock, or space railed off for prisoners: opposite, a window breast-high at which an Inspector always presides day and night to hear charges. Passing by a corner-door into his office on the other side of this window, we find it much like any other office – inky, dull, and quiet – papers stuck against the walls – perfect library of old charges on shelves overhead – stools and desks – a hall-porter's chair, little used – gaslights – fire – sober clock. At one desk stands a policeman, duly coated and caped, looking stiffly over his glazed stock at a handbill he is copying. Two Inspectors sit near, working away at a great rate with noisy pens that sound like little rattles.

The clock points a quarter before nine. One of the Inspectors takes under his arm a slate, the night's muster roll, and an orderly book. He proceeds to the Yard. The gas jet, shining from the office through its window, and a couple of street lamps indistinctly light the place.

On the appearance of the inspecting officer in the yard, and at the sound of the word 'Attention!' about seventy white faces, peering out above half-a-dozen parallel lines of dark figures, fall into military ranks in 'open order.' A man from each section – a Serjeant – comes forward to form the staff of the commanding officer. The roll is called over, and certain men are told off as a Reserve, to remain at the station for any exigencies that may arise. The book is then opened, and the Inspector reads aloud a series of warnings. P. C. John Jones, J, No. 202, was discovered drunk on duty on such a day, and dismissed the force. Serjeant Jenkins did not report that a robbery had been complained of in such a street, and is suspended for a month. The whole division are then enlightened as to the names, addresses, ages, and heights,

of all persons who have been 'missing' from a radius of fifteen miles
from Charing Cross (the police definition of the Metropolis) since the
previous night; as to the colours of their hair, eyes, and clothes; as to
the cut of their coats, the fashion and material of their gowns, the shape
of their hats or bonnets, the make of their boots. So minute and definite
are all these personal descriptions, that a P. C. (the official ellipsis for
Police Constable) must be very sleepy, or unusually dull of observation, if, in the event of his meeting with any of these missing individuals, he does not put them in train of restoration to their anxious friends.
Lost articles of property are then enumerated and described with equal
exactness. When we reflect that the same routine is being performed at
the same moment at the head of every police regiment or division in
the Metropolis, it seems extraordinary how any thing or person *can* be
lost in London. Among the trifles enumerated as 'found,' are a horse
and cart, a small dog, a brooch, a baby, and a firkin of butter.

Emotion is no part of a policeman's duty. If felt, it must be suppressed: he listens as stolidly to the following account of the baby, as
to the history of the horse and cart, the little dog, the brooch, and the
butter.

S. DIVISION. Found, at Eight and a quarter P.M., on the 2nd instant
by [a gentleman named], of Bayham Street, Camden Town, on the
step of his door, the body of a new-born Infant, tied up in a Holland
Bag. Had on a Calico Bed-gown and Muslim Cap, trimmed with
Satin Ribbon. Also a Note, stating, 'Any one who finds this precious burthen, pay him the last duties which a Mother – much in
distress and trouble of mind – is unable to do. May the blessing of
God be on you!'

The book is closed. The mother 'much in distress and trouble of mind,'
is shut up with it; and the Inspector proceeds to make his inspection.
He marches past each rank. The men, one by one, produce their kit;
consisting of lantern, rattle, and staff. He sees that each man is clean
and properly provided for the duties of the night. Returning to his former
station amidst the serjeants, he gives the word 'Close up!'

The men now form a compact body, and the serjeants take their
stand at the head of their respective ranks. But, before this efficient

body of troops deploy to their various beats, they are addressed by the
superior officer much as a colonel harangues his regiment before going
into action. The Inspector's speech – sharp and pithily delivered – is
something to this effect:

'Now, men, I must again beg of you to be very careful in your
examination of empty houses. See that the doors are fast; and, if not,
search for any persons unlawfully concealed therein. Number nineteen
section will allow no destitute parties to herd together under the Adelphi
arches. Section Number twenty-four will be very particular in insisting
on all gentlemen's carriages [it is an opera night] keeping the rank,
close to the kerb-stone, and in cautioning the coachmen not to leave
their horses. Be sure and look sharp after flower-girls. Offering flowers
for sale is a pretence. The girls are either beggars or thieves; but you
must exercise great caution. You must not interfere with them unless
you actually hear them asking charity, or see them trying pockets, or
engaged in actual theft. The chief thing, however, is the empty houses;
thieves get from them into the adjoining premises, and then there's a
burglary. – 'Tention, to the left face, march!'

The sections march off in Indian file, and the Inspector returns to
his office by one door, while the half-dozen 'Reserves' go into the
outer-room by another. The former, now buttons on his great coat: and,
after supper, will visit every beat in the division, to see that the men
are at their duties. The other Inspector remains, to take the charges.

A small man, who gives his name, Mr Spills, (or for whom that
name will do in this place as well as another), presents himself at the
half-open window to complain of a gentleman now present, who is
stricken in years, bald, well dressed, staid in countenance respectable
in appearance, and exceedingly drunk. He gazes at his accuser from
behind the dock, with lack-lustre penitence, as that gentleman elab-
orates his grievance to the patient Inspector; who, out of a tangle of
digressions and innuendoes dashed with sparkling scraps of club-room
oratory, extracts – not without difficulty – the substance of the complaint, and reduces it to a charge of 'drunk and disorderly.' The culprit,
it seems, not half an hour ago – purely by accident – found his way
into Craven Street, Strand. Though there are upwards of forty doors in
Craven street, he *would* kick, and thump, and batter the complainant's
door. No other door would do. The complainant don't know why; the

delinquent don't know why; nobody knows why. No entreaty, no ex-
postulation, no threat, could induce him to transfer his favours to any
other door in the neighbourhood. He was a perfect stranger to Mr Spills;
yet, when Mr Spills presented himself at the gate of his castle in answer
to the thundering summons, the prisoner insisted on finishing the evening
at the domestic supper-table of the Spills family. Finally, the prisoner
emphasised his claim on Mr Spills's hospitality by striking Mr Spills
on the mouth. This led to his being immediately handed over to the
custody of a P. C.

The defendant answers the usual questions as to name and condition, with a drowsy indifference peculiar to the muddled. But, when the
Inspector asks his age, a faint ray of his spirit shines through him.
What is that to the police? Have they anything to do with the census?
They may lock him up, fine him, put him in jail, work him on the
tread-mill, if they like. All this is in their power; he knows the law
well enough, Sir; but they can't make him tell his age – and he won't
– won't do it, Sir! – At length, after having been mildly pressed, and
cross-examined, and coaxed, he passes his fingers through the few grey
hairs that fringe his bad head, and suddenly roars:

'Well then: Five-and-twenty!'

All the policemen laugh. The prisoner – but now triumphant in his
retort – checks himself, endeavours to stand erect, and surveys them
with defiance.

'Have you anything about you, you would like us to take care of?'
This is the usual apology for searching a drunken prisoner: searches
cannot be enforced except in cases of felony.

Before the prisoner can answer, one of the Reserves eases him of his
property. Had his adventures been produced in print, they could scarcely
have been better described than by the following articles: a pen-knife,
an empty sandwich-box, a bunch of keys, a bird's-eye handkerchief, a
sovereign, fivepence in half-pence, a tooth-pick, and a pocket-book.
From his neck is drawn a watch-guard, cut through, – *no* watch.

When he is sober, he will be questioned as to his loss; a description
of the watch, with its maker's name and number will be extracted from
him; it will be sent round to every station; and, by this time to-morrow
night, every pawnbroker in the Metropolis will be asked whether such
a watch has been offered as a pledge? Most probably it will be re-

covered and restored before he has time to get tipsy again – and when he has, he will probably lose it again.

'When shall I have to appear before the magistrate?' asks the prosecutor.

'At ten o'clock to-morrow morning,' – and so ends that case.

There is no peace for the Inspector. During the twenty-four hours he is on duty, his window is constantly framing some new picture. For some minutes, a brown face with bright black eyes has been peering impatiently from under a quantity of tangled black hair and a straw hat behind Mr Spills. It now advances to the window.

'Have you got e'er a gipsy woman here, sir?'

'No gipsy woman to-night.'

'Thank'ee, sir:' and the querist retires to repeat this new reading of 'Shepherds, I have lost my love,' at every other station-house, till he finds her – and bails her.

Most of the constables who have been relieved from duty by the nine o'clock men have now dropped in, and are detailing anything worthy of a report to their respective serjeants. The serjeants enter these occurrences on a printed form. Only one is presented, now:

P. C. 67 reports that, at 5½ P.M., a boy, named Philip Isaac was knocked down, in Bow Street, by a horse belonging to Mr Parks, a Newsvender. He was taken to Charing X Hospital, and sent home, slightly bruised.

The Inspector has not time to file this document before an earnest-looking man comes to the window. Something has happened which evidently causes him more pain than resentment.

'I am afraid we have been robbed. My name is Parker, of the firm of Parker and Tide, Upholsterers. This afternoon at three o'clock, our clerk handed to a young man who is our collector, (he is only nineteen), about ninety-six pounds, to take to the bank. He ought to have been back in about fifteen minutes; but he hadn't come back at six o'clock. I went to the bank to see if the cash had been paid in, and it had *not*.'

'Be good enough to describe his person and dress, sir,' says the Inspector, taking out a printed form called 'a Route.'

These are minutely detailed and recorded. 'Has he any friends or relatives in London?'

The applicant replies by describing the residence and condition of
the youth's father and uncle. The Inspector orders 'Ninety-two' (one of
the Reserves) to go with the gentleman, 'and see what he can make of
it.' The misguided delinquent's chance of escape will be lessened every
minute. Not only will his usual haunts be visited in the course of the
night by Ninety-two; but his description will be known, before morning, by *every* police officer on duty. This Route, – which is now being
copied by a Reserve into a book – will be passed on, presently, to the
next station. There, it will again be copied; passed on to the next; copied; forwarded – and so on until it shall have made the circuit of all the
Metropolitan stations. In the morning, that description will be read to
the men going on duty. 'Long neck, light hair, brown clothes, low
crowned hat,' and so on.

A member of the E division throws a paper on the window-sill,
touches his hat, exclaims, 'Route, sir!' and departs.

The Routes are coming in all night long. A lady has lost her purse in
an omnibus. Here is a description of the supposed thief – a woman
who sat next to the lady – and here are the dates and numbers of the
bank notes, inscribed on the paper with exactness. On the back, is an
entry of the hour at which the paper was received at, and sent away
from, every station to which it has yet been. A Reserve is called in to
book the memorandum; and in a quarter of an hour he is off with it to
the station next on the Route. Not only are these notices read to the
men at each relief, but the most important of them are inserted in the
Police Gazette, the especial literary organ of the Force, which is edited
by one of its members.

A well dressed youth about eighteen years of age, now leans over
the window to bring himself as near to the Inspector as possible. He
whispers in a broad Scotch accent:

'I am destitute. I came up from Scotland to find one Saunders M'Alpine,
and I *can't* find him, and I have spent all my money. I have not a
farthing left. I want a night's lodging.'

'Reserve!' The Inspector wastes no words in a case like this.

'Sir.'

'Go over to the relieving officer and ask him to give this young man
a night in the casual ward.'

The policeman and the half-shamed suppliant go out together.

'That is a genuine tale,' remarks the Inspector.

'Evidently a fortune-seeking young Scotchman,' we venture to con-
jecture, 'who has come to London upon too slight an invitation, and
with too slender a purse. He has an honest face, and won't know want
long. He may die Lord Mayor.'

The Inspector is not sanguine in such cases. 'He *may*,' he says.

There is a great commotion in the outer office. Looking through the
window, we see a stout bustling woman who announces herself as a
complainant, three female witnesses, and two policemen. This solemn
procession moves towards the window; yet we look in vain for a prisoner. The prisoner is in truth invisible on the floor of the dock, so one
of his guards is ordered to mount him on a bench. He is a handsome,
dirty, curly-headed boy about the age of seven, though he says he is
nine. The prosecutrix makes her charge.

'Last Sunday, sir, (if you please, sir, I keep a cigar and stationer's
shop), this here little creetur breaks one of my windows, and the moment after, I loses a box of paints –'

'Value?' asks the Inspector, already entering the charge, after one
sharp look at the child.

'Value, sir? Well, I'll say eight-pence. Well, sir, to-night again, just
before shutting up, I hears another pane go smash. I looks out, and I
sees this same little creetur a running aways. I runs after him, and
hands him over to the police.'

The child does not exhibit the smallest sign of fear or sorrow. He
does not even whimper. He tells his name and address, when asked
them, in a straightforward business-like manner, as if he were quite
used to the whole proceeding. He is locked up; and the prosecutrix is
desired to appear before the Magistrate in the morning to substantiate
her charge.

'A child so young, a professional thief!'

'Ah! These are the most distressing cases we have to deal with. The
number of children brought here, either as prisoners, or as having been
lost, is from five to six thousand per annum. Juvenile crime and its
forerunner – the neglect of children by their parents – is still on the
increase. That's the experience of the whole Force.'

'If some place were provided at which neglected children could be
made to pass their time, instead of in the market and streets – say, in

industrial schools provided by the nation – juvenile delinquency would very much decrease? –'

'I believe, sir, (and I speak the sentiments of many experienced officers in the Force,) that it would be much lessened, and that the expense of such establishments would be saved in a very short time out of the police and county rates. Let alone morality altogether.'

And the Inspector resumes his writing. For a little while we are left to think, to the ticking of the clock.

There are six hundred and fifty-six gentlemen in the English House of Commons assembling in London. There is not one of those gentlemen who may not, in one week, if he choose, acquire as dismal a knowledge of the Hell upon earth in which he lives, in regard of these children, as this Inspector has – as we have – as no man can by possibility shut out, who will walk this town with open eyes observant of what is crying to GOD in the streets. If we were one of those six hundred and fifty-six, and had the courage to declare that we know the day *must come* when these children must be taken, by the strong hand, out of our shameful public ways, and must be rescued – when the State must (no will, or will not, in the case, but must) take up neglected and ignorant children wheresoever they are found, severely punishing the parents when they can be found, too, and forcing them, if they have any means of existence, to contribute something towards the reclamation of their offspring, but never again entrusting them with the duties they have abandoned; – if we were to say this, and were to add that as the day must come, it cannot come too soon, and had best come now – Red Tape would arise against us in ten thousand shapes of virtuous opposition, and cocks would crow, and donkeys would bray, and owls would hoot, and strangers would be espied, and houses would be counted out, and we should be satisfactorily put down. Meanwhile, in Aberdeen, the horror has risen to that height, that against the law, the authorities have by force swept their streets clear of these unchristian objects, and have, to the utmost extent of their illegal power, successfully done this very thing. Do none of the six hundred and fifty-six know of it – do none of them look into it – do none of them lay down their newspapers when they read of a baby sentenced for the third, fourth, fifth, sixth, seventh time to imprisonment and whipping, and ask themselves the question, 'Is there any earthly thing this child can

The discovery of a suicide – an illustration by Henry Aneley

do when this new sentence is fulfilled, but steal again, and be again imprisoned and again flogged, until, a precocious human devil, it is shipped away to corrupt a new world?' Do none of the six hundred and fifty-six, care to walk from Charing Cross to Whitechapel – to look into Wentworth Street – to stray into the lanes of Westminster – to go into a prison almost within the shadow of their own Victoria Tower – to see with their eyes and hear with their ears, what such childhood is, and what escape it has from being what it is? Well! Red Tape is easier, and tells for more in blue books, and will give you a committee five years long if you like, to enquire whether the wind ever blows, or the rain ever falls – and then you can talk about it, and do nothing.

Our meditations are suddenly interrupted.

'Here's a pretty business!' cries a pale man in a breathless hurry, at the window. 'Somebody has been tampering with my door-lock!'

'How do you mean, sir?'

'Why, I live round the corner, and I had been to the Play, and I left my door on the lock (it's a Chubb!) and I come back, and the lock won't act. It has been tampered with. There either are, or have been, thieves in the place!'

'Reserve!'

'Sir!'

'Take another man with you, and a couple of ladders, and see to this gentleman's house.'

A sallow anxious little man rushes in.

'O! you haven't seen anything of such a thing as a black and tan spaniel, have you?'

'Is it a spaniel dog we have got in the yard?' the Inspector inquires of the jailer.

'No, sir, it's a brown tarrier?'

'O! It can't be my dog then. A brown tarrier? O! Good night, gentlemen! Thank you.'

'Good night, sir.'

The Reserve just now dispatched with the other man and the two ladders, returns, gruff-voiced and a little disgusted.

'Well? what's up round the corner?'

'Nothing the matter with the lock, sir. I opened it with the key directly!'

We fall into a doze before the fire. Only one little rattle of a pen is springing now, for the other Inspector has put on his great-coat and gone out, to make the round of his beat and look after his men. We become aware in our sleep of a scuffling on the pavement outside. It approaches, and becomes noisy and hollow on the boarded floor within. We again repair to the window.

A very ill-looking woman in the dock. A very stupid little gentleman, very much overcome with liquor, and with his head extremely towzled, endeavouring to make out the meaning of two immoveable Policemen, and indistinctly muttering a desire to know 'war it's awr abow.'

'Well?' says the Inspector, possessed of the case in a look.

'I was on duty, sir, in Lincoln's Inn Fields just now,' says one of the Policemen, 'when I see this gent' –

Here, 'this gent,' with an air of great dignity, again observers, 'Mirrer Insperrer, I requesherknow war it's awr ABOW.'

'We'll hear you presently, sir. Go on!'

– 'when I see this gent, in conversation against the railings with this woman. I requested him to move on, and observed his watch-guard hanging loose out of his pocket. "You've lost your watch," I said. Then I turned to her! "And you've got it," I said. "I an't," she said. Then she said, turning to him, "You know you've been in company with many others to-night, flower-girls, and a lot more." "I shall take *you*," I said, anyhow. Then I turned my lantern on her, and saw this silver watch, with the glass broke, lying behind her on the stones. Then I took her into custody, and the other constable brought the gent along.'

'Jailer!' says the Inspector.

'Sir!'

'Keep your eye on her. Take care she don't make away with anything – and send for Mrs Green.'

The accused sits in a corner of the dock, quite composed, with her arms under her dirty shawl, and says nothing. The Inspector folds a charge-sheet, and dips his pen in the ink.

'Now, sir, your name, if you please?'

'Ba – a.'

'*That* can't be your name, sir. What name does he say, Constable?'

The second Constable 'seriously inclines his ear;' the gent being a

short man, and the second constable a tall one. 'He says his name's
Bat, sir.' (Getting at it after a good deal of trouble.)

'Where do you live, Mr Bat?'

'Lamber.'

'And what are you? – what business are you, Mr Bat?'

'Fesher,' says Mr Bat, again collecting dignity.

'Profession, is it? Very good, sir. What's your profession?'

'Solirrer,' returns Mr Bat.

'Solicitor, of Lambeth. Have you lost anything besides your watch sir?'

'I am nor aware – lost – any – arrickle – prorrery,' says Mr Bat.

The Inspector has been looking at the watch.

'What do you value this watch at, sir?'

'Ten pound,' says Mr Bat, with unexpected promptitude.

'Hardly worth so much as that, I should think?'

'Five pound five,' says Mr Bat. 'I doro how much. I'm not par-
TICK-ler,' this word costs Mr Bat a tremendous effort, 'abow the war.
It's not my war. It's a frez of my.'

'If it belongs to a friend of yours, you wouldn't like to lose it, I
suppose?'

'I doro,' says Mr Bat, 'I'm nor any ways par-TICK-ler abow the war.
It's a frez of my;' which he afterwards repeats at intervals, scores of
times. Always as an entirely novel idea.

Inspector writes. Brings charge-sheet to window. Reads same to Mr Bat.

'You charge this woman, sir,' – her name, age, and address have
been previously taken – 'with robbing you of your watch. I won't trouble
you to sign the sheet, as you are not in good writing order. You'll have
to be here this morning – it's now two – at a quarter before ten.'

'Never get up 'till har par,' says Mr Bat, with decision.

'You'll have to be here this morning,' repeats the Inspector placidly,
'at a quarter before ten. If you don't come, we shall have to send for
you, and that might be unpleasant. Stay a bit. Now, look here. I have
written it down. "Mr Bat to be in Bow Street, quarter before ten." Or
I'll even say to make it easier to you, a quarter past. There! "Quarter
past ten." Now, let me fold this up and put it in your pocket; and when
your landlady, or whoever it is at home, finds it there, she'll take care
to call you.'

All of which is elaborately done for Mr Bat. A constable who has skilfully taken a writ out of the unconscious Mr Bat's pocket in the meantime, and has discovered from the indorsement that he has given his name and address correctly, receives instructions to put Mr Bat into a cab and send him home.

'And, Constable,' says the Inspector to the first man, musing over the watch as he speaks, 'do you go back to Lincoln's Inn Fields, and look about, and you'll find, somewhere, the little silver pin belonging to the handle. She has done it in the usual way, and twisted the pin right out.'

'What mawrer is it?' says Mr Bat, staggering back again, 'T'morrow-mawrer?'

'Not to-morrow morning. This morning.'

'*This* mawrer?' says Mr Bat. 'How can it be this mawrer? *War* is this aur abow?'

As there is no present probability of his discovering 'what it is all about,' he is conveyed to his cab; and a very indignant matron with a very livid face, a trembling lip, and a violently heaving breast, presents herself.

'Which I wishes to complain immediate on Pleeseman forty-two and fifty-three and insists on the charge being took; and that I will sub-stantiate before the magistrates to-morrow morning, and what is more will prove and which is saying a great deal sir!'

'You needn't be in a passion, you know, here, ma'am. Everything will be done correct.'

'Which I *am* not in a passion sir and everythink shalt be done correct, if you please!' drawing herself up with a look designed to freeze the whole division. 'I make a charge immediate,' very rapidly, 'against pleese-men forty-two and fifty-three, and insists on the charge being took.'

'I can't take it till I know what it is,' returns the patient Inspector, leaning on the window-sill, and making no hopeless effort, as yet, to write it down. 'How was it, ma'am?'

'This is how it were, sir. I were standing at the door of my own 'ouse.'

'Where is your house, ma'am?'

'*Where* is my house, sir?' with the freezing look.

'Yes, ma'am. Is it in the Strand, for instance.'

'No, sir,' with indignant triumph. 'It is *not* in the Strand!'

'Where then, ma'am?'

'Where then, sir?' with severe sarcasm.

'I *ope* it is in Doory Lane.'

'In Drury Lane. And what is your name, ma'am?'

'*My* name, sir?' with inconceivable scorn. 'My name is Megby.'

'Mrs Megby?'

'Sir, I *ope* so!' with the previous sarcasm. Then, very rapidly, 'I keep a Coffee house, as I will substantiate to-morrow morning and what is more will prove and that is saying a great deal.' Then, still more rapidly, 'I wish to make a charge immediate against pleesemen forty-two and fifty-three!'

'Well, ma'am, be so good as make it.'

'I were standing at my door,' falling of a sudden into a genteel and impressive slowness, 'in conversation with a friend, a gentleman from the country which his name is Henery Lupvitch, *Es*-quire –'

'Is he here, ma'am?'

'No, sir,' with surpassing scorn. 'He is *not* here!'

'Well, ma'am?'

'With Henery Lupvitch *Es*-quire, and which I had just been hissuing directions to two of my servants, when here come between us a couple of female persons which I know to be the commonest dirt, and pushed against me.'

'Both of them pushed against you?'

'No sir,' with scorn and triumph, 'they did *not*! *One* of 'em pushed against me' – A dead stoppage, expressive of implacable gentility.

'Well, ma'am – did you say anything then?'

'I ask your parding. Did I which, sir?' As compelling herself to fortitude under great provocation.

'Did you say anything?'

'I *ope* I did. I says, how dare you do that ma'am?'

Stoppage again. Expressive of a severe desire that those words be instantly taken down.

'You said how dare you do that?'

' "Nobody," continuing to quote with a lofty and abstracted effort of memory, "never interfered with you." She replies, "That's nothink to you, ma'am. Never you mind." '

Another pause, expressive of the same desire as before. Much incensed at nothing resulting.

'She then turns back between me and Henery Lupvitch *Es*-quire, and commits an assault upon me, which I am not a acquisition and will not endoor or what is more submit to.'

What Mrs Megby means by the particular expression that she is not an acquisition, does not appear; but she turns more livid, and not only her lip but her whole frame trembles as she solemnly repeats, 'I am not a acquisition.'

'Well, ma'am. Then forty-two and fifty-three came up –'

'No they did *not*, sir; nothink of the sort! – I called 'em up.'

'And you said?'

'Sir?' with tremendous calmness.

'You said?' –

'*I made the observation*,' with strong emphasis and exactness, 'I give this person in charge for assaulting of me. Forty-two says, 'O you're not hurt. Don't make a disturbance here. Fifty-three likewys declines to take the charge. Which,' with greater rapidity than ever, 'is the two pleesemen I am here to appear against; and will be here at nine to-morrow morning, or at height if needful, or at sivin – hany hour – and as a ouseholder demanding the present charge to be regularly hentered against pleesemen respectually numbered forty-two and fifty-three, which shall be substantiated by day or night or morning – which is more – for I am not a acquisition, and what those pleesemen done sir they shall answer!'

The Inspector – whose patience is not in the least affected – being now possessed of the charge, reduces it to a formal accusation against two P. C.'s, for neglect of duty, and gravely records it in Mrs Megby's own words – with such fidelity that, at the end of every sentence when it is read over, Mrs Megby, comparatively softened, repeats, 'Yes, sir, which it is correct!' and afterwards signs, as if her name were not half long enough for her great revenge.

On the removal of Mrs Megby's person, Mr Bat, to our great amazement, is revealed behind her.

'I say! Is it t'morrow mawrer?' asks Mr Bat in confidence.

'He has got out of the cab,' says the Inspector, whom nothing surprises, 'and will be brought in, in custody, presently! No. This morning. Why don't you go home?'

'*This* mawrer!' says Mr Bat, profoundly reflecting. 'How car it be *this* mawrer. It must be yesserday mawrer.'

'You had better make the best of your way home, sir,' says the Inspector.

'No offence is interrer,' says Mr Bat. 'I happened to be passing – this dirrertion – when – saw door open – kaymin. It's a frez of my – I am nor –' he is quite unequal to the word particular now, so concludes with 'you no war I me! – I am aw ri! I shall be here in the mawrer!' and stumbles out again.

The watch stealer, who has been removed, is now brought back. Mrs Green (the searcher) reports to have found upon her some half-pence, two pawnbroker's duplicates, and a comb. All produced.

'Very good. You can lock her up now, jailer. – What does she say?'

'She says can she have her comb, sir?'

'Oh yes. She can have her comb. Take it!' And away she goes to the cells, a dirty unwholesome object, designing, no doubt, to comb herself out for the magisterial presence in the morning.

'O! Please sir, you have got two French ladies here, in brown shot silk?' says a woman with a basket. (We have changed the scene to the Vine Street Station House, but its general arrangement is just the same.)

'Yes.'

'Will you send 'em in, this fowl and bread for supper, please?'

'They shall have it. Hand it in.'

'Thank'ee, sir. Good night, sir!'

The Inspector has eyed the woman, and now eyes the fowl. He turns it up, opens it neatly with his knife, takes out a little bottle of brandy artfully concealed within it, puts the brandy on a shelf as confiscated, and sends in the rest of the supper.

What is this very neat new trunk in a corner, carefully corded?

It is here on a charge of 'drunk and incapable.' It was found in Piccadilly to-night (with a young woman sitting on it) and is full of good clothes, evidently belonging to a domestic servant. Those clothes will be rags soon, and the drunken woman will die of gin, or be drowned in the river.

We are dozing by the fire again, and it is past three o'clock when the stillness (only invaded at intervals by the head voices of the two French ladies talking in their cell – no other prisoners seem to be awake,) is broken by the complaints of a woman and the cries of a child. The outer door opens noisily, and the complaints and the cries come nearer, and come into the dock.

'What's this?' says the Inspector, putting up the window. 'Don't cry there, don't cry!'

A rough-headed miserable little boy of four or five years old stops in his crying and looks frightened.

'This woman,' says a wet constable, glistening in the gaslight, 'has been making a disturbance in the street for hours, on and off. She says she wants relief. I have warned her off my beat over and over again, sir; but it's of no use. She took at last to rousing the whole neighbourhood.'

'You hear what the constable says. What did you do that for?'

'Because I want relief, sir.'

'If you want relief, why don't you go to the relieving-officer?'

'I've been, sir, God knows; but I couldn't get any. I haven't been under a blessed roof for three nights; but have been prowling the streets the whole night long, sir. And I can't do it any more, sir. And my husband has been dead these eight months, sir. And I've nobody to help me to a shelter or a bit of bread, God knows!'

'You haven't been drinking, have you?'

'Drinking, sir? Me, sir?'

'I am afraid you have. Is that your own child?'

'O yes, sir, he's my child!'

'*He* hasn't been with you in the streets three nights, has he?'

'No, sir. A friend took him in for me, sir; but couldn't afford to keep him any longer, sir, and turned him on my hands this afternoon, sir.'

'You didn't fetch him away yourself, to have him to beg with, I suppose?'

'O no, sir! Heavens knows I didn't, sir!'

'Well!' writing on a slip of paper, 'I shall send the child to the workhouse until the morning, and keep you here. And then, if your story is true, you can tell it to the magistrate, and it will be inquired into.'

'Very well, sir. And God knows I'll be thankful to have it inquired into!'

'Reserve!'

'Sir!'

'Take this child to the workhouse. Here's the order. You go along with this man, my little fellow, and they'll put you in a nice warm bed, and give you some breakfast in the morning. There's a good boy!'

The wretched urchin parts from his mother without a look, and trots contentedly away with the constable. There would be no very strong ties to break here if the constable were taking him to an industrial school. Our honourable friend the member for Red Tape voted for breaking stronger ties than these in workhouses once upon a time. And we seem faintly to remember that he glorified himself upon that measure very much!

We shift the scene to Southwark. It is much the same. We return to Bow Street. Still the same. Excellent method, carefully administered, vigilant in all respects except this main one: prevention of ignorance, remedy for unnatural neglect of children, punishment of wicked parents, interposition of the State, as a measure of human policy, if not of human pity and accountability, at the very source of crime.

Our Inspectors hold that drunkenness as a cause of crime, is in the ratio of two to one greater than any other cause. We doubt if they make due allowance for the cases in which it is the consequence or companion of crime, and not the cause; but, we do not doubt its extensive influence as a cause alone. Of the seven thousand and eighteen charges entered in the books of Bow Street station during 1850, at least half are against persons of both sexes, for being 'drunk and incapable.' If offences be included which have been indirectly instigated by intoxication the proportion rises to at least seventy-five per cent. As a proof of this, it can be demonstrated from the books at head quarters (Scotland Yard) that there was a great and sudden diminution of charges after the wise measure of shutting up public houses at twelve o'clock on Saturday nights.

Towards five o'clock, the number of cases falls off, and the business of the station dwindles down to charges against a few drunken women. We have seen enough, and we retire.

We have not wearied the reader, whom we now discharge, with more than a small part of our experience; we have not related how the two respectable tradesmen, 'happening' to get drunk at 'the House they used,' first fought with one another, then 'dropped into' a policeman; as that witness related in evidence, until admonished by his Inspector concerning the Queen's English: nor how one young person resident near Covent Garden, reproached another young person in a loud tone of voice at three o'clock in the morning, with being 'a shilling minx' – nor how that young person retorted that, allowing herself for the sake of argument to be a minx, she must yet prefer a claim to be a pound minx rather than a shilling one, and so they fell to fighting and were taken into custody – nor how the first minx, piteously declaring that she had 'left her place without a bit of key,' was consoled, before having the police-key turned upon herself, by the dispatch of a trusty constable to secure her goods and chattels from pillage: nor how the two smiths taken up for 'larking' on an extensive scale, were sorely solicitous about 'a centre-punch' which one of them had in his pocket; and which, on being searched (according to custom) for knives, they expected never to see more: nor how the drunken gentleman of independent property – who being too drunk to be allowed to buy a railway ticket, and being most properly refused, most improperly 'dropped into' the Railway authorities – complained to us, visiting his cell, that he was locked up on a foul charge at which humanity revolted, and was not allowed to send for bail, and was *this* the Bill of Rights? We have seen that an incessant system of communication, day and night, is kept up between every station of the force; we have seen, not only crime speedily detected, but distress quickly relieved; we have seen regard paid to every application, whether it be an enquiry after a gipsy woman, or a black-and-tan spaniel, or a frivolous complaint against a constable; we have seen that everything that occurs is written down, to be forwarded to head quarters; we have seen an extraordinary degree of patience habitually exercised in listening to prolix details, in relieving the kernel of a case from its almost impenetrable husk; we have seen how impossible it is for anything of a serious, of even an unusual, nature to happen without being reported; and that if reported, additional force can be immediately supplied from each station; where from twenty to thirty men are always collected while off duty. We have seen that the whole system is well, intelligently, zealously worked; and we have seen, finally, that the addition of a few extra men will be all-sufficient for any exigencies which may arise from the coming influx of visitors.

Believe us, nervous old lady, dyspeptic half-pay, suspicious quidnunc, plot-dreading diplomatist, you may sleep in peace! As for you, trembling rate-payer, it is not to be doubted that, after what you have read, you will continue to pay your eightpence in the pound without a grudge.

And if, either you nervous old lady, or you dyspeptic half-pay, or you suspicious quidnunc, or you plot-dreading diplomatist, or you ungrudging rate-payer, have ever seen or heard, or read of, a vast city which a solitary watcher might traverse in the dead of night as he may traverse London, you are far wiser than we. It is daybreak on this third morning of our vigil – on, it may be, the three thousandth morning of our seeing the pale dawn in these hushed and solemn streets. Sleep in peace! If you have children in your houses, wake to think of, and to act for, the doomed childhood that encircles you out of doors, from the rising up of the sun unto the going down of the stars, and sleep in greater peace. There is matter enough for real dread there. It is a higher cause than the cause of any rotten government on the Continent of Europe, that, trembling, hears the Marseillaise in every whisper, and dreads a barricade in every gathering of men!

EIGHT

On Duty with Inspector Field

How goes the night? Saint Giles's clock is striking nine. The weather is dull and wet, and the long lines of street lamps are blurred, as if we saw them through tears. A damp wind blows and rakes the pieman's fire out, when he opens the door of his little furnace, carrying away an eddy of sparks.

Saint Giles's clock strikes nine. We are punctual. Where is Inspector Field? Assistant Commissioner of Police is already here, enwrapped in oil-skin cloak, and standing in the shadow of Saint Giles's steeple. Detective Sergeant, weary of speaking French all day to foreigners unpacking at the Great Exhibition, is already here. Where is Inspector Field?

Inspector Field is, to-night, the guardian genius of the British Museum. He is bringing his shrewd eye to bear on every corner of its solitary galleries, before he reports 'all right.' Suspicious of the Elgin marbles, and not to be done by cat-faced Egyptian giants with their hands upon their knees, Inspector Field, sagacious, vigilant, lamp in hand, throwing monstrous shadows on the walls and ceilings, passes through the spacious rooms. If a mummy trembled in an atom of its dusty covering, Inspector Field would say, 'Come out of that, Tom Green. I know you!' If the smallest 'Gonoph' about town were crouching at the bottom of a classic bath, Inspector Field would nose him with a finer scent than the ogre's, when adventurous Jack lay trembling in his kitchen copper. But all is quiet, and Inspector Field goes warily on, making little outward show of attending to anything in particular, just recognising the Ichthyosaurus as a familiar acquaintance, and wondering, perhaps, how the detectives did it in the days before the Flood.

Will Inspector Field be long about this work? He may be half-an-hour longer. He sends his compliments by Police Constable, and proposes that we meet at St Giles's Station House, across the road. Good. It were as well to stand by the fire, there, as in the shadow of Saint Giles's steeple.

Anything doing here to-night? Not much. We are very quiet. A lost boy, extremely calm and small, sitting by the fire, whom we now confide to a constable to take home, for the child says that if you show him Newgate Street, he can show you where he lives – a raving drunken woman in the cells, who has screeched her voice away, and has hardly power enough left to declare, even with the passionate help of her feet and arms, that she is the daughter of a British officer, and, strike her blind and dead, but she'll write a letter to the Queen! but who is soothed with a drink of water – in another cell, a quiet woman with a child at her breast, for begging – in another, her husband in a smock-frock, with a basket of watercresses – in another, a pickpocket – in another, a meek tremulous old pauper man who has been out for a holiday 'and has took but a little drop, but it has overcome him after so many months in the house' – and that's all as yet. Presently, a sensation at the Station House door. Mr Field, gentlemen!

Inspector Field comes in, wiping his forehead, for he is of a burly figure, and has come fast from the ores and metals of the deep mines of the earth, and from the Parrot Gods of the South Sea Islands, and from the birds and beetles of the tropics, and from the Arts of Greece and Rome, and from the Sculptures of Nineveh, and from the traces of an elder world, when these were not. Is Rogers ready? Rogers is ready, strapped and great-coated, with a flaming eye in the middle of his waist, like a deformed Cyclops. Lead on, Rogers, to Rats' Castle!

How many people may there be in London, who, if we had brought them deviously and blindfold, to this street, fifty paces from the Station House, and within call of Saint Giles's church, would know it for a not remote part of the city in which their lives are passed? How many, who amidst this compound of sickening smells, these heaps of

Inspector Field confronted with an unexpected clue. Anonymous illustration

filth, these tumbling houses, with all their vile contents, animate, and inanimate, slimily overflowing into the black road, would believe that they breathe *this* air? How much Red Tape may there be, that could look round on the faces which now hem us in – for our appearance here has caused a rush from all points to a common centre – the lowering foreheads, the sallow cheeks, the brutal eyes, the matted hair, the infected, vermin-haunted heaps of rags – and say, 'I have thought of this. I have not dismissed the thing. I have neither blustered it away, nor frozen it away, nor tied it up and put it away, nor smoothly said pooh, pooh! to it when it has been shown to me?'

This is not what Rogers wants to know, however. What Rogers wants to know, is, whether you *will* clear the way here, some of you, or whether you won't; because if you don't do it right on end, he'll lock you up! 'What! *You* are there, are you, Bob Miles? You haven't had enough of it yet, haven't you? You want three months more, do you? Come away from that gentleman! What are you creeping round there for?'

'What am I a doing, thinn, Mr Rogers?' says Bob Miles, appearing, villainous, at the end of a lane of light, made by the lantern.

'I'll let you know pretty quick, if you don't hook it. WILL you hook it?'

A sycophantic murmur rises from the crowd. 'Hook it, Bob, when Mr Rogers and Mr Field tells you! Why don't you hook it, when you are told to?'

The most importunate of the voices strikes familiarly on Mr Rogers's ear. He suddenly turns his lantern on the owner.

'What! *You* are there, are you, Mister Click? You hook it too – come!'

'What for?' says Mr Click, discomfited.

'You hook it, will you!' says Mr Rogers with stern emphasis.

Both Click and Miles *do* 'hook it,' without another word, or, in plainer English, sneak away.

'Close up there, my men!' says Inspector Field to two constables on duty who have followed. 'Keep together, gentlemen; we are going down here. Heads!'

Saint Giles's church strikes half-past ten. We stoop low, and creep down a precipitous flight of steps into a dark close cellar. There is a fire. There is a long deal table. There are benches. The cellar is full of company, chiefly very young men in various conditions of dirt and raggedness. Some are eating supper. There are no girls or women present. Welcome to Rats' Castle, gentlemen, and to this company of noted thieves!

'Well, my lads! How are you, my lads? What have you been doing to-day? Here's some company come to see you, my lads! *There's* a plate of beefsteak, sir, for the supper of a fine young man! And there's a mouth for a steak, sir! Why, I should be too proud of such a mouth as that, if I had it myself! Stand up and show it, sir! Take off your cap. There's a fine young man for a nice little party, sir! An't he?'

Inspector Field is the bustling speaker. Inspector Field's eye is the roving eye that searches every corner of the cellar as he talks. Inspector Field's hand is the well-known hand that has collared half the people here, and motioned their brothers, sisters, fathers, mothers, male and female friends, inexorably to New South Wales. Yet Inspector Field stands in this den, the Sultan of the place. Every thief here cowers before him, like a schoolboy before his schoolmaster. All watch him, all answer when addressed, all laugh at his jokes, all seek to propitiate him. This cellar company alone – to say nothing of the crowd surrounding the entrance from the street above, and making the steps shine with eyes – is strong enough to murder us all, and willing enough to do it; but, let Inspector Field have a mind to pick out one thief here, and take him; let him produce that ghostly truncheon from his pocket, and say, with his business-air, 'My lad, I want you!' and all Rats' Castle shall be stricken with paralysis, and not a finger move against him, as he fits the handcuffs on!

Where's the Earl of Warwick? – Here he is, Mr Field! Here's the Earl of Warwick, Mr Field! – O there you are, my Lord. Come for'ard. There's a chest, sir, not to have a clean shirt on. An't it? Take your hat off, my Lord. Why, I should be ashamed if I was you – and an Earl, too – to show myself to a gentleman with my hat on! – The Earl of Warwick laughs and uncovers. All the company laugh. One pickpocket, especially, laughs with great enthusiasm. O what a jolly game it is, when Mr Field comes down – and don't want nobody!

So, *you* are here, too, are you, you tall, grey, soldierly-looking, grave man, standing by the fire? – Yes, sir. Good evening, Mr Field! – Let us see. You lived servant to a nobleman once? – Yes, Mr Field. – And what is it you do how; I forget? – Well, Mr Field, I job about as well as I can. I left my employment on account of delicate health. The family is still kind to me. Mr Wix of Piccadilly is also very kind to me when I am hard up. Likewise Mr Nix of Oxford Street. I get a trifle from them occasionally, and rub on as well as I can, Mr Field. Mr Field's eye rolls enjoyingly, for this man is a notorious begging-letter writer. – Good night, my lads! – Good night, Mr Field, and thank'ee, sir!

Clear the street here, half a thousand of you! Cut it, Mrs Stalken – none of that – we don't want you! Rogers of the flaming eye, lead on to the tramps' lodging-house!

A dream of baleful faces attends to the door. Now, stand back all of you! In the rear Detective Sergeant plants himself, composedly whistling, with his strong right arm across the narrow passage. Mrs Stalker, I am something'd that need not be written here, if you won't get yourself into trouble, in about half a minute, if I see that face of yours again!

Saint Giles's church clock, striking eleven, hums through our hand from the dilapidated door of a dark outhouse as we open it, and are stricken back by the pestilent breath that issues from within. Rogers to the front with the light, and let us look!

Ten, twenty, thirty – who can count them! Men, women, children, for the most part naked, heaped upon the floor like maggots in a cheese! Ho! In that dark corner yonder! Does anybody lie there? Me sir, Irish me, a widder, with six children. And yonder? Me sir, Irish me, with me wife and eight poor babes. And to the left there? Me sir, Irish me, along with two more Irish boys as is me friends. And to the right there? Me sir and the Murphy fam'ly, numbering five blessed souls. And what's this, coiling, now, about my foot? Another Irish me, pitifully in want of shaving, whom I have awakened from sleep – and across my other foot lies his wife – and by the shoes of Inspector Field lie their three eldest – and their three youngest are at present squeezed between the open door and the wall. And why is there no one on that little mat before the sullen fire? Because O'Donovan, with his wife and daughter, is not come in from selling Lucifers! Nor on the bit of sacking in the nearest corner? Bad luck! Because that Irish family is late to-night, a-cadging in the streets!

They are all awake now, the children excepted, and most of them sit up, to stare. Wheresoever Mr Rogers turns the flaming eye, there is a spectral figure rising, unshrouded, from a grave of rags. Who is the landlord here? – I am, Mr Field! says a bundle of ribs and parchment against the wall, scratching itself. – Will you spend this money fairly, in the morning, to buy coffee for 'em all? – Yes, sir, I will! – O he'll do it, sir, he'll do it fair. He's honest! cry the spectres. And with thanks and Good Night sink into their graves again.

Thus, we make our New Oxford Streets, and our other new streets, never heeding, never asking, where the wretches whom we clear out, crowd. With such scenes at our doors, with all the plagues of Egypt tied up with bits of cobweb in kennels so near our homes, we timorously make our Nuisance Bills and Boards of Health, nonentities, and think to keep away the Wolves of Crime and Filth, by our electioneering ducking to little vestrymen and our gentlemanly handling of Red Tape!

Intelligence of the coffee-money has got abroad. The yard is full, and Rogers of the flaming eye is beleaguered with entreaties to show other Lodging Houses. Mine next! Mine! Mine! Rogers, military, obdurate, stiff-necked, immovable, replies not, but leads away; all falling back before him. Inspector Field follows. Detective Sergeant, with his barrier of arm across the little passage, deliberately waits to close the procession. He sees behind him, without any effort, and exceedingly disturbs one individual far in the rear by coolly calling out, 'It won't do, Mr Michael! Don't try it!'

After council holden in the street, we enter other lodging-houses, public-houses, many lairs and holes; all noisome and offensive; none so filthy and so crowded as where Irish are. In one, The Ethiopian party are expected home presently – were in Oxford Street when last heard of – shall be fetched, for our delight, within ten minutes. In another, one of the two or three Professors who draw Napoleon Buonaparte and a couple of mackerel, on the pavement, and then let the work of art out to a speculator, is refreshing after his labours. In another, the vested interest of the profitable nuisance has been in one family for a hundred years, and the landlord drives in comfortably from the country to his snug little stew in town. In all, Inspector Field is received with warmth. Coiners and smashers droop before him; pickpockets defer to him; the gentle sex (not very gentle here) smile upon him. Half-drunken hags check themselves in the midst of pots of beer, or pints of gin, to drink to Mr Field, and pressingly to ask the honour of his finishing the draught. One beldame in rusty black has such admiration for him, that she runs a whole street's length to shake him by the hand; tumbling into a heap of mud by the way, and still pressing her attentions when her very form has ceased to be distinguishable through it. Before the power of the law, the power of superior sense – for common thieves are fools beside these men – and the power of a perfect mastery of their character, the garrison of Rats' Castle and the adjacent Fortresses make but a skulking show indeed when reviewed by Inspector Field.

Saint Giles's clock says it will be midnight in half-an-hour, and Inspector Field says we must hurry to the Old Mint in the Borough. The cab-driver is low-spirited, and has a solemn sense of his responsibility. Now, what's your fare, my lad? – O *you* know, Inspector Field, what's the good of asking *me*!

Say, Parker, strapped and great-coated, and waiting in dim Borough doorway by appointment, to replace the trusty Rogers whom we left deep in Saint Giles's, are you ready? Ready, Inspector Field, and at a motion of my wrist behold my flaming eye.

This narrow street, sir, is the chief part of the Old Mint, full of low lodging-houses, as you see by the transparent canvas-lamps and blinds, announcing beds for travellers! But it is greatly changed, friend Field, from my former knowledge of it; it is infinitely quieter and more subdued than when I was here last, some seven years ago? O yes! Inspector Haynes, a first-rate man, is on this station now and plays the Devil with them!

Well, my lads! How are you to-night, my lads? Playing cards here, eh? Who wins? – Why, Mr Field, I, the sulky gentleman with the damp flat side-curls, rubbing my bleared eye with the end of my neckerchief which is like a dirty eel-skin, am losing just at present, but I suppose I must take my pipe out of my mouth, and be submissive to *you* – I hope I see you well, Mr Field? – Aye, all right, my lad. Deputy, who have you got up-stairs? Be pleased to show the rooms!

Why Deputy, Inspector Field can't say. He only knows that the man who takes care of the beds and lodgers is always called so. Steady, O Deputy, with the flaring candle in the blacking-bottle, for this is a slushy back-yard, and the wooden staircase outside the house creaks and has holes in it.

Again, in these confined intolerable rooms, burrowed out like the holes of rats or the nests of insect-vermin, but fuller of intolerable smells, are crowds of sleepers, each on his foul truckle-bed coiled up beneath a rug. Halloa here! Come! Let us see you! Show your face! Pilot Parker goes from bed to bed and turns their slumbering heads towards us, as a salesman might turn sheep. Some wake up with an execration and a threat. – What! who spoke? O! If it's the accursed glaring eye that fixes me, go where I will, I am helpless. Here! I sit up to be looked at. Is it me you want? Not you, lie down again! and I lie down, with a woful growl.

Wherever the turning lane of light becomes stationary for a moment, some sleeper appears at the end of it, submits himself to be scrutinised, and fades away into the darkness.

There should be strange dreams here, Deputy. They sleep sound enough, says Deputy, taking the candle out of the blacking-bottle, snuffing it with his fingers, throwing the snuff into the bottle, and corking it up with the candle; that's all *I* know. What is the inscription, Deputy, on all the discoloured sheets? A precaution against loss of linen. Deputy turns down the rug of an unoccupied bed and discloses it. STOP THIEF!

To lie at night, wrapped in the legend of my slinking life; to take the cry that pursues me, waking, to my breast in sleep; to have it staring at me, and clamouring for me, as soon as consciousness returns; to have it for my first-foot on New-Year's day, my Valentine, my Birthday salute, my Christmas greeting, my parting with the old year. STOP THIEF!

And to know that I *must* be stopped, come what will. To know that I am no match for this individual energy and keenness, or this organised and steady system! Come across the street, here, and, entering by a little shop, and yard, examine these intricate passages and doors, contrived for escape, flapping and counter-flapping, like the lids of the conjurer's boxes. But what avail they? Who gets in by a nod, and shows their secret working to us? Inspector Field.

Don't forget the old Farm House, Parker! Parker is not the man to forget it. We are going there, now. It is the old Manor-House of these parts, and stood in the country once. Then, perhaps, there was something, which was not the beastly street, to see from the shattered low fronts of the overhanging wooden houses we are passing under – shut up now, pasted over with bills about the literature and drama of the

Mint, and mouldering away. This long paved yard was a paddock or a garden once, or a court in front of the Farm House. Perchance, with a dovecot in the centre, and fowls pecking about – with fair elm trees, then, where discoloured chimney-stacks and gables are now – noisy, then, with rooks which have yielded to a different sort of rookery. It's likelier than not, Inspector Field thinks, as we turn into the common kitchen, which is in the yard, and many paces from the house.

Well my lads and lasses, how are you all? Where's Blackey, who has stood near London Bridge these five-and-twenty years, with a painted skin to represent disease? – Here he is, Mr Field! – How are you, Blackey? – Jolly, sa! Not playing the fiddle to-night, Blackey? – Not a night, sa! A sharp, smiling youth, the wit of the kitchen, interposes. He an't musical to-night, sir. I've been giving him a moral lecture; I've been a talking to him about his latter end, you see. A good many of these are my pupils, sir. This here young man (smoothing down the hair of one near him, reading a Sunday paper) is a pupil of mine. I'm a teaching of him to read, sir. He's a promising cove, sir. He's a smith, he is, and gets his living by the sweat of the brow, sir. So do I, myself, sir. This young woman is my sister, Mr Field. *She's* getting on very well too. I've a deal of trouble with 'em, sir, but I'm richly rewarded, now I see 'em all a doing so well, and growing up so creditable. That's a great comfort, that is, an't it, sir? – In the midst of the kitchen (the whole kitchen is in ecstasies with this impromptu 'chaff') sits a young, modest, gentle-looking creature, with a beautiful child in her lap. She seems to belong to the company, but is so strangely unlike it. She has such a pretty, quiet face and voice, and is so proud to hear the child admired – thinks you would hardly believe that he is only nine months old! Is she as bad as the rest, I wonder? Inspectorial experience does not engender a belief contrariwise, but prompts the answer, Not a ha'porth of difference!

There is a piano going in the old Farm House as we approach. It stops. Landlady appears. Has no objections, Mr Field, to gentlemen being brought, but wishes it were at earlier hours, the lodgers complaining of ill-conwenience. Inspector Field is polite and soothing – knows his woman and the sex. Deputy (a girl in this case) shows the way up a heavy broad old staircase, kept very clean, into clean rooms where many sleepers are, and where painted panels of an older time look strangely on the truckle beds. The sight of whitewash and the smell of soap – two things we seem by this time to have parted from in infancy – make the old Farm House a phenomenon, and connect themselves with the so curiously misplaced picture of the pretty mother and child long after we have left it, – long after we have left, besides, the neighbouring nook with something of a rustic flavour in it yet, where once, beneath a low wooden colonnade still standing as of yore, the eminent Jack Sheppard condescended to regale himself, and where, now, two old bachelor brothers in broad hats (who are whispered in the Mint to have made a compact long ago that if either should ever marry, he must forfeit his share of the joint property) still keep a sequestered tavern, and sit o' nights smoking pipes in the bar, among ancient bottles and glasses, as our eyes behold them.

How goes the night now? Saint George of Southwark answers with twelve blows upon his bell. Parker, good night, for Williams is already waiting over in the region of Ratcliffe Highway, to show the houses where the sailors dance.

I should like to know where Inspector Field was born. In Ratcliffe Highway, I would have answered with confidence, but for his being equally at home wherever we go. *He* does not trouble his head as I do, about the river at night. *He* does not care for its creeping, black and silent, on our right there, rushing through sluice-gates, lapping at piles and posts and iron rings, hiding strange things in its mud, running away with suicides and accidentally drowned bodies faster than midnight funeral should, and acquiring such various experience between its cradle and its grave. It has no mystery for *him*. Is there not the Thames Police!

Accordingly, Williams leads the way. We are a little late, for some of the houses are already closing. No matter. You show us plenty. All the landlords know Inspector Field. All pass him, freely and good-humouredly, wheresoever he wants to go. So thoroughly are all these houses open to him and our local guide, that, granting that sailors must be entertained in their own way – as I suppose they must, and have a right to be – I hardly know how such places could be better regulated. Not that I call the company very select, or the dancing very graceful – even so graceful as that of the German Sugar Bakers, whose assembly, by the Minories, we stopped to visit – but there is watchful maintenance

of order in every house, and swift expulsion where need is. Even in
the midst of drunkenness, both of the lethargic kind and the lively,
there is sharp landlord supervision, and pockets are in less peril than
out of doors. These houses show, singularly, how much of the pictur-
esque and romantic there truly is in the sailor, requiring to be especially
addressed. All the songs (sung in a hailstorm of halfpence, which are
pitched at the singer without the least tenderness for the time or tune –
mostly from great rolls of copper carried for the purpose – and which
he occasionally dodges like shot as they fly near his head) are of the
sentimental sea sort. All the rooms are decorated with nautical subjects. Wrecks, engagements, ships on fire, ships passing lighthouses on
iron-bound coasts, ships blowing up, ships going down, ships running
ashore, men lying out upon the main-yard in a gale of wind, sailors
and ships in every variety of peril, constitute the illustrations of fact.
Nothing can be done in the fanciful way, without a thumping boy upon
a scaly dolphin.

How goes the night now? Past one. Black and Green are waiting in
Whitechapel to unveil the mysteries of Wentworth Street. Williams,
the best of friends must part. Adieu!

Are not Black and Green ready at the appointed place? O yes! They
glide out of shadow as we stop. Imperturbable Black opens the cab-
door; Imperturbable Green takes a mental note of the driver. Both Green
and Black then open, each his flaming eye, and marshal us the way
that we are going.

The lodging-house we want is hidden in a maze of streets and courts.
It is fast shut. We knock at the door, and stand hushed looking up for
a light at one or other of the begrimed old lattice windows in its ugly
front, when another constable comes up – supposes that we want 'to
see the school.' Detective Sergeant meanwhile has got over a rail, opened
a gate, dropped down an area, overcome some other little obstacles,
and tapped at a window. Now returns. The landlord will send a deputy
immediately.

Deputy is heard to stumble out of bed. Deputy lights a candle, draws
back a bolt or two, and appears at the door. Deputy is a shivering shirt
and trousers by no means clean, a yawning face, a shock head much
confused externally and internally. We want to look for some one. You
may go up with the light, and take 'em all, if you like, says Deputy,

resigning it, and sitting down upon a bench in the kitchen with his ten fingers sleepily twisting in his hair.

Halloa here! Now then! Show yourselves. That'll do. It's not you. Don't disturb yourself any more! So on, through a labyrinth of airless rooms, each man responding, like a wild beast, to the keeper who has tamed him, and who goes into his cage. What, you haven't found him, then? says Deputy, when we came down. A woman mysteriously sitting up all night in the dark by the smouldering ashes of the kitchen fire, says it's only tramps and cadgers here; it's gonophs over the way. A man mysteriously walking about the kitchen all night in the dark, bids her hold her tongue. We come out. Deputy fastens the door and goes to bed again.

Black and Green, you know Bark, lodging-house keeper and receiver of stolen goods? – O yes, Inspector Field. – Go to Bark's next.

Bark sleeps in an inner wooden hutch, near his street door. As we parley on the step with Bark's Deputy, Bark growls in his bed. We enter, and Bark flies out of bed. Bark is a red villain and a wrathful, with a sanguine throat that looks very much as if it were expressly made for hanging, as he stretches it out, in pale defiance, over the half-door of his hutch. Bark's parts of speech are of an awful sort – principally adjectives. I won't, says Bark, have no adjective police and adjective strangers in my adjective premises! I won't, by adjective and substantive! Give me my trousers, and I'll send the whole adjective police to adjective and substantive! Give me, says Bark, my adjective trousers! I'll put an adjective knife in the whole bileing of 'em. I'll punch their adjective heads. I'll rip up their adjective substantives. Give me my adjective trousers! says Bark, and I'll spile the bileing of 'em!

Now, Bark, what's the use of this? Here's Black and Green, Detective Sergeant, and Inspector Field. You know we will come in. – I know you won't! says Bark. Somebody give me my adjective trousers! Bark's trousers seem difficult to find. He calls for them as Hercules might for his club. Give me my adjective trousers! says Bark, and I'll spile the bileing of 'em.

Inspector Field holds that its all one whether Bark likes the visit or don't like it. He, Inspector Field, is an Inspector of the Detective Police, Detective Sergeant *is* Detective Sergeant, Black and Green are constables in uniform. Don't you be a fool, Bark, or you know it will be the worse for you. – I don't care, says Bark. Give me my adjective trousers!

At two o'clock in the morning, we descend into Bark's low kitchen, leaving Bark to foam at the mouth above, and Imperturbable Black and Green to look at him. Bark's kitchen is crammed full of thieves, holding a *conversazione* there by lamp-light. It is by far the most dangerous assembly we have seen yet. Stimulated by the ravings of Bark, above, their looks are sullen, but not a man speaks. We ascend again. Bark has got his trousers, and is in a state of madness in the passage with his back against a door that shuts off the upper staircase. We observe, in other respects, a ferocious individuality in Bark. Instead of 'STOP THIEF!' on his linen, he prints 'STOLEN FROM Bark's!'

Now, Bark, we are going up-stairs! – No, you ain't! – You refuse admission to the Police, do you, Bark? – Yes, I do! I refuse it to all the adjective police, and to all the adjective substantives. If the adjective coves in the kitchen was men, they'd come up now, and do for you! Shut me that there door! says Bark, and suddenly we are enclosed in the passage. They'd come up and do for you! cries Bark, and waits. Not a sound in the kitchen! They'd come up and do for you! cries Bark again, and waits. Not a sound in the kitchen! We are shut up, half-a-dozen of us, in Bark's house in the innermost recesses of the worst part of London, in the dead of the night – the house is crammed with notorious robbers and ruffians – and not a man stirs. No, Bark. They know the weight of the law, and they know Inspector Field and Co. too well.

We leave bully Bark to subside at leisure out of his passion and his trousers, and, I dare say, to be inconveniently reminded of this little brush before long. Black and Green do ordinary duty here, and look serious.

As to White, who waits on Holborn Hill to show the courts that are eaten out of Rotten Gray's Inn Lane, where other lodging-houses are, and where (in one blind alley) the Thieves' Kitchen and Seminary for the teaching of the art to children, is, the night has so worn away, being now

almost at odds with morning, which is which,

that they are quiet, and no light shines through the chinks in the shutters. As undistinctive Death will come here, one day, sleep comes now. The wicked cease from troubling sometimes, even in this life.

[NINE]

Down with the Tide

A very dark night it was, and bitter cold; the east wind blowing bleak, and bringing with it stinging particles from marsh, and moor, and fen – from the Great Desert and Old Egypt, maybe. Some of the component parts of the sharp-edged vapour that came flying up the Thames at London might be mummy-dust, dry atoms from the Temple at Jerusalem, camels' foot-prints, crocodiles' hatching places, loosened grains of expression from the visages of blunt-nosed sphynxes, waifs and strays from caravans of turbaned merchants, vegetation from jungles, frozen snow from the Himalayas. O! It was very very dark upon the Thames, and it was bitter bitter cold.

'And yet,' said the voice within the great pea-coat at my side, 'you'll have seen a good many rivers too, I dare say?'

'Truly,' said I, 'when I come to think of it, not a few. From the Niagara, downward to the mountain rivers of Italy, which are like the national spirit – very tame, or chafing suddenly and bursting bounds, only to dwindle away again. The Moselle, and the Rhine, and the Rhone; and the Seine, and the Saone; and the St Lawrence, Mississippi, and Ohio; and the Tiber, the Po, and the Arno; and the –'

Peacoat coughing as if he had had enough of that, I said no more. I could have carried the catalogue on to a teasing length, though, if I had been in the cruel mind.

'And after all,' said he, 'this looks so dismal?'

137

'So awful,' I returned, 'at night. The Seine at Paris is very gloomy too, at such a time, and is probably the scene of far more crime and greater wickedness; but this river looks so broad and vast, so murky and silent, seems such an image of death in the midst of the great city's life, that –'

That Peacoat coughed again. He *could not* stand my holding forth.

We were in a four-oared Thames Police Galley, lying on our oars in the deep shadow of Southwark Bridge – under the corner arch on the Surrey side – having come down with the tide from Vauxhall. We were fain to hold on pretty tight, though close in shore, for the river was swollen and the tide running down very strong. We were watching certain water-rats of human growth, and lay in the deep shade as quiet as mice; our light hidden and our scraps of conversation carried on in whispers. Above us, the massive iron girders of the arch were faintly visible, and below us its ponderous shadow seemed to sink down to the bottom of the stream.

We had been lying here some half-an-hour. With our backs to the wind, it is true; but the wind being in a determined temper blew straight through us, and would not take the trouble to go round. I would have boarded a fireship to get into action, and mildly suggested as much to my friend Pea.

'No doubt,' says he as patiently as possible; 'but shore-going tactics wouldn't do with us. River thieves can always get rid of stolen property in a moment by dropping it overboard. We want to take them *with* the property, so we lurk about and come out upon 'em sharp. If they see us or hear us, over it goes.'

Pea's wisdom being indisputable, there was nothing for it but to sit there and be blown through, for another half-hour. The water-rats thinking it wise to abscond at the end of that time without commission of felony, we shot out, disappointed, with the tide.

'Grim they look, don't they?' said Pea, seeing me glance over my shoulder at the lights upon the bridge, and downward at their long crooked reflections in the river.

'Very,' said I, 'and make one think with a shudder of Suicides. What a night for a dreadful leap from that parapet!'

'Aye, but Waterloo's the favourite bridge for making holes in the water from,' returned Pea. 'By the bye – avast pulling, lads! – would you like to speak to Waterloo on the subject?'

My face confessing a surprised desire to have some friendly conversation with Waterloo Bridge, and my friend Pea being the most obliging of men, we put about, pulled out of the force of the stream, and in place of going at great speed with the tide, began to strive against it, close in shore again. Every colour but black seemed to have departed from the world. The air was black, the water was black, the barges and hulks were black, the piles were black, the buildings were black, the shadows were only a deeper shade of black upon a black ground. Here and there, a coal fire in an iron cresset blazed upon a wharf; but, one knew that it too had been black a little while ago, and would be black again soon. Uncomfortable rushes of water suggestive of gurgling and drowning, ghostly rattlings of iron chains, dismal clankings of discordant engines, formed the music that accompanied the dip of our oars and their rattling in the rullocks. Even the noises had a black sound to me – as the trumpet sounded red to the blind man.

Our dexterous boat's crew made nothing of the tide, and pulled us gallantly up to Waterloo Bridge. Here Pea and I disembarked, passed under the black stone archway, and climbed the steep stone steps. Within a few feet of their summit, Pea presented me to Waterloo (or an eminent toll-taker representing that structure), muffled up to the eyes in a thick shawl, and amply great-coated and fur-capped.

Waterloo received us with cordiality, and observed of the night that it was 'a Searcher.' He had been originally called the Strand Bridge, he informed us, but had received his present name at the suggestion of the proprietors, when Parliament had resolved to vote three hundred thousand pound for the erection of a monument in honour of the victory. Parliament took the hint (said Waterloo, with the least flavour of misanthropy) and saved the money. Of course the late Duke of Wellington was the first passenger, and of course he paid his penny, and of course a noble lord preserved it evermore. The treadle and index at the tollhouse (a most ingenious contrivance for rendering fraud impossible), were invented by Mr Lethbridge, then property-man at Drury Lane Theatre.

Was it suicide, we wanted to know about? said Waterloo. Ha! Well, he had seen a good deal of that work, he did assure us. He had prevented some. Why, one day a woman, poorish looking, came in between the hatch, slapped down a penny, and wanted to go on without the change! Waterloo suspected this, and says to his mate, 'Give an eye to the gate,' and bolted after her. She had got to the third seat between the piers, and was on the parapet just a-going over, when he caught her and gave her in charge. At the police office next morning, she said it was along of trouble and a bad husband.

'Likely enough,' observed Waterloo to Pea and myself, as he adjusted his chin in his shawl. 'There's a deal of trouble about, you see – and bad husbands too!'

Another time, a young woman at twelve o'clock in the open day, got through, darted along; and, before Waterloo could come near her, jumped upon the parapet, and shot herself over sideways. Alarm given, watermen put off, lucky escape. – Clothes buoyed her up.

'This is where it is,' said Waterloo. 'If people jump off straight for-wards from the middle of the parapet of the bays of the bridge, they are seldom killed by drowning, but are smashed, poor things; that's what *they* are; they dash themselves upon the buttress of the bridge. But you jump off,' said Waterloo to me, putting his fore-finger in a button-hole of my great-coat; 'you jump off from the side of the bay, and you'll tumble, true, into the stream under the arch. What you have got to do, is to mind how you jump in! There was poor Tom Steele from Dublin. Didn't dive! Bless you, didn't dive at all! Fell down so flat into the water, that he broke his breast-bone, and lived two days!'

I asked Waterloo if there were a favourite side of his bridge for this dreadful purpose? He reflected, and thought yes, there was. He should say the Surrey side.

Three decent-looking men went through one day, soberly and quietly, and went on abreast for about a dozen yards: when the middle one, he sung out, all of a sudden, 'Here goes Jack!' and was over in a minute. Body found? Well. Waterloo didn't rightly recollect about that. They were compositors, *they* were.

He considered it astonishing how quick people were! Why, there was a cab came up one Boxing-night, with a young woman in it, who looked, according to Waterloo's opinion of her, a little the worse for liquor; very handsome she was too – very handsome. She stopped the cab at the gate, and said she'd pay the cabman then, which she did, though there was a little hankering about the fare, because at first she didn't seem quite to know where she wanted to be drove to. However, she paid the man, and the toll too, and looking Waterloo in the face (he thought she knew him, don't you see!) said, 'I'll finish it some-how!' Well, the cab went off, leaving Waterloo a little doubtful in his mind, and while it was going on at full speed the young woman jumped out, never fell, hardly staggered, ran along the bridge pavement a little way, passing several people, and jumped over from the second open-ing. At the inquest it was giv' in evidence that she had been quarrel-ling at the Hero of Waterloo, and it was brought in jealousy. (One of the results of Waterloo's experience was, that there was a deal of jeal-ousy about.)

'Do we ever get madmen?' said Waterloo, in answer to an inquiry of mine. 'Well, we *do* get madmen. Yes, we have had one or two; escaped from 'Sylums, I suppose. One hadn't a halfpenny; and because I wouldn't let him through, he went back a little way, stooped down, took a run, and butted at the hatch like a ram. He smashed his hat rarely, but his head didn't seem no worse – in my opinion on account of his being wrong in it afore. Sometimes people haven't got a half-penny. If they are really tired and poor we give 'em one and let 'em through. Other people will leave things – pocket-handkerchiefs mostly. I *have* taken cravats and gloves, pocket-knives, tooth-picks, studs, shirt-pins, rings (generally from young gents, early in the morning), but handkerchiefs is the general thing.'

'Regular customers?' said Waterloo. 'Lord, yes! We have regular customers. One, such a worn-out used-up old file as you can scarcely picter, comes from the Surrey side as regular as ten o'clock at night comes; and goes over, *I* think, to some flash house on the Middlesex side. He comes back, he does, as reg'lar as the clock strikes three in the morning, and then can hardly drag one of his old legs after the other. He always turns down the water-stairs, comes up again, and then goes on down the Waterloo Road. He always does the same thing, and never varies a minute. Does it every night – even Sundays.'

I asked Waterloo if he had given his mind to the possibility of this particular customer going down the water-stairs at three o'clock in some morning, and never coming up again? He didn't think *that* of him, he replied. In fact, it was Waterloo's opinion, founded on his observation of that file, that he know'd a trick worth two of it.

'There's another queer old customer,' said Waterloo, 'comes over, as punctual as the almanack, at eleven o'clock on the sixth of January, at eleven o'clock on the fifth of April, at eleven o'clock on the sixth of July, at eleven o'clock on the tenth of October. Drives a shaggy little, rough pony, in a sort of a rattle-trap arm-chair sort of a thing. White hair he has, and white whiskers, and muffles himself up with all manner of shawls. He comes back again the same afternoon, and we never see more of him for three months. He is a captain in the navy – retired – wery old – wery odd – and served with Lord Nelson. He is particular about drawing his pension at Somerset House afore the clock strikes twelve every quarter. I *have* heerd say that he thinks it wouldn't be according to the Act of Parliament, if he didn't draw it afore twelve.'

Having related these anecdotes in a natural manner, which was the best warranty in the world for their genuine nature, our friend Waterloo was sinking deep into his shawl again, as having exhausted his communicative powers and taken in enough east wind, when my other friend Pea in a moment brought him to the surface by asking whether he had not been occasionally the subject of assault and battery in the execution of his duty? Waterloo recovering his spirits, instantly dashed into a new branch of his subject. We learnt how 'both these teeth' – here he pointed to the places where two front teeth were not – were knocked out by an ugly customer who one night made a dash at him (Waterloo) while his (the ugly customer's) pal and coadjutor made a dash at the toll-taking apron where the money-pockets were; how Waterloo, letting the teeth go (to Blazes, he observed indefinitely), grappled with the apron-seizer, permitting the ugly one to run away; and how he saved the bank, and captured his man, and consigned him to fine and imprisonment. Also how, on another night, 'a Cove' laid hold of Waterloo, then presiding at the horse gate of his bridge, and threw him unceremoniously over his knee, having first cut his head open with his whip. How Waterloo 'got right,' and started after the Cove all down the Waterloo Road, through Stamford Street, and round to the foot of Blackfriars Bridge, where the Cove 'cut into' a public-house. How Waterloo cut in too; but how an aider and abettor of the Cove's, who happened to be taking a promiscuous drain at the bar, stopped Waterloo; and the Cove cut out again, ran across the road down Holland Street, and where not, and into a beer-shop. How Water-

A narrow escape on the Thames – an illustration by George Cruikshank

loo breaking away from his detainer was close upon the Cove's heels,
attended by no end of people who, seeing him running with the blood
streaming down his face, thought something worse was 'up,' and roared
Fire! and Murder! on the hopeful chance of the matter in hand being
one or both. How the Cove was ignominiously taken, in a shed where
he had run to hide, and how at the Police Court they at first wanted to
make a sessions job of it; but eventually Waterloo was allowed to be
'spoke to,' and the Cove made it square with Waterloo by paying his
doctor's bill (W. was laid up for a week) and giving him 'Three, ten.'
Likewise we learnt what we had faintly suspected before, that your
sporting amateur on the Derby day, albeit a captain, can be – 'if he
be,' as Captain Bobadil observes, 'so generously minded' – anything
but a man of honour and a gentleman; not sufficiently gratifying his
nice sense of humour by the witty scattering of flour and rotten eggs
on obtuse civilians, but requiring the further excitement of 'bilking the
toll,' and 'pitching into' Waterloo, and 'cutting him about the head
with his whip;' finally being, when called upon to answer for the assault, what Waterloo described as 'Minus,' or, as I humbly conceived
it, not to be found. Likewise did Waterloo inform us, in reply to my
inquiries, admiringly and deferentially preferred through my friend Pea,
that the takings at the Bridge had more than doubled in amount, since
the reduction of the toll one half. And being asked if the aforesaid
takings included much bad money, Waterloo responded, with a look
far deeper than the deepest part of the river, *he* should think not! – and
so retired into his shawl for the rest of the night.

Then did Pea and I once more embark in our four-oared galley, and
glide swiftly down the river with the tide. And while the shrewd East
rasped and notched us, as with jagged razors, did my friend Pea impart
to me confidences of interest relating to the Thames Police; we be-
tween-whiles finding 'duty boats' hanging in dark corners under banks,
like weeds – our own was a 'supervision boat' – and they, as they
reported 'all right!' flashing their hidden light on us, and we flashing
ours on them. These duty boats had one sitter in each: an Inspector:
and were rowed 'Ran-dan,' which – for the information of those who
never graduated, as I was once proud to do, under a fireman-waterman
and winner of Kean's Prize Wherry: who, in the course of his tuition,
took hundreds of gallons of rum and egg (at my expense) at the vari-

ous houses of note above and below bridge; not by any means because
he liked it, but to cure a weakness in his liver, for which the faculty
had particularly recommended it – may be explained as rowed by three
men, two pulling an oar each, and one a pair of sculls.

Thus, floating down our black highway, sullenly frowned upon by
the knitted brows of Blackfriars, Southwark, and London, each in his
lowering turn, I was shown by my friend Pea that there are, in the
Thames Police Force, whose district extends from Battersea to Barking
Creek, ninety-eight men, eight duty boats, and two supervision boats;
and that these go about so silently, and lie in wait in such dark places,
and so seem to be nowhere, and so may be anywhere, that they have
gradually become a police of prevention, keeping the river almost clear
of any great crimes, even while the increased vigilance on shore has
made it much harder than of yore to live by 'thieving' in the streets.
And as to the various kinds of water-thieves, said my friend Pea, there
were the Tier-rangers, who silently dropped alongside the tiers of shipping in the Pool, by night, and who, going to the companion-head,
listened for two snores – snore number one, the skipper's; snore number
two, the mate's – mates and skippers always snoring great guns, and
being dead sure to be hard at it if they had turned in and were asleep.
Hearing the double fire, down went the Rangers into the skippers'
cabins; groped for the skippers' inexpressibles, which it was the custom
of those gentlemen to shake off, watch, money, braces, boots, and all
together, on the floor; and therewith made off as silently as might be.
Then there were the Lumpers, or labourers employed to unload vessels.
They wore loose canvas jackets with a broad hem in the bottom, turned
inside, so as to form a large circular pocket in which they could conceal, like clowns in pantomimes, packages of surprising sizes. A great
deal of property was stolen in this manner (Pea confided to me) from
steamers; first, because steamers carry a larger number of small packages than other ships; next, because of the extreme rapidity with which
they are obliged to be unladen for their return voyages. The Lumpers
dispose of their booty easily to marine-store dealers, and the only remedy to be suggested is that marine-store shops should be licensed, and
thus brought under the eye of the police as rigidly as public-houses.
Lumpers also smuggle goods ashore for the crews of vessels. The smug-
gling of tobacco is so considerable, that it is well worth the while of

the sellers of smuggled tobacco to use hydraulic presses, to squeeze a single pound into a package small enough to be contained in an ordinary pocket. Next, said my friend Pea, there were the Truckers – less thieves than smugglers, whose business it was to land more considerable parcels of goods than the Lumpers could manage. They sometimes sold articles of grocery and so forth, to the crews, in order to cloak their real calling, and get aboard without suspicion. Many of them had boats of their own, and made money. Besides these, there were the Dredgermen, who, under pretence of dredging up coals and such like from the bottom of the river, hung about barges and other undecked craft, and when they saw an opportunity, threw any property they could lay their hands on overboard: in order slyly to dredge it up when the vessel was gone. Sometimes, they dexterously used their dredges to whip away anything that might lie within reach. Some of them were mighty neat at this, and the accomplishment was called dry dredging. Then, there was a vast deal of property, such as copper nails, sheathing, hardwood, &c., habitually brought away by shipwrights and other workmen from their employers' yards, and disposed of to marine-store dealers, many of whom escaped detection through hard swearing, and their extraordinary artful ways of accounting for the possession of stolen property. Likewise, there were special-pleading practitioners, for whom barges 'drifted away of their own selves' – they having no hand in it, except first cutting them loose, and afterwards plundering them – innocents, meaning no harm, who had the misfortune to observe those foundlings wandering about the Thames.

We were now going in and out, with little noise and great nicety, among the tiers of shipping, whose many hulls, lying close together, rose out of the water like black streets. Here and there, a Scotch, an Irish, or a foreign steamer, getting up her steam as the tide made, looked, with her great chimney and high sides, like a quiet factory among the common buildings. Now, the streets opened into clearer spaces, now contracted in alleys; but the tiers were so like houses, in the dark, that I could almost have believed myself in the narrower by-ways of Venice. Everything was wonderfully still; for, it wanted full three hours of flood, and nothing seemed awake but a dog here and there.

So we took no Tier-rangers captive, nor any Lumpers, nor Truckers, nor Dredgermen, nor other evil-disposed person or persons; but went

ashore at Wapping, where the old Thames Police office is now a station-house, and where the old Court, with its cabin windows looking
on the river, is a quaint charge room: with nothing worse in it usually
than a stuffed cat in a glass case, and a portrait, pleasant to behold, of
a rare old Thames Police officer, Mr Superintendent Evans, now succeeded by his son. We looked over the charge books, admirably kept,
and found the prevention so good that there were not five hundred
entries (including drunken and disorderly) in a whole year. Then, we
looked into the store-room; where there was an oakum smell, and a
nautical seasoning of dreadnought clothing, rope yarn, boat hooks, sculls
and oars, spare stretchers, rudders, pistols, cutlasses, and the like. Then,
into the cell, aired high up in the wooden wall through an opening like
a kitchen plate-rack: wherein there was a drunken man, not at all warm,
and very wishful to know if it were morning yet. Then, into a better
sort of watch and ward room, where there was a squadron of stone
bottles drawn up, ready to be filled with hot water and applied to any
unfortunate creature who might be brought in apparently drowned. Finally, we shook hands with our worthy friend Pea, and ran all the way
to Tower Hill, under strong Police suspicion occasionally, before we
got warm.

TEN

Inspector Bucket's Job

Mr Bucket and his fat forefinger are much in consultation together under existing circumstances. When Mr Bucket has a matter of this pressing interest under his consideration, the fat forefinger seems to rise to the dignity of a familiar demon. He puts it to his ears, and it whispers information; he puts it to his lips, and its enjoins him to secrecy; he rubs it over his nose, and it sharpens his scent; he shakes it before a guilty man, and it charms him to his destruction. The Augurs of the Detective Temple invariably predict, that when Mr Bucket and that finger are in much conference, a terrible avenger will be heard of before long.

Otherwise mildly studious in his observation of human nature, on the whole a benignant philosopher not disposed to be severe upon the follies of mankind, Mr Bucket pervades a vast number of houses, and strolls about an infinity of streets: to outward appearance rather languishing for want of an object. He is in the friendliest condition towards his species, and will drink with most of them. He is free with his money, affable in his manners, innocent in his conversation – but, through the placid stream of his life, there glides an under-current of forefinger.

Time and place cannot bind Mr Bucket. Like man in the abstract, he is here to-day and gone to-morrow – but, very unlike man indeed, he is here again the next day. This evening he will be casually looking into the iron extinguishers at the door of Sir Leicester Dedlock's house in town; and to-morrow morning he will be walking on the leads at Chesney Wold, where erst the old man walked whose ghost is propitiated with a hundred guineas. Drawers, desks, pockets, all things belonging to him, Mr Bucket examines. A few hours afterwards, he and the Roman will be alone together, comparing forefingers.

It is likely that these occupations are irreconcilable with home enjoyment, but it is certain that Mr Bucket at present does not go home. Though in general he highly appreciates the society of Mrs Bucket – a lady of a natural detective genius, which, if it had been improved by professional exercise, might have done great things, but which has paused at the level of a clever amateur – he holds himself aloof from that dear solace. Mrs Bucket is dependent on their lodger (fortunately an amiable lady in whom she takes an interest) for companionship and conversation.

A great crowd assembles in Lincoln's Inn Fields on the day of the funeral. Sir Leicester Dedlock attends the ceremony in person; strictly speaking, there are only three other human followers, that is to say, Lord Doodle, William Buffy, and the debilitated cousin (thrown in as a makeweight), but the amount of inconsolable carriages is immense. The Peerage contributes more four-wheeled affliction than has ever been seen in that neighborhood. Such is the assemblage of armorial bearings on coach panels, that the Heralds' College might be supposed to have lost its father and mother at a blow. The Duke of Foodle sends a splendid pile of dust and ashes, with silver wheelboxes, patent axles, all the last improvements, and three bereaved worms, six feet high, holding on behind, in a bunch of woe. All the state coachmen in London seem plunged into mourning; and if that dead old man of the rusty garb be not beyond a taste in horseflesh (which appears impossible), it must be highly gratified this day.

Quiet among the undertakers and the equipages, and the calves of so many legs all steeped in grief, Mr Bucket sits concealed in one of the inconsolable carriages, and at his ease surveys the crowd through the lattice blinds. He has a keen eye for a crowd – as for what not? – and looking here and there, now from this side of the carriage, now from the other, now up at the house windows, now along the people's heads, nothing escapes him.

'And there you are, my partner, eh?' says Mr Bucket to himself, apostrophizing Mrs Bucket, stationed, by his favor, on the steps of the deceased's house. 'And so you are! And so you are! And very well indeed you are looking, Mrs Bucket!'

The procession has not started yet, but is waiting for the cause of its assemblage to be brought out. Mr Bucket, in the foremost emblazoned carriage, uses his two fat forefingers to hold the lattice a hair's breadth open while he looks.

And it says a great deal for his attachment, as a husband, that he is still occupied with Mrs B. 'There you are, my partner, eh?' he murmuringly repeats. 'And our lodger with you. I'm taking notice of you, Mrs Bucket; I hope you're all right in your health, my dear!'

Not another word does Mr Bucket say; but sits with most attentive eyes until the sacked depository of noble secrets is brought down—— Where are all those secrets now? Does he keep them yet? Did they fly with him on that sudden journey? – and until the procession moves, and Mr Bucket's view is changed. After which he composes himself for an easy ride; and takes note of the fittings of the carriage, in case he should ever find such knowledge useful.

Contrast enough between Mr Tulkinghorn shut up in his dark carriage, and Mr Bucket shut up in *his*. Between the immeasurable track of space beyond the little wound that has thrown the one into the fixed sleep which jolts so heavily over the stones of the streets, and the narrow track of blood which keeps the other in the watchful state expressed in every hair of his head! But it is all one to both; neither is troubled about that.

Mr Bucket sits out the procession in his own easy manner, and glides from the carriage when the opportunity he has settled with himself arrives. He makes for Sir Leicester Dedlock's, which is at present a sort of home to him, where he comes and goes as he likes at all hours, where he is always welcome and made much of, where he knows the whole establishment, and walks in an atmosphere of mysterious greatness.

No knocking or ringing for Mr Bucket. He has caused himself to be provided with a key, and can pass at his pleasure. As he is crossing the hall, Mercury informs him, 'Here's another letter for you, Mr Bucket, come by post,' and gives it to him.

'Another one, eh?' says Mr Bucket.

If Mercury should chance to be possessed by any lingering curiosity as to Mr Bucket's letters, that wary person is not the man to gratify it.

Mr Bucket looks at him as if his face were a vista of some miles in length, and he were leisurely contemplating the same.

'Do you happen to carry a box?' says Mr Bucket.

Unfortunately Mercury is no snuff-taker.

'Could you fetch me a pinch from anywheres?' says Mr Bucket. 'Thankee. It don't matter what it is; I'm not particular as to the kind. Thankee!'

Having leisurely helped himself from a canister borrowed from some-body downstairs for the purpose, and having made a considerable show of tasting it, first with one side of his nose and then with the other, Mr Bucket, with much deliberation, pronounces it of the right sort, and goes on, letter in hand.

Now, although Mr Bucket walks upstairs to the little library within the larger one, with the face of a man who receives some scores of letters every day, it happens that much correspondence is not incidental to his life. He is no great scribe; rather handling his pen like the pocket-staff he carries about with him always convenient to his grasp; and discourages correspondence with himself in others, as being too artless and direct a way of doing delicate business. Further, he often sees dam-aging letters produced in evidence, and has occasion to reflect that it was a green thing to write them. For these reasons he has very little to do with letters, either as sender or receiver. And yet he has received a round half-dozen within the last twenty-four hours.

'And this,' says Mr Bucket, spreading it out on the table, 'is in the same hand, and consists of the same two words.'

What two words?

He turns the key in the door, ungirdles his black pocket-book (book of fate to many), lays another letter by it, and reads, boldly written in each, 'LADY DEDLOCK.'

'Yes, yes,' says Mr Bucket. 'But I could have made the money without this anonymous information.'

Having put the letters in his book of fate, and girdling it up again, he unlocks the door just in time to admit his dinner, which is brought upon a goodly tray, with a decanter of sherry. Mr Bucket frequently observes, in friendly circles where there is no restraint, that he likes a toothful of your fine old brown East Inder sherry better than anything you can offer him. Consequently he fills and empties his glass, with a smack of his lips; and is proceeding with his refreshment, when an idea enters his mind.

Mr Bucket softly opens the door of communication between that room and the next, and looks in. The library is deserted, and the fire is sinking low. Mr Bucket's eye, after taking a pigeon-flight around the room, alights upon a table where letters are usually put as they arrive. Several letters for Sir Leicester are upon it. Mr Bucket draws near and examines the directions. 'No,' he says, 'there's none in that hand. It's only me as is written to. I can break it to Sir Leicester Dedlock, Baronet, to-morrow.'

With that he returns to finish his dinner with a good appetite; and after a light nap, is summoned into the drawing-room. Sir Leicester has received him there these several evenings past, to know whether he has anything to report. The debilitated cousin (much exhausted by the funeral), and Volumnia, are in attendance.

Mr Bucket makes three distinctly different bows to these three people. A bow of homage to Sir Leicester, a bow of gallantry to Volumnia, and a bow of recognition to the debilitated cousin; to whom it airily says, 'You are a swell about town, and you know me, and I know you.' Having distributed these little specimens of his tact, Mr Bucket rubs his hands.

'Have you anything new to communicate, officer?' inquires Sir Leicester. 'Do you wish to hold any conversation with me in private?'

'Why – not to-night, Sir Leicester Dedlock, Baronet.'

'Because my time,' pursues Sir Leicester, 'is wholly at your disposal, with a view to the vindication of the outraged majesty of the law.'

Mr Bucket coughs and glances at Volumnia, rouged and necklaced, as though he would respectfully observe, 'I do assure you, you're a pretty creetur. I've seen hundreds worse-looking at your time of life, I have indeed.'

The fair Volumnia, not quite unconscious perhaps of the humanizing influence of her charms, pauses in the writing of cocked-hat notes, and meditatively adjusts the pearl necklace. Mr Bucket prices that decoration in his mind, and thinks it as likely as not that Volumnia is writing poetry.

'If I have not,' pursues Sir Leicester, 'in the most emphatic manner, adjured you, officer, to exercise your utmost skill in this atrocious case, I particularly desire to take the present opportunity of rectifying any omission I may have made. Let no expense be a consideration. I am prepared to defray all charges. You can incur none, in pursuit of the object you have undertaken, that I shall hesitate for a moment to bear.'

Mr Bucket made Sir Leicester's bow again, as a response to this liberality.

'My mind,' Sir Leicester adds, with generous warmth, 'has not, as may be easily supposed, recovered its tone since the late diabolical occurrence. It is not likely ever to recover its tone. But it is full of indignation to-night, after undergoing the ordeal of consigning to the tomb the remains of a faithful, a zealous, a devoted adherent.'

Sir Leicester's voice trembles, and his gray hair stirs upon his head. Tears are in his eyes; the best part of his nature is aroused.

'I declare,' he says, 'I solemnly declare that until this crime is discovered and, in the course of justice, punished, I almost feel as if there were a stain upon my name. A gentleman who has devoted a large portion of his life to me, a gentleman who has devoted the last day of his life to me, a gentleman who has constantly sat at my table and slept under my roof, goes from my house to his own, and is struck down within an hour of his leaving my house. I cannot say but that he may have been followed from my house, watched at my house, even first marked because of his association with my house – which may have suggested his possessing greater wealth, and being altogether of greater importance than his own retiring demeanor would have indicated. If I cannot, with my means and influence, and my position, bring all the perpetrators of such a crime to light, I fail in the assertion of my respect for that gentleman's memory, and of my fidelity towards one who was ever faithful to me.'

While he makes this protestation with great emotion and earnestness, looking round the room as if he were addressing an assembly, Mr Bucket glances at him with an observant gravity in which there might be, but for the audacity of the thought, a touch of compassion.

'The ceremony of to-day,' continues Sir Leicester, 'strikingly illustrative of the respect in which my deceased friend;' he lays a stress upon the word, for death levels all distinction; 'was held by the flower of the land, has, I say, aggravated the shock I have received from this most horrible and audacious crime. If it were my brother who had committed it, I would not spare him.'

Mr Bucket looks very grave. Volumnia remarks of the deceased that he was the trustiest and dearest person!

'You must feel it as a deprivation to you, miss,' replied Mr Bucket, soothingly, 'no doubt. He was calculated to *be* a deprivation, I'm sure he was.'

Volumnia gives Mr Bucket to understand, in reply, that her sensitive mind is fully made up never to get the better of it as long as she lives; that her nerves are unstrung for ever; and that she has not the least expectation of ever smiling again. Meanwhile she folds up a cocked hat for that redoubtable old general at Bath, descriptive of her melancholy condition.

'It gives a start to a delicate female,' says Mr Bucket, sympathetically, 'but it'll wear off.'

Volumnia wishes of all things to know what is doing? Whether they are going to convict, or whatever it is, that dreadful soldier? Whether he had any accomplices, or whatever the thing is called in the law? And a great deal more to the like artless purpose.

'Why, you see, miss,' returns Mr Bucket, bringing the finger into persuasive action – and such is his natural gallantry, that he had almost said, my dear; 'it ain't easy to answer those questions at the present moment. Not at the present moment. I've kept myself on this case, Sir Leicester Dedlock, Baronet,' whom Mr Bucket takes into the conversation in right of his importance, 'morning, noon, and night. But for a glass or two of sherry, I don't think I could have had my mind so much upon the stretch as it has been. I *could* answer your question, miss, but duty forbids it. Sir Leicester Dedlock, Baronet, will very soon be made acquainted with all that has been traced. And I hope that he may find it;' Mr Bucket again looks grave; 'to his satisfaction.'

The debilitated cousin only hopes some fler'll be executed – zample. Thinks more interest's wanted – get man hanged presentime – than get man place ten thousand a year. Hasn't a doubt – zample – far better hang wrong fler than no fler.

'*You* know life, you know, sir,' says Mr Bucket, with a complimentary twinkle of his eye and crook of his finger, 'and you can confirm what I've mentioned to this lady. *You* don't want to be told, that, from information I have received, I have gone to work. You're up to what a lady can't be expected to be up to. Lord! especially in your elevated station of society, miss,' says Mr Bucket, quite reddening at another narrow escape from my dear.

'The officer, Volumnia,' observes Sir Leicester, 'is faithful to his duty, and perfectly right.'

Mr Bucket murmurs, 'Glad to have the honor o' your approbation, Sir Leicester Dedlock, Baronet.'

'In fact, Volumnia,' proceeds Sir Leicester, 'it is not holding up a good model for imitation, to ask the officer any such questions as you have put to him. He is the best judge of his own responsibility; he acts upon his responsibility. And it does not become us, who assist in making the laws, to impede or interfere with those who carry them into execution. Or,' says Sir Leicester, somewhat sternly, for Volumnia was going to cut in before he had rounded his sentence; 'or who vindicate their outraged majesty.'

Volumnia with all humility explains that she has not merely the plea of curiosity to urge (in common with the giddy youth of her sex in general), but that she is perfectly dying with regret and interest for the darling man whose loss they all deplore.

'Very well, Volumnia,' returns Sir Leicester. 'Then you cannot be too discreet.'

Mr Bucket takes the opportunity of a pause to be heard again.

'Sir Leicester Dedlock, Baronet, I have no objections to telling this lady, with your leave and among ourselves, that I look upon the case as pretty well complete. It is a beautiful case – a beautiful case – and what little is wanting to complete it, I expect to be able to supply in a few hours.'

'I am very glad indeed to hear it,' says Sir Leicester. 'Highly creditable to you.'

'Sir Leicester Dedlock, Baronet,' returns Mr Bucket, very seriously, 'I hope it may at one and the same time do me credit, and prove satisfactory to all. When I depict it as a beautiful case, you see, miss,' Mr Bucket goes on, glancing gravely at Sir Leicester, 'I mean from my point of view. As considered from other points of view, such cases will always involve more or less unpleasantness. Very strange things comes to our knowledge in families, miss; bless your heart, what you would think to be phenomenons, quite.'

Volumnia, with her innocent little scream, supposes so.

'Aye, and even in gen-teel families, in high families, in great families,' says Mr Bucket, again gravely eying Sir Leicester aside. 'I have had the honor of being employed in high families before; and you have no idea – come, I'll go so far as to say not even *you* have any idea, sir,' this to the debilitated cousin, 'what games goes on!'

The cousin, who has been casting sofa-pillows on his head, in a prostration of boredom, yawns, 'Vayli' – being the used-up for 'very likely.'

Sir Leicester, deeming it time to dismiss the officer, here majestically interposes with the words, 'Very good. Thank you!' and also with a wave of his hand, implying not only that there is an end of the discourse, but that if high families fall into low habits they must take the consequences. 'You will not forget, officer,' he adds, with condescension, 'that I am at your disposal when you please.'

Mr Bucket (still grave) inquires if to-morrow morning, now, would suit, in case he should be as for'ard as he expects to be? Sir Leicester replies, 'All times are alike to me.' Mr Bucket makes his three bows, and is withdrawing, when a forgotten point occurs to him.

'Might I ask, by-the-bye,' he says, in a low voice, cautiously returning, 'who posted the reward-bill on the staircase.'

'*I* ordered it to be put up there,' replies Sir Leicester.

'Would it be considered a liberty, Sir Leicester Dedlock, Baronet, if I was to ask you why?'

'Not at all. I chose it as a conspicuous part of the house. I think it cannot be too prominently kept before the whole establishment. I wish my people to be impressed with the enormity of the crime, the determination to punish it, and the hopelessness of escape. At the same time, officer, if you in your better knowledge of the subject see any objection –'

Mr Bucket sees none now; the bill having been put up, had better not be taken down. Repeating his three bows he withdraws: closing the door on Volumnia's little scream, which is a preliminary to her remarking that that charmingly horrible person is a perfect Blue Chamber.

In his fondness for society, and his adaptability to all grades, Mr Bucket is presently standing before the hall-fire – bright and warm on the early winter night – admiring Mercury.

'Why, you're six foot two, I suppose?' says Mr Bucket.

'Three,' says Mercury.

'Are you so much? But then, you see, you're broad in proportion, and don't look it. You're not one of the weak-legged ones, you ain't. Was you ever modeled now?' Mr Bucket asks, conveying the expression of an artist into the turn of his eye and head.

Mercury never was modeled.

'Then you ought to be, you know,' says Mr Bucket; 'and a friend of mine that you'll hear of one day as a Royal Academy sculptor, would stand something handsome to make a drawing of your proportions for the marble. My Lady's out, ain't she?'

'Out to dinner.'

'Goes out pretty well every day, don't she?'

'Yes.'

'Not to be wondered at!' says Mr Bucket. 'Such a fine woman as her, so handsome and so graceful and so elegant, is like a fresh lemon on a dinner-table, ornamental wherever she goes. Was your father in the same way of life as yourself?'

Answer in the negative.

'Mine was,' says Mr Bucket. 'My father was first a page, then a footman, then a butler, then a steward, then an innkeeper. Lived universally respected, and died lamented. Said with his last breath that he considered service the most honorable part of his career, and so it was. I've a brother in the service, *and* a brother-in-law. My Lady a good temper?'

Mercury replies, 'As good as you can expect.'

'Ah!' says Mr Bucket, 'a little spoilt? A little capricious? Lord! What can you anticipate when they are so handsome as that? And we like 'em all the better for it, don't we?'

Mercury, with his hands in the pockets of his bright peach-blossom small-clothes, stretches his symmetrical silk legs with the air of a man of gallantry, and can't deny it. Come the roll of wheels, and a violent ringing at the bell.

'Talk of the angels,' says Mr Bucket. 'Here she is!'

The doors are thrown open, and she passes through the hall. Still very pale, she is dressed in slight mourning, and wears two beautiful bracelets. Either their beauty, or the beauty of her arms, is particularly attractive to Mr Bucket. He looks at them with an eager eye, and rattles something in his pockets – halfpence perhaps.

Noticing him at his distance, she turns an inquiring look on the other Mercury who has brought her home.

'Mr Bucket, my Lady.'

Mr Bucket makes a leg, and comes forward, passing his familiar demon over the region of his mouth.

'Are you waiting to see Sir Leicester?'

'No, my Lady, I've seen him!'

'Have you anything to say to me?'

'Not just at present, my Lady.'

'Have you made any new discoveries?'

'A few, my Lady.'

This is merely in passing. She scarcely makes a stop, and sweeps upstairs alone. Mr Bucket, moving towards the staircase foot, watches her as she goes up the steps the old man came down to his grave; past murderous groups of statuary, repeated with their shadowy weapons on the wall; past the printed bill, which she looks at going by; out of view.

'She's a lovely woman, too, she really is,' says Mr Bucket, coming back to Mercury. 'Don't look quite healthy though.'

Is not quite healthy, Mercury informs him. Suffers much from headaches.

Really? That's a pity! Walking Mr Bucket would recommend for that. Well, she tries walking, Mercury rejoins. Walks sometimes for two hours, when she has them bad. By night too.

'Are you sure you're quite so much as six foot three?' asks Mr Bucket, 'begging your pardon for interrupting you a moment?'

Not a doubt about it.

'You're so well put together that I shouldn't have thought it. But the household troops, though considered fine men, are built so straggling. – Walks by night, does she? When it's moonlight, though?'

O yes. When it's moonlight! Of course. O, of course! Conversational and acquiescent on both sides.

'I suppose you ain't in the habit of walking yourself?' says Mr Bucket. 'Not much time for it, I should say?'

Besides which, Mercury don't like it. Prefers carriage exercise.

'To be sure,' says Mr Bucket. 'That makes a difference. Now I think of it,' says Mr Bucket, warming his hands, and looking pleasantly at the blaze, 'she went out walking, the very night of this business.'

'To be sure she did! I let her into the garden over the way.'

'And left her there. Certainly you did. I saw you doing it.'

'I didn't see *you*,' says Mercury.

'I was rather in a hurry,' returns Mr Bucket, 'for I was going to visit a aunt of mine that lives at Chelsea – next door but two to the old original Bun House – ninety year old the old lady is, a single woman, and got a little property. Yes, I chanced to be passing at the time. Let's see. What time might it be? It wasn't ten.'

'Half-past nine.'

'You're right. So it was. And if I don't deceive myself, my Lady was muffled in a loose black mantle, with a deep fringe to it?'

'Of course she was.'

Of course she was. Mr Bucket must return to a little work he has to get on with upstairs; but he must shake hands with Mercury, in acknowledgment of his agreeable conversation, and will he – this is all he asks – will he, when he has a leisure half-hour, think of bestowing it on that Royal Academy sculptor, for the advantage of both parties?

Refreshed by sleep, Mr Bucket rises betimes in the morning, and prepares for a field-day. Smartened up by the aid of a clean shirt, and a wet hairbrush, with which instrument, on occasions of ceremony, he lubricates such thin locks as remain to him after his life of severe study, Mr Bucket lays in a breakfast of two mutton chops as a foundation to work upon, together with tea, eggs, toast, and marmalade on a corresponding scale. Having much enjoyed these strengthening matters, and having held subtle conference with his familiar demon, he confidently instructs Mercury 'just to mention quietly to Sir Leicester Dedlock, Baronet, that whatever he's ready for me, I'm ready for him.' A gracious message being returned that Sir Leicester will expedite his dressing and join Mr Bucket in the library within ten minutes, Mr Bucket repairs to that apartment; and stands before the fire, with his finger on his chin, looking at the blazing coals.

Thoughtful Mr Bucket is; as a man may be, with weighty work to do; but composed, sure, confident. From the expression of his face, he might be a famous whist-player for a large stake – say a hundred guineas

Inspector Bucket, 'the first significant detective in English literature', as drawn by E. G. Dalziel for *Bleak House*

certain – with the game in his hand, but with a high reputation involved in his playing his hand out to the last card, in a masterly way. Not in the least anxious or disturbed is Mr Bucket when Sir Leicester appears; but he eyes the baronet aside as he comes slowly to his easy-chair, with that observant gravity of yesterday, in which there might have been, but for the audacity of the idea, a touch of compassion.

'I am sorry to have kept you waiting, officer, but I am rather later than my usual hour this morning. I am not well. The agitation, and the indignation from which I have recently suffered, have been too much for me. I am subject to – gout;' Sir Leicester was going to say indisposition, and would have said it to anybody else, but Mr Bucket palpably knows all about it; 'and recent circumstances have brought it on.'

As he takes his seat with some difficulty, and with an air of pain, Mr Bucket draws a little nearer, standing with one of his large hands on the library-table.

'I am not aware, officer,' Sir Leicester observes, raising his eyes to his face, 'whether you wish us to be alone; but that is entirely as you please. If you do, well and good. If not, Miss Dedlock would be interested –'

'Why, Sir Leicester Dedlock, Baronet,' returns Mr Bucket, with his head persuasively on one side, and his forefinger pendant at one ear like an ear-ring, 'we can't be too private just at present. You will presently see that we can't be too private. A lady, under the circumstances, and especially in Miss Dedlock's elevated station of society, can't but be agreeable to me; but speaking without a view to myself, I will take the liberty of assuring you that *I* know we can't be too private.'

'That is enough.'

'So much so, Sir Leicester Dedlock, Baronet,' Mr Bucket resumes, 'that I was on the point of asking your permission to turn the key in the door.'

'By all means.' Mr Bucket skillfully and softly takes that precaution; stooping on his knee for a moment, from mere force of habit, so to adjust the key in the lock as that no one shall peep in from the outer side.

'Sir Leicester Dedlock, Baronet, I mentioned yesterday evening, that I wanted but a very little to complete this case. I have now completed it, and collected proof against the person who did this crime.'

'Against the soldier?'

'No, Sir Leicester Dedlock; not the soldier.'

Sir Leicester looks astounded, and inquires, 'Is the man in custody?'

Mr Bucket tells him, after a pause, 'It was a woman.'

Sir Leicester leans back in his chair, and breathlessly ejaculates, 'Good Heaven!'

'Now, Sir Leicester Dedlock, Baronet,' Mr Bucket begins, standing over him with one hand spread out on the library-table, and the forefinger of the other in impressive use, 'it's my duty to prepare you for a train of circumstances that may, and I go so far as to say that will, give you a shock. But, Sir Leicester Dedlock, Baronet, you are a gentleman; and I know what a gentleman is, and what a gentleman is capable of. A gentleman can bear a shock, when it must come, boldly and steadily. A gentleman can make up his mind to stand up against almost any blow. Why, take yourself, Sir Leicester Dedlock, Baronet. If there's a blow to be inflicted on you, you naturally think of your family. You ask yourself, how would all them ancestors of yours, away to Julius Cæsar – not to go beyond him at present – have borne that blow; you remember scores of them that would have borne it well; and you bear it well on their accounts, and to maintain the family credit. That's the way you argue, and that's the way you act, Sir Leicester Dedlock, Baronet.'

Sir Leicester, leaning back in his chair, and grasping the elbows, sits looking at him with a stony face.

'Now, Sir Leicester Dedlock,' proceeds Mr Bucket, 'thus preparing you, let me beg of you not to trouble your mind, for a moment, as to anything having come to *my* knowledge. I know so much about so many characters, high and low, that a piece of information more or less, don't signify a straw. I don't suppose there's a move on the board that would surprise *me*; and as to this or that move having taken place, why, my knowing it is no odds at all; any possible move whatever (provided it's in a wrong direction) being a probable move according to my experience. Therefore, what I say to you, Sir Leicester Dedlock, Baronet, is, don't you go and let yourself be put out of the way, because of my knowing anything of your family affairs.'

'I thank you for your preparation,' returns Sir Leicester, after a silence, without moving hand, foot, or feature; 'which I hope is not necessary, though I give it credit for being well intended. Be so good as to go on.

Also;' Sir Leicester seems to shrink in the shadow of his figure; 'also take a seat, if you have no objection.'

None at all. Mr Bucket brings a chair, and diminishes his shadow. 'Now, Sir Leicester Dedlock, Baronet, with this short preface I come to the point. Lady Dedlock –'

Sir Leicester raises himself in his seat, and stares at him fiercely. Mr Bucket brings the finger into play as an emollient.

'Lady Dedlock, you see she's universally admired. That's what her Ladyship is; she's universally admired,' says Mr Bucket.

'I would greatly prefer, officer,' Sir Leicester returns, stiffly, 'my Lady's name being entirely omitted from this discussion.'

'So would I, Sir Leicester Dedlock, Baronet, but – it's impossible.'

'Impossible?'

Mr Bucket shakes his relentless head.

'Sir Leicester Dedlock, Baronet, it's altogether impossible. What I have got to say is about her Ladyship. She is the pivot it all turns on.'

'Officer,' retorts Sir Leicester, with a fiery eye, and a quivering lip, 'you know your duty. Do your duty; but be careful not to overstep it. I would not suffer it. I would not endure it. You bring my Lady's name into this communication, upon your responsibility – upon your responsibility. My Lady's name is not a name for common persons to trifle with!'

'Sir Leicester Dedlock, Baronet, I say what I must say; and no more.'

'I hope it may prove so. Very well. Go on. Go on, sir!'

Glancing at the angry eyes which now avoid him, and at the angry figure trembling from head to foot, yet striving to be still, Mr Bucket feels his way with his forefinger, and in a low voice proceeds.

'Sir Leicester Dedlock, Baronet, it becomes my duty to tell you that the deceased Mr Tulkinghorn long entertained mistrust and suspicions of Lady Dedlock.'

'If he had dared to breathe them to me, sir – which he never did – I would have killed him myself!' exclaims Sir Leicester, striking his hand upon the table. But in the very heat and fury of the act, he stops, fixed by the knowing eyes of Mr Bucket, whose forefinger is slowly going, and who, with mingled confidence and patience, shakes his head.

'Sir Leicester Dedlock, the deceased Mr Tulkinghorn was deep and close; and what he fully had in his mind in the very beginning, I can't

take upon myself to say. But I know from his lips, that he long ago
suspected Lady Dedlock of having discovered, through the sight of
some hand-writing – in this very house, and when you yourself, Sir
Leicester Dedlock, were present – the existence, in great poverty, of a
certain person, who had been her lover before you courted her, and
who ought to have been her husband;' Mr Bucket stops, and deliberately repeats, 'ought to have been her husband; not a doubt about it. I
know from his lips, that when that person soon afterwards died, he
suspected Lady Dedlock of visiting his wretched lodging, and his wretched
grave alone, and in secret. I know from my own inquiries, and through
my eyes and ears, that Lady Dedlock did make such visit, in the dress
of her own maid; for the deceased Mr Tulkinghorn employed me to
reckon up her Ladyship – if you'll excuse my making use of the term
we commonly employ – and I reckoned her up, so far, completely. I
confronted the maid, in the chambers in Lincoln's Inn Fields, with a
witness who had been Lady Dedlock's guide; and there couldn't be the
shadow of a doubt that she had worn the young woman's dress, unknown
to her. Sir Leicester Dedlock, Baronet, I did endeavor to pave the way
a little towards these unpleasant disclosures, yesterday, by saying that
very strange things happened even in high families sometimes. All this,
and more, has happened in your own family, and to and through your
own Lady. It is my belief that the deceased Mr Tulkinghorn followed
up these inquiries to the hour of his death; and that he and Lady Dedlock
even had bad blood between them upon the matter that very night.
Now, only you put that to Lady Dedlock, Sir Leicester Dedlock, Baronet;
and ask her Ladyship whether, even after he had left here, she didn't
go down to his chambers with the intention of saying something further to him, dressed in a loose black mantle with a deep fringe to it.'

Sir Leicester sits like a statue, gazing at the cruel finger that is prob-
ing the life-blood of his heart.

'You put that to her Ladyship, Sir Leicester Dedlock, Baronet, from
me, Inspector Bucket of the Detective. And if her Ladyship makes any
difficulty about admitting of it, you tell her that it's no use; that Inspector Bucket knows it, and knows that she passed the soldier as you
called him (though he's not in the army now), and knows that she
knows she passed him, on the staircase. Now, Sir Leicester Dedlock,
Baronet, why do I relate all this?'

Sir Leicester, who has covered his face with his hands, uttering a single groan, requests him to pause for a moment. By-and-by he takes his hands away; and so preserves his dignity and outward calmness, though there is no more color in his face than in his white hair, that Mr Bucket is a little awed by him. Something frozen and fixed is upon his manner, over and above its usual shell of haughtiness; and Mr Bucket soon detects an unusual slowness in his speech, with now and then a curious trouble in beginning, which occasions him to utter inarticulate sounds. With such sounds, he now breaks silence; soon, however, controlling himself to say, that he does not comprehend why a gentleman so faithful and zealous as the late Mr Tulkinghorn should have communicated to him nothing of this painful, this distressing, this unlooked-for, this overwhelming, this incredible intelligence.

'Again, Sir Leicester Dedlock, Baronet,' returns Mr Bucket, 'put it to her Ladyship to clear that up. Put it to her Ladyship, if you think it right, from Inspector Bucket of the Detective. You'll find, or I'm much mistaken, that the deceased Mr Tulkinghorn had the intention of communicating the whole to you, as soon as he considered it ripe; and further, that he had given her Ladyship so to understand. Why, he might have been going to reveal it the very morning when I examined the body! You don't know what I'm going to say and do, five minutes from this present time, Sir Leicester Dedlock, Baronet; and supposing I was to be picked off now, you might wonder why I hadn't done it, don't you see?'

Sir Leicester seems to wake, though his eyes have been wide open; and he looks intently at Mr Bucket, as Mr Bucket refers to his watch.

'The party to be apprehended is now in this house,' proceeds Mr Bucket, putting up his watch with a steady hand, and with rising spirits, 'and I'm about to take her into custody in your presence. Sir Leicester Dedlock, Baronet, don't you say a word, nor yet stir. There'll be no noise, and no disturbance at all. I'll come back in the course of the evening, if agreeable to you, and endeavor to meet your wishes respecting this unfortunate family matter, and the nobbiest way of keeping it quiet. Now, Sir Leicester Dedlock, Baronet, don't you be nervous on account of the apprehension at present coming off. You shall see the whole case clear, from first to last.'

Mr Bucket rings, goes to the door, briefly whispers Mercury, shuts

the door, and stands behind it with his arms folded. After a suspense of
a minute or two, the door slowly opens, and a Frenchwoman enters.
Mademoiselle Hortense.

The moment she is in the room, Mr Bucket claps the door to, and
puts his back up against it. The suddenness of the noise occasions her
to turn; and then, for the first time she sees Sir Leicester Dedlock in
his chair.

'I ask you pardon,' she mutters hurriedly. 'They tell me there was
no one here.'

Her step towards the door brings her front to front with Mr Bucket.
Suddenly a spasm shoots across her face, and she turns deadly pale.

'This is my lodger, Sir Leicester Dedlock,' says Mr Bucket, nodding
at her. 'This foreign young woman has been my lodger for some weeks
back.'

'What do Sir Leicester care for that, you think, my angel?' returns
Mademoiselle, in a jocular strain.

'Why, my angel,' returns Mr Bucket, 'we shall see.'

Mademoiselle Hortense eyes him with a scowl upon her tight face,
which generally changes into a smile of scorn. 'You are very mysterieuse.
Are you drunk?'

'Tolerable sober, my angel,' returns Mr Bucket.

'I come from arriving at this so detestable house with your wife.
Your wife have left me since some minutes. They tell me downstairs
that your wife is here. I come here, and your wife is not here. What is
the intention of this fool's play, say then?' Mademoiselle demands,
with her arms composedly crossed, but with something in her dark
cheek beating like a clock.

Mr Bucket merely shakes the finger at her.

'Ah, my God, you are an unhappy idiot!' cries Mademoiselle, with a
toss of her head and a laugh. – 'Leave me to pass downstairs, great
pig.' With a stamp of her foot, and a menace.

'Now, Mademoiselle,' says Mr Bucket, in a cool determined way,
'you go and sit down upon that sofy.'

'I will not sit down upon nothing,' she replies, with a shower of
nods.

'Now, Mademoiselle,' repeats Mr Bucket, making no demonstration,
except with the finger, 'you sit down upon that sofy.'

'Why?'

'Because I take you into custody on the charge of murder, and you don't need to be told it. Now, I want to be polite to one of your sex and a foreigner, if I can. If I can't, I must be rough; and there's rougher ones outside. What I am to be depends on you. So I recommend you, as a friend, afore another half a blessed moment has passed over your head, to go and sit down upon the sofy.'

Mademoiselle complies, saying in a concentrated voice, while that something in her check beats fast and hard, 'You are a Devil.'

'Now, you see,' Mr Bucket proceeds approvingly, 'you're comfortable, and conducting yourself as I should expect a foreign young woman of your sense to do. So I'll give you a piece of advice, and it's this, Don't you talk too much. You're not expected to say anything here, and you can't keep too quiet a tongue in you head. In short, the less you Parlay, the better, you know.' Mr Bucket is very complacent over this French explanation.

Mademoiselle, with that tigerish expansion of the mouth, and her black eyes darting fire upon him, sits upright on the sofa in a rigid state, with her hands clenched – and her feet too, one might suppose – muttering, 'O, you Bucket, you are a Devil!'

'Now, Sir Leicester Dedlock, Baronet,' says Mr Bucket, and from this time forth the finger never rests, 'this young woman, my lodger, was her Ladyship's maid at the time I have mentioned to you; and this young woman, besides being extraordinary vehement and passionate against her Ladyship after being discharged –'

'Lie!' cries Mademoiselle. 'I discharged myself.'

'Now, why don't you take my advice?' returns Mr Bucket, in an impressive, almost in an imploring tone. 'I'm surprised at the indiscreetness you commit. You'll say something that'll be used against you, you know. You're sure to come to it. Never you mind what I say till it's given in evidence. It is not addressed to you.'

'Discharge, too!' cries Mademoiselle, furiously, 'by her Ladyship! Eh, my faith, a pretty Ladyship! Why, I r-r-r-ruin my character by remaining with a Ladyship so infame!'

'Upon my soul I wonder at you!' Mr Bucket remonstrates. 'I thought the French were a polite nation, I did, really. Yet to hear a female going on like that, before Sir Leicester Dedlock, Baronet!'

'He is a poor abused!' cries Mademoiselle. 'I spit upon his house, upon his name, upon his imbecility,' all of which she makes the carpet represent. 'Oh, that he is a great man! O yes, superb! O Heaven! Bah!'

'Well, Sir Leicester Dedlock,' proceeds Mr Bucket, 'this intemperate foreigner also angrily took it into her head that she established a claim upon Mr Tulkinghorn, deceased, by attending on the occasion I told you of, at his chambers; though she was liberally paid for her time and trouble.'

'Lie!' cries Mademoiselle. 'I ref-use his money altogezzer.'

('If you *will* Parlay, you know,' says Mr Bucket, parenthetically, 'you must take the consequences.) Now, whether she became my lodger, Sir Leicester Dedlock, with any deliberate intention then of doing this deed and blinding me, I give no opinion on; but she lived in my house, in that capacity, at the time that she was hovering about the chambers of the deceased Mr Tulkinghorn with a view to a wrangle, and likewise persecuting and half frightening the life out of an unfortunate stationer.'

'Lie!' cries Mademioselle. 'All lie!'

'The murder was committed, Sir Leicester Dedlock, Baronet, and you know under what circumstances. Now, I beg of you to follow me close with your attention for a minute or two. I was sent for, and the case was intrusted to me. I examined the place, and the body, and the papers, and everything. From information I received (from a clerk in the same house) I took George into custody, as having been seen hanging about there, on the night, and at very nigh the time, of the murder, also, as having been overheard in high words with the deceased on former occasions – even threatening him, as the witness made out. If you ask me, Sir Leicester Dedlock, whether from the first I believed George to be the murderer, I tell you candidly No; but he might be, notwithstanding; and there was enough against him to make it my duty to take him, and get him kept under remand. Now, observe!'

As Mr Bucket bends forward in some excitement – for him – and inaugurates what he is going to say with one ghostly beat of his forefinger in the air, Mademoiselle Hortense fixes her black eyes upon him with a dark frown, and sets her dry lips closely and firmly together.

'I went home, Sir Leicester Dedlock, Baronet, at night, and found this young woman having supper with my wife, Mrs Bucket. She had made a mighty show of being fond of Mrs Bucket from her first offering herself as our lodger, but that night she made more than ever – in fact, overdid it. Likewise, she overdid her respect, and all that, for the lamented memory of the deceased Mr Tulkinghorn. By the living Lord, it flashed upon me, as I sat opposite to her at the table and saw her with a knife in her hand, that she had done it!'

Mademoiselle is hardly audible, in straining through her teeth and lips the words 'You are a Devil.'

'Now where,' pursues Mr Bucket, 'had she been on the night of the murder? She had been to the theayter. (She really was there, I have since found, both before the deed and after it.) I knew I had an artful customer to deal with, and that proof would be very difficult; and I laid a trap for her – such a trap as I never laid yet, and such a venture as I never made yet. I worked it out in my mind while I was talking to her at supper. When I went upstairs to bed, our house being small and this young woman's ears sharp, I stuffed the sheet into Mrs Bucket's mouth that she shouldn't say a word of surprise, and told her all about it. – My dear, don't you give your mind to that again, or I shall link your feet together at the ankles.' Mr Bucket, breaking off, has made a noiseless descent upon Mademoiselle, and laid his heavy hand upon her shoulder.

'What is the matter with you now?' she asked him.

'Don't you think any more,' returns Mr Bucket, with admonitory finger, 'of throwing yourself out of window. That's what's the matter with me. Come! Just take my arm. You needn't get up; I'll sit down by you. Now take my arm, will you? I'm a married man, you know; you're acquainted with my wife. Just take my arm.'

Vainly endeavoring to moisten those dry lips, with a painful sound, she struggles with herself and complies.

'Now we're all right again. Sir Leicester Dedlock, Baronet, this case could never have been the case it is, but for Mrs Bucket, who is a woman in fifty thousand – in a hundred and fifty thousand! To throw this young woman off her guard, I have never set foot in our house since; though I've communicated with Mrs Bucket, in the baker's loaves and in the milk, as often as required. My whispered words to Mrs Bucket, when she had the sheet in her mouth, were, "My dear, can you throw her off continually with natural accounts of my suspicions against

George, and this, and that, and t'other? Can you do without rest, and keep watch upon her, night and day? Can you undertake to say, She shall do nothing without my knowledge, she shall be my prisoner without suspecting it, she shall no more escape from me than from death, and her life shall be my life, and her soul my soul, till I have got her, if she did this murder?" Mrs Bucket says to me, as well as she could speak, on account of the sheet, "Bucket, I can!" And she has acted up to it glorious!'

'Lies!' Mademoiselle interposes. 'All lies, my friend!'

'Sir Leicester Dedlock, Baronet, how did my calculations come out under these circumstances? When I calculated that this impetuous young woman would overdo it in new directions, was I wrong or right? I was right. What does she try to do? Don't let it give you a turn? To throw the murder on her Ladyship?'

Sir Leicester rises from his chair, and staggers down again.

'And she got encouragement in it from hearing that I was always here, which was done a' purpose. Now, open that pocket-book of mine, Sir Leicester Dedlock, if I may take the liberty of throwing it towards you, and look at the letters sent to me, each with two words, LADY DEDLOCK, in it. Open the one directed to yourself, which I stopped this very morning, and read the three words, LADY DEDLOCK, MURDERESS, in it. These letters have been falling about like a shower of lady-birds. What do you say now to Mrs Bucket, from her spy-place, having seen them all written by this young woman? What do you say to Mrs Bucket having, within this half-hour, secured the corresponding ink and paper, fellow half-sheets and what not? What do you say to Mrs Bucket having watched the posting of 'em every one by this young woman, Sir Leicester Dedlock, Baronet?' Mr Bucket asks, triumphant in his admiration of his lady's genius.

Two things are especially observable, as Mr Bucket proceeds to a conclusion. First, that he seems imperceptibly to establish a dreadful right of property in Mademoiselle. Secondly, that the very atmosphere she breathes seems to narrow and contract about her, as if a close net, or a pall, were being drawn nearer and yet nearer around her breathless figure.

'There is no doubt that her Ladyship was on the spot at the eventful period,' says Mr Bucket; 'and my foreign friend here saw her, I believe, from the upper part of the staircase. Her Ladyship and George and my foreign friend were all pretty close on one another's heels. But that don't signify any more, so I'll not go into it. I found the wadding of the pistol with which the deceased Mr Tulkinghorn was shot. It was a bit of the printed description of your house at Chesney Wold. Not much in that, you'll say, Sir Leicester Dedlock, Baronet. No. But when my foreign friend here is so thoroughly off her guard as to think it a safe time to tear up the rest of the leaf, and when Mrs Bucket puts the pieces together and finds the wadding wanting, it begins to look like Queer Street.'

'These are very long lies,' Mademoiselle interposes. 'You prose great deal. Is it that you have almost all finished, or are you speaking always?'

'Sir Leicester Dedlock, Baronet,' proceeds Mr Bucket, who delights in a full title, and does violence to himself when he dispenses with any fragment of it, 'the last point in the case which I am now going to mention, shows the necessity of patience in our business, and never doing a thing in a hurry. I watched this young woman yesterday, without her knowledge, when she was looking at the funeral, in company with my wife, who planned to take her there; and I had so much to convict her, and I saw such an expression in her face, and my mind so rose against her malice towards her Ladyship, and the time was altogether such a time for bringing down what you may call retribution upon her, that if I had been a younger hand with less experience, I should have taken her, certain. Equally, last night, when her Ladyship, as is so universally admired I am sure, come home, looking – why, Lord! a man might almost say like Venus rising from the ocean, it was so unpleasant and inconsistent to think of her being charged with a murder of which she was innocent, that I felt quite to want to put an end to this job. What should I have lost? Sir Leicester Dedlock, Baronet, I should have lost the weapon. My prisoner here proposed to Mrs Bucket, after the departure of the funeral, that they should go, per bus, a little ways into the country, and take tea at a very decent house of entertainment. Now, near that house of entertainment there's a piece of water. At tea, my prisoner got up to fetch her pocket-handkercher from the bedroom where the bonnets was; she was rather a long time gone, and came back a little out of wind. As soon as they came home this was reported to me by Mrs Bucket, along with her observations and suspicions. I

had the piece of water dragged by moonlight, in presence of a couple
of our men, and the pocket-pistol was brought up before it had been
there a half a dozen hours. Now, my dear, put your arm a little further
through mine, and hold it steady, and I shan't hurt you!'

In a trice Mr Bucket snaps a handcuff on her wrist. 'That's one,'
says Mr Bucket. 'Now the other, darling. Two, and all told!'

He rises; she rises too. 'Where,' she asks him, darkening her large
eyes until their drooping lids almost conceal them – and yet they stare,
'where is your false, your treacherous and cursed wife?'

'She's gone for'ard to the Police Office,' returns Mr Bucket. 'You'll
see her there, my dear.'

'I would like to kiss her!' exclaims Mademoiselle Hortense, panting
tigress-like.

'You'd bite her, I suspect,' says Mr Bucket.

'I would!' making her eyes very large. 'I would love to tear her,
limb from limb.'

'Bless you, darling,' says Mr Bucket, with the greatest composure;
'I am fully prepared to hear that. Your sex have such a surprising
animosity against one another, when you do differ. You don't mind me
half so much, do you?'

'No. Though you are a devil still.'

'Angel and devil by turns, eh?' cried Mr Bucket. 'But I am in my
regular employment, you must consider. Let me put your shawl tidy.
I've been lady's maid to a good many before now. Anything wanting
to the bonnet? There's a cab at the door.'

Mademoiselle Hortense, casting an indignant eye at the glass, shakes
herself perfectly neat in one shake, and looks, to do her justice, un-
commonly genteel.

'Listen then, my angel,' says she, after several sarcastic nods: 'You
are very spiritual. But can you restore him back to life?'

Mr Bucket answers, 'Not exactly.'

'That is droll. Listen yet one time. You are very spiritual. Can you
make an honorable lady of Her?'

'Don't be so malicious,' says Mr Bucket.

'Or a haughty gentleman of *Him*?' cries Mademoiselle, referring to
Sir Leicester with ineffable disdain. 'Eh! O then regard him! The poor
infant! Ha! ha! ha!'

'Come, come, why, this is worse parlaying than the other,' says Mr
Bucket. 'Come along!'

'You cannot do these things? Then you can do as you please with
me. It is but the death, it is all the same. Let us go, my angel. Adieu
you old man, gray. I pity you, and I des-pise you!'

With these last words, she snaps her teeth together, as if her mouth
closed with a spring. It is impossible to describe how Mr Bucket gets
her out, but he accomplishes that feat in a manner so peculiar to himself; enfolding and pervading her like a cloud, and hovering away with
her as if he were a homely Jupiter, and she the object of his affections.

Sir Leicester, left alone, remains in the same attitude, as though he
were still listening, and his attention were still occupied. At length he
gazes round the empty room, and finding it deserted, rises unsteadily
to his feet, pushes back his chair, and walks a few steps, supporting
himself by the table. Then he stops; and, with more of those inarticulate sounds, lifts up his eyes and seems to stare at something.

Heaven knows what he sees. The green, green woods of Chesney
Wold, the noble house, the pictures of his forefathers, strangers defac-
ing them, officers of police coarsely handling his most precious heir-
looms, thousands of fingers pointing at him, thousands of faces sneering
at him. But if such shadows flit before him to his bewilderment, there
is one other shadow which he can name with something like distinct-
ness even yet, and to which alone he addresses his tearing of his white
hair, and his extended arms.

It is she, in association with whom, saving that she has been for
years a main fiber of the root of his dignity and pride, he has never
had a selfish thought. It is she whom he has loved, admired, honored,
and set up for the world to respect. It is she, who, at the core of all the
constrained formalities and conventionalities of his life, has been a stock
of living tenderness and love, susceptible as nothing else is of being
struck with the agony he feels. He sees her, almost to the exclusion of
himself; and cannot bear to look upon her cast down from the high
place she has graced so well.

And, even to the point of his sinking on the ground oblivious of his
suffering, he can yet pronounce her name with something like distinct-
ness in the midst of those intrusive sounds, and in a tone of mourning
and compassion rather than reproach.

ELEVEN

Hunted Down

I

Most of us see some romances in life. In my capacity as Chief Manager of a Life Assurance Office, I think I have within the last thirty years seen more romances than the generality of men, however unpromising the opportunity may, at first sight, seem.

As I have retired, and live at my ease, I possess the means that I used to want, of considering what I have seen, at leisure. My experiences have a more remarkable aspect, so reviewed, than they had when they were in progress. I have come home from the Play now, and can recall the scenes of the Drama upon which the curtain has fallen, free from the glare, bewilderment, and bustle of the Theatre.

Let me recall one of these Romances of the real world.

There is nothing truer than physiognomy, taken in connection with manner. The art of reading that book of which Eternal Wisdom obliges every human creature to present his or her own page with the individual character written on it, is a difficult one, perhaps, and is little studied. It may require some natural aptitude, and it must require (for everything does) some patience and some pains. That these are not usually given to it, – that numbers of people accept a few stock common-place expressions of the face as the whole list of characteristics, and neither seek nor know the refinements that are truest, – that You, for instance, give a great deal of time and attention to the reading of music, Greek, Latin, French, Italian, Hebrew, if you please, and do not qualify yourself to read the face of the master or mistress looking over your shoulder teaching it to you, – I assume to be five hundred times more probable than improbable. Perhaps a little self-sufficiency may be at the bottom of this; facial expression requires no study from you, you think; it comes by nature to you to know enough about it, and you are not to be taken in.

I confess, for my part, that I *have* been taken in, over and over again. I have been taken in by acquaintances, and I have been taken in (of course) by friends; far oftener by friends than by any other class of persons. How came I to be so deceived? Had I quite misread their faces?

No. Believe me, my first impression of those people, founded on face and manner alone, was invariably true. My mistake was in suffering them to come nearer to me and explain themselves away.

II

The partition which separated my own office from our general outer office in the City was of thick plate-glass. I could see through it what passed in the outer office, without hearing a word. I had it put up in place of a wall that had been there for years, – ever since the house was built. It is no matter whether I did or did not make the change in order that I might derive my first impression of strangers, who came to us on business, from their faces alone, without being influenced by anything they said. Enough to mention that I turned my glass partition to that account, and that a Life Assurance Office is at all times exposed to be practised upon by the most crafty and cruel of the human race.

It was through my glass partition that I first saw the gentleman whose story I am going to tell.

He had come in without my observing it, and had put his hat and umbrella on the broad counter, and was bending over it to take some papers from one of the clerks. He was about forty or so, dark, exceedingly well dressed in black, – being in mourning, – and the hand he extended with a polite air, had a particularly well-fitting black-kid glove upon it. His hair, which was elaborately brushed and oiled, was parted straight up the middle; and he presented this parting to the clerk, exactly (to my thinking) as if he had said, in so many words: 'You must take me, if you please, my friend, just as I show myself. Come straight up here, follow the gravel path, keep off the grass, I allow no trespassing.'

I conceived a very great aversion to that man the moment I thus saw him.

He had asked for some of our printed forms, and the clerk was giving them to him and explaining them. An obliged and agreeable smile was on his face, and his eyes met those of the clerk with a sprightly look. (I have known a vast quantity of nonsense talked about bad men not looking you in the face. Don't trust that conventional idea. Dishonesty will stare honesty out of countenance, any day in the week, if there is anything to be got by it.)

I saw, in the corner of his eyelash, that he became aware of my looking at him. Immediately he turned the parting in his hair toward the glass partition, as if he said to me with a sweet smile, 'Straight up here, if you please. Off the grass!'

In a few moments he had put on his hat and taken up his umbrella, and was gone.

I beckoned the clerk into my room, and asked, 'Who was that?'

He had the gentleman's card in his hand. 'Mr Julius Slinkton, Middle Temple.'

'A barrister, Mr Adams?'

'I think not, sir.'

'I should have thought him a clergyman, but for his having no Reverend here,' said I.

'Probably, from his appearance,' Mr Adams replied, 'he is reading for orders.'

I should mention that he wore a dainty white cravat, and dainty linen altogether.

'What did he want, Mr Adams?'

'Merely a form of proposal, sir, and form of reference.'

'Recommended here? Did he say?'

'Yes, he said he was recommended here by a friend of yours. He noticed you, but said that as he had not the pleasure of your personal acquaintance he would not trouble you.'

'Did he know my name?'

'O yes, sir! He said, "There *is* Mr Sampson, I see!"'

'A well-spoken gentleman, apparently?'

'Remarkably so, sir.'

'Insinuating manners, apparently?'

'Very much so, indeed, sir.'

'Hah!' said I. 'I want nothing at present, Mr Adams.'

Within a fortnight of that day I went to dine with a friend of mine, a merchant, a man of taste, who buys pictures and books; and the first man I saw among the company was Mr Julius Slinkton. There he was, standing before the fire, with good large eyes and an open expression of face; but still (I thought) requiring everybody to come at him by the prepared way he offered, and by no other.

I noticed him ask my friend to introduce him to Mr Sampson, and my friend did so. Mr Slinkton was very happy to see me. Not too happy; there was no over-doing of the matter; happy in a thoroughly well-bred, perfectly unmeaning way.

'I thought you had met,' our host observed.

'No,' said Mr Slinkton. 'I did look in at Mr Sampson's office, on your recommendation; but I really did not feel justified in troubling Mr Sampson himself, on a point in the everyday routine of an ordinary clerk.'

I said I should have been glad to show him any attention on our friend's introduction.

'I am sure of that,' said he, 'and am much obliged. At another time, perhaps, I may be less delicate. Only, however, if I have real business; for I know, Mr Sampson, how precious business time is, and what a vast number of impertinent people there are in the world.'

I acknowledged his consideration with a slight bow. 'You were thinking,' said I, 'of effecting a policy on your life.'

'O dear no! I am afraid I am not so prudent as you pay me the compliment of supposing me to be, Mr Sampson. I merely inquired for a friend. But you know what friends are in such matters. Nothing may ever come of it. I have the greatest reluctance to trouble men of business with inquiries for friends, knowing the probabilities to be a thousand to one that the friends will never follow them up. People are so fickle, so selfish, so inconsiderate. Don't you, in your business, find them so every day, Mr Sampson?'

I was going to give a qualified answer; but he turned his smooth, white parting on me with its 'Straight up here, if you please!' and I answered 'Yes.'

'I hear, Mr Sampson,' he resumed presently, for our friend had a new cook, and dinner was not so punctual as usual, 'that your profession has recently suffered a great loss.'

'In money?' said I.

He laughed at my ready association of loss with money, and replied, 'No, in talent and vigour.'

Not at once following out his allusion, I considered for a moment. '*Has* it sustained a loss of that kind?' said I. 'I was not aware of it.'

'Understand me, Mr Sampson. I don't imagine that you have retired. It is not so bad as that. But Mr Meltham –'

'O, to be sure!' said I. 'Yes! Mr Meltham, the young actuary of the "Inestimable."'

'Just so,' he returned in a consoling way.

'He is a great loss. He was at once the most profound, the most original, and the most energetic man I have ever known connected with Life Assurance.'

I spoke strongly; for I had a high esteem and admiration for Meltham; and my gentleman had indefinitely conveyed to me some suspicion that he wanted to sneer at him. He recalled me to my guard by presenting that trim pathway up his head, with its infernal 'Not on the grass, if you please – the gravel.'

'You knew him, Mr Slinkton.'

'Only by reputation. To have known him as an acquaintance, or as a friend, is an honour I should have sought if he had remained in society, though I might never have had the good fortune to attain it, being a man of far inferior mark. He was scarcely above thirty, I suppose?'

'About thirty.'

'Ah!' he sighed in his former consoling way. 'What creatures we are! To break up, Mr Sampson, and become incapable of business at that time of life! – Any reason assigned for the melancholy fact?'

('Humph!' thought I, as I looked at him. 'But I WON'T go up the track, and I WILL go on the grass.')

'What reason have you heard assigned, Mr Slinkton?' I asked, point-blank.

'Most likely a false one. You know what Rumour is, Mr Sampson. I never repeat what I hear; it is the only way of paring the nails and shaving the head of Rumour. But when *you* ask me what reason I have heard assigned for Mr Meltham's passing away from among men, it is another thing. I am not gratifying idle gossip then. I was told, Mr Sampson, that Mr Meltham had relinquished all his avocations and all his prospects, because he was, in fact, broken-hearted. A disappointed attachment I heard, – though it hardly seems probable, in the case of a man so distinguished and so attractive.'

'Attractions and distinctions are no armour against death,' said I.

'O, she died? Pray pardon me. I did not hear that. That, indeed, makes it very, very sad. Poor Mr Meltham! She died? Ah, dear me! Lamentable, lamentable!'

I still thought his pity was not quite genuine, and I still suspected an unaccountable sneer under all this, until he said, as we were parted, like the other knots of talkers, by the announcement of dinner:

'Mr Sampson, you are surprised to see me so moved on behalf of a man whom I have never known. I am not so disinterested as you may suppose. I have suffered, and recently too, from death myself. I have lost one of two charming nieces, who were my constant companions. She died young – barely three-and-twenty; and even her remaining sister is far from strong. The world is a grave!'

He said this with deep feeling, and I felt reproached for the coldness of my manner. Coldness and distrust had been engendered in me, I knew, by my bad experiences; they were not natural to me; and I often thought how much I had lost in life, losing trustfulness, and how little I had gained, gaining hard caution. This state of mind being habitual to me, I troubled myself more about this conversation than I might have troubled myself about a greater matter. I listened to his talk at dinner, and observed how readily other men responded to it, and with what a graceful instinct he adapted his subjects to the knowledge and habits of those he talked with. As, in talking with me, he had easily started the subject I might be supposed to understand best, and to be the most interested in, so, in talking with others, he guided himself by the same rule. The company was of a varied character; but he was not at fault, that I could discover, with any member of it. He knew just as much of each man's pursuit as made him agreeable to that man in reference to it, and just as little as made it natural in him to seek modestly for information when the theme was broached.

As he talked and talked – but really not too much, for the rest of us seemed to force it upon him – I became quite angry with myself. I took his face to pieces in my mind, like a watch, and examined it in detail. I could not say much against any of his features separately; I could say even less against them when they were put together. 'Then is it not monstrous,' I asked myself, 'that because a man happens to part his hair straight up the middle of his head, I should permit myself to suspect, and even to detest him?'

(I may stop to remark that this was no proof of my sense. An observer of men who finds himself steadily repelled by some apparently trifling thing in a stranger is right to give it great weight. It may be the clue to the whole mystery. A hair or two will show where a lion is hidden. A very little key will open a very heavy door.)

I took my part in the conversation with him after a time, and we got on remarkably well. In the drawing-room I asked the host how long he had known Mr Slinkton. He answered, not many months; he had met him at the house of a celebrated painter then present, who had known him well when he was travelling with his nieces in Italy for their health. His plans in life being broken by the death of one of them, he was reading with the intention of going back to college as a matter of form, taking his degree, and going into orders. I could not but argue with myself that here was the true explanation of his interest in poor Meltham, and that I had been almost brutal in my distrust on that simple head.

III

On the very next day but one I was sitting behind my glass partition, as before, when he came into the outer office, as before. The moment I saw him again without hearing him, I hated him worse than ever.

It was only for a moment that I had this opportunity; for he waved his tight-fitting black glove the instant I looked at him, and came straight in.

'Mr Sampson, good-day! I presume, you see, upon your kind permission to intrude upon you. I don't keep my word in being justified by business, for my business here – if I may so abuse the word – is of the slightest nature.'

I asked, was it anything I could assist him in?

'I thank you, no. I merely called to inquire outside whether my dilatory friend had been so false to himself as to be practical and sensible. But, of course, he has done nothing. I gave him your papers with my own hand, and he was hot upon the intention, but of course he has done nothing. Apart from the general human disinclination to do anything that ought to be done, I dare say there is a specialty about assuring one's life. You find it like will-making. People are so superstitious, and take it for granted they will die soon afterwards.'

'Up here, if you please; straight up here, Mr Sampson. Neither to the right nor to the left.' I almost fancied I could hear him breathe the words as he sat smiling at me, with that intolerable parting exactly opposite the bridge of my nose.

'There is such a feeling sometimes, no doubt,' I replied; 'but I don't think it obtains to any great extent.'

'Well,' said he, with a shrug and a smile, 'I wish some good angel would influence my friend in the right direction. I rashly promised his mother and sister in Norfolk to see it done, and he promised them that he would do it. But I suppose he never will.'

He spoke for a minute or two on indifferent topics, and went away.

I had scarcely unlocked the drawers of my writing-table next morning, when he reappeared. I noticed that he came straight to the door in the glass partition, and did not pause a single moment outside.

'Can you spare me two minutes, my dear Mr Sampson?'

'By all means.'

'Much obliged,' laying his hat and umbrella on the table; 'I came early, not to interrupt you. That fact is, I am taken by surprise in reference to this proposal my friend has made.'

'Has he made one?' said I.

'Ye-es,' he answered, deliberately looking at me; and then a bright idea seemed to strike him – 'or he only tells me he has. Perhaps that may be a new way of evading the matter. By Jupiter, I never thought of that!'

Mr Adams was opening the morning's letters in the outer office. 'What is the name, Mr Slinkton?' I asked.

'Beckwith.'

I looked out at the door and requested Mr Adams, if there were a proposal in that name, to bring it in. He had already laid it out of his hand on the counter. It was easily selected from the rest, and he gave it me. Alfred Beckwith. Proposal to effect a policy with us for two thousand pounds. Dated yesterday.

'From the Middle Temple, I see, Mr Slinkton.'

'Yes. He lives on the same staircase with me; his door is opposite. I never thought he would make me his reference though.'

'It seems natural enough that he should.'

'Quite so, Mr Sampson; but I never thought of it. Let me see.' He took the printed paper from his pocket. 'How am I to answer all these questions?'

'According to the truth, of course,' said I.

'O, of course!' he answered, looking up from the paper with a smile; 'I meant they were so many. But you do right to be particular. It stands to reason that you must be particular. Will you allow me to use your pen and ink?'

'Certainly.'

'And your desk?'

'Certainly.'

He had been hovering about between his hat and his umbrella for a place to write on. He now sat down in my chair, at my blotting-paper and inkstand, with the long walk up his head in accurate perspective before me, as I stood with my back to the fire.

Before answering each question he ran over it aloud, and discussed it. How long had he known Mr Alfred Beckwith? That he had to calculate by years upon his fingers. What were his habits? No difficulty about them; temperate in the last degree, and took a little too much exercise, if anything. All the answers were satisfactory. When he had written them all, he looked them over, and finally signed them in a very pretty hand. He supposed he had now done with the business. I told him he was not likely to be troubled any farther. Should he leave the papers there? If he pleased. Much obliged. Good-morning.

I had had one other visitor before him; not at the office, but at my own house. That visitor had come to my bedside when it was not yet daylight, and had been seen by no one else but by my faithful confidential servant.

A second reference paper (for we required always two) was sent down into Norfolk, and was duly received back by post. This, likewise, was satisfactorily answered in every respect. Our forms were all complied with; we accepted the proposal, and the premium for one year was paid.

IV

For six or seven months I saw no more of Mr Slinkton. He called once at my house, but I was not at home; and he once asked me to dine with him in the Temple, but I was engaged. His friend's assurance was effected in March. Late in September or early in October I was down at Scarborough for a breath of sea-air, where I met him on the beach. It was a hot evening; he came toward me with his hat in his hand; and there was the walk I had felt so strongly disinclined to take in perfect order again, exactly in front of the bridge of my nose.

He was not alone, but had a young lady on his arm.

She was dressed in mourning, and I looked at her with great interest. She had the appearance of being extremely delicate, and her face was remarkably pale and melancholy; but she was very pretty. He introduced her as his niece, Miss Niner.

'Are you strolling, Mr Sampson? Is it possible you can be idle?'

It *was* possible, and I *was* strolling.

'Shall we stroll together?'

'With pleasure.'

The young lady walked between us, and we walked on the cool sea sand, in the direction of Filey.

'There have been wheels here,' said Mr Slinkton. 'And now I look again, the wheels of a hand-carriage! Margaret, my love, your shadow without doubt!'

'Miss Niner's shadow?' I repeated, looking down at it on the sand.

'Not that one,' Mr Slinkton returned, laughing. 'Margaret, my dear, tell Mr Sampson.'

'Indeed,' said the young lady, turning to me, 'there is nothing to tell – except that I constantly see the same invalid old gentleman at all times, wherever I go. I have mentioned it to my uncle, and he calls the gentleman my shadow.'

'Does he live in Scarborough?' I asked.

'He is staying here.'

'Do you live in Scarborough?'

'No, I am staying here. My uncle has placed me with a family here, for my health.'

'And your shadow?' said I, smiling.

'My shadow,' she answered, smiling too, 'is – like myself – not very robust, I fear; for I lose my shadow sometimes, as my shadow loses me at other times. We both seem liable to confinement to the house. I have not seen my shadow for days and days; but it does oddly happen, occasionally, that wherever I go, for many days together, this gentleman goes. We have come together in the most unfrequented nooks on this shore.'

'Is this he?' said I, pointing before us.

The wheels had swept down to the water's edge, and described a great loop on the sand in turning. Bringing the loop back towards us, and spinning it out as it came, was a hand-carriage, drawn by a man.

'Yes,' said Miss Niner, 'this really is my shadow, uncle.'

As the carriage approached us and we approached the carriage, I saw within it an old man, whose head was sunk on his breast, and who was enveloped in a variety of wrappers. He was drawn by a very quiet but very keen-looking man, with iron-gray hair, who was slightly lame. They had passed us, when the carriage stopped, and the old gentleman within, putting out his arm, called to me by my name. I went back, and was absent from Mr Slinkton and his niece for about five minutes.

When I rejoined them, Mr Slinkton was the first to speak. Indeed, he said to me in a raised voice before I came up with him:

'It is well you have not been longer, or my niece might have died of curiosity to know who her shadow is, Mr Sampson.'

'An old East India Director,' said I. 'An intimate friend of our friend's, at whose house I first had the pleasure of meeting you. A certain Major Banks. You have heard of him?'

'Never.'

'Very rich, Miss Niner; but very old, and very crippled. An amiable man, sensible – much interested in you. He has just been expatiating on the affection that he has observed to exist between you and your uncle.'

Mr Slinkton was holding his hat again, and he passed his hand up the straight walk, as if he himself went up it serenely, after me.

'Mr Sampson,' he said, tenderly pressing his niece's arm in his, 'our affection was always a strong one, for we have had but few near ties. We have still fewer now. We have associations to bring us together, that are not of this world, Margaret.'

'Dear uncle!' murmured the young lady, and turned her face aside to hide her tears.

'My niece and I have such remembrances and regrets in common, Mr Sampson,' he feelingly pursued, 'that it would be strange indeed if the relations between us were cold or indifferent. If I remember a conversation we once had together, you will understand the reference I make. Cheer up, dear Margaret. Don't droop, don't droop. My Margaret! I cannot bear to see you droop!'

The poor young lady was very much affected, but controlled herself. His feelings, too, were very acute. In a word, he found himself under such great need of a restorative, that he presently went away, to take a bath of sea-water, leaving the young lady and me sitting by a point of rock, and probably presuming – but that you will say was a pardonable indulgence in a luxury – that she would praise him with all her heart.

She did, poor thing! With all her confiding heart, she praised him to me, for his care of her dead sister, and for his untiring devotion in her last illness. The sister had wasted away very slowly, and wild and terrible fantasies had come over her toward the end, but he had never been impatient with her, or at a loss; had always been gentle, watchful, and self-possessed. The sister had known him, as she had known him, to be the best of men, the kindest of men, and yet a man of such admirable strength of character, as to be a very tower for the support of their weak natures while their poor lives endured.

'I shall leave him, Mr Sampson, very soon,' said the young lady; 'I know my life is drawing to an end; and when I am gone, I hope he will marry and be happy. I am sure he has lived single so long, only for my sake, and for my poor, poor sister's.'

The little hand-carriage had made another great loop on the damp sand, and was coming back again, gradually spinning out a slim figure of eight, half a mile long.

'Young lady,' said I, looking around, laying my hand upon her arm,

and speaking in a low voice, 'time presses. You hear the gentle murmur of that sea?'

She looked at me with the utmost wonder and alarm, saying,
'Yes!'

'And you know what a voice is in it when the storm comes?'
'Yes!'

'You see how quiet and peaceful it lies before us, and you know
what an awful sight of power without pity it might be, this very night!'
'Yes!'.

'But if you had never heard or seen it, or heard of it in its cruelty,
could you believe that it beats every inanimate thing in its way to
pieces, without mercy, and destroys life without remorse?'

'You terrify me, sir, by these questions!'

'To save you, young lady, to save you! For God's sake, collect your
strength and collect your firmness! If you were here alone, and hemmed
in by the rising tide on the flow to fifty feet above your head, you
could not be in greater danger than the danger you are now to be saved
from.'

The figure on the sand was spun out, and straggled off into a crooked
little jerk that ended at the cliff very near us.

'As I am, before Heaven and the judge of all mankind, your friend,
and your dear sister's friend, I solemnly entreat you, Miss Niner, without one moment's loss of time, to come to this gentleman with me!'

If the little carriage had been less near to us, I doubt if I could have
got her away; but it was so near that we were there before she had
recovered the hurry of being urged from the rock. I did not remain
there with her two minutes. Certainly within five, I had the inexpress-
ible satisfaction of seeing her – from the point we had sat on, and to
which I had returned – half supported and half carried up some rude
steps notched in the cliff, by the figure of an active man. With that
figure beside her, I knew she was safe anywhere.

I sat alone on the rock, awaiting Mr Slinkton's return. The twilight
was deepening and the shadows were heavy, when he came round the
point, with his hat hanging at his button-hole, smoothing his wet hair
with one of his hands, and picking out the old path with the other and
a pocket-comb.

'My niece not here, Mr Sampson?' he said, looking about.

'Miss Niner seemed to feel a chill in the air after the sun was down, and has gone home.'

He looked surprised, as though she were not accustomed to do anything without him; even to originate so slight a proceeding.

'I persuaded Miss Niner,' I explained.

'Ah!' said he. 'She is easily persuaded – for her good. Thank you, Mr Sampson; she is better within doors. The bathing-place was farther than I thought, to say the truth.'

'Miss Niner is very delicate,' I observed.

He shook his head and drew a deep sigh. 'Very, very, very. You may recollect my saying so. The time that has since intervened has not strengthened her. The gloomy shadow that fell upon her sister so early in life seems, in my anxious eyes, to gather over her, ever darker, ever darker. Dear Margaret, dear Margaret! But we must hope.'

The hand-carriage was spinning away before us at a most indecorous pace for an invalid vehicle, and was making most irregular curves upon the sand. Mr Slinkton, noticing it after he had put his handkerchief to his eyes, said:

'If I may judge from appearances, your friend will be upset, Mr Sampson.'

'It looks probable, certainly,' said I.

'The servant must be drunk.'

'The servants of old gentlemen will get drunk sometimes,' said I.

'The major draws very light, Mr Sampson.'

'The major does draw light,' said I.

By this time the carriage, much to my relief, was lost in the darkness. We walked on for a little, side by side over the sand, in silence. After a short while he said, in a voice still affected by the emotion that his niece's state of health had awakened in him,

'Do you stay here long, Mr Sampson?'

'Why, no. I am going away to-night.'

'So soon? But business always holds you in request. Men like Mr Sampson are too important to others, to be spared to their own need of relaxation and enjoyment.'

'I don't know about that,' said I. 'However, I am going back.'

'To London?'

'To London.'

'I shall be there too, soon after you.'

I knew that as well as he did. But I did not tell him so. Any more than I told him what defensive weapon my right hand rested on in my pocket, as I walked by his side. Any more than I told him why I did not walk on the sea side of him with the night closing in.

We left the beach, and our ways diverged. We exchanged good-night, and had parted indeed, when he said, returning,

'Mr Sampson, *may* I ask? Poor Meltham, whom we spoke of, – dead yet?'

'Not when I last heard of him; but too broken a man to live long, and hopelessly lost to his old calling.'

'Dear, dear, dear!' said he, with great feeling. 'Sad, sad, sad! The world is a grave!' And so went his way.

It was not his fault if the world were not a grave; but I did not call that observation after him, any more than I had mentioned those other things just now enumerated. He went his way, and I went mine with all expedition. This happened, as I have said, either at the end of September or beginning of October. The next time I saw him, and the last time, was late in November.

V

I had a very particular engagement to breakfast in the Temple. It was a bitter north-easterly morning, and the sleet and slush lay inches deep in the streets. I could get no conveyance, and was soon wet to the knees; but I should have been true to that appointment, though I had to wade to it up to my neck in the same impediments.

The appointment took me to some chambers in the Temple. They were at the top of a lonely corner house overlooking the river. The name, MR ALFRED BECKWITH, was painted on the outer door. On the door opposite, on the same landing, the name MR JULIUS SLINKTON. The doors of both sets of chambers stood open, so that anything said aloud in one set could be heard in the other.

I had never been in those chambers before. They were dismal, close, unwholesome, and oppressive; the furniture, originally good, and not yet old, was faded and dirty, – the rooms were in great disorder; there was a strong prevailing smell of opium, brandy, and tobacco; the grate and fire-irons were splashed all over with unsightly blotches of rust; and on a sofa by the fire, in the room where breakfast had been prepared, lay the host, Mr Beckwith, a man with all the appearances of the worst kind of drunkard, very far advanced upon his shameful way to death.

'Slinkton is not come yet,' said this creature, staggering up when I went in; 'I'll call him. – Halloa! Julius Cæsar! Come and drink!' As he hoarsely roared this out, he beat the poker and tongs together in a mad way, as if that were his usual manner of summoning his associate.

The voice of Mr Slinkton was heard through the clatter from the opposite side of the staircase, and he came in. He had not expected the pleasure of meeting me. I have seen several artful men brought to a stand, but I never saw a man so aghast as he was when his eyes rested on mine.

'Julius Cæsar,' cried Beckwith, staggering between us, 'Mist' Sampson! Mist' Sampson, Julius Cæsar! Julius, Mist' Sampson, is the friend of my soul. Julius keeps me plied with liquor, morning, noon, and night. Julius is a real benefactor. Julius threw the tea and coffee out of window when I used to have any. Julius empties all the water-jugs of their contents, and fills 'em with spirits. Julius winds me up and keeps me going. – Boil the brandy, Julius!'

There was a rusty and furred saucepan in the ashes, – the ashes looked like the accumulation of weeks, – and Beckwith, rolling and staggering between us as if he were going to plunge headlong into the fire, got the saucepan out, and tried to force it into Slinkton's hand.

'Boil the brandy, Julius Cæsar! Come! Do your usual office. Boil the brandy!'

He became so fierce in his gesticulations with the saucepan, that I expected to see him lay open Slinkton's head with it. I therefore put out my hand to check him. He reeled back to the sofa, and sat there panting, shaking, and red-eyed, in his rags of dressing-gown, looking at us both. I noticed then that there was nothing to drink on the table but brandy, and nothing to eat but salted herrings, and a hot, sickly, highly-peppered stew.

'At all events, Mr Sampson,' said Slinkton, offering me the smooth gravel path for the last time, 'I thank you for interfering between me and this unfortunate man's violence. However you came here, Mr Sampson, or with whatever motive you came here at least I thank you for that.'

'Boil the brandy,' muttered Beckwith.

Without gratifying his desire to know how I came there, I said, quietly, 'How is your niece, Mr Slinkton?'

He looked hard at me, and I looked hard at him.

'I am sorry to say, Mr Sampson, that my niece has proved treacherous and ungrateful to her best friend. She left me without a word of notice or explanation. She was misled, no doubt, by some designing rascal. Perhaps you may have heard of it?'

'I did hear that she was misled by a designing rascal. In fact, I have proof of it.'

'Are you sure of that?' said he.

'Quite.'

'Boil the brandy,' muttered Beckwith. 'Company to breakfast, Julius Cæsar. Do your usual office, – provide the usual breakfast, dinner, tea, and supper. Boil the brandy!'

The eyes of Slinkton looked from him to me, and he said, after a moment's consideration,

'Mr Sampson, you are a man of the world, and so am I. I will be plain with you.'

'O no, you won't,' said I, shaking my head.

'I tell you, sir, I will be plain with you.'

'And I tell you you will not,' said I. 'I know all about you. *You* plain with any one? Nonsense, nonsense!'

'I plainly tell you, Mr Sampson,' he went on, with a manner almost composed, 'that I understand your object. You want to save your funds, and escape from your liabilities; these are old tricks of trade with you Office-gentlemen. But you will not do it, sir; you will not succeed. You have not an easy adversary to play against, when you play against me. We shall have to inquire, in due time, when and how Mr Beckwith fell into his present habits. With that remark, sir, I put this poor creature, and his incoherent wanderings of speech, aside, and wish you a good morning and a better case next time.'

While he was saying this, Beckwith had filled a half-pint glass with brandy. At this moment, he threw the brandy at his face, and threw the glass after it. Slinkton put his hands up, half blinded with the spirit, and cut with the glass across the forehead. At the sound of the break-age, a fourth person came into the room, closed the door, and stood at it; he was a very quiet but very keen-looking man, with iron-gray hair, and slightly lame.

Slinkton pulled out his handkerchief, assuaged the pain in his smart-ing eyes, and dabbled the blood on his forehead. He was a long time about it, and I saw that in the doing of it, a tremendous change came over him, occasioned by the change in Beckwith, – who ceased to pant and tremble, sat upright, and never took his eyes off him. I never in my life saw a face in which abhorrence and determination were so forcibly painted as in Beckwith's then.

'Look at me, you villain,' said Beckwith, 'and see me as I really am. I took these rooms, to make them a trap for you. I came into them as a drunkard, to bait the trap for you. You fell into the trap, and you will never leave it alive. On the morning when you last went to Mr Sampson's office, I had seen him first. Your plot has been known to both of us, all along, and you have been counterplotted all along. What? Having been cajoled into putting the prize of two thousand pounds in your power, I was to be done to death with brandy, and, brandy not proving quick enough, with something quicker? Have I never seen you, when you thought my senses gone, pouring from your little bottle into my glass? Why, you Murderer and Forger, alone here with you in the dead of night, as I have so often been, I have had my hand upon the trigger of a pistol, twenty times, to blow your brains out!'

This sudden starting up of the thing that he had supposed to be his imbecile victim into a determined man, with a settled resolution to hunt him down and be the death of him, mercilessly expressed from head to foot, was, in the first shock, too much for him. Without any figure of speech, he staggered under it. But there is no greater mistake than to suppose that a man who is a calculating criminal, is, in any phase of his guilt, otherwise than true to himself, and perfectly consistent with his whole character. Such a man commits murder, and murder is the natural culmination of his course; such a man has to outface murder, and will do it with hardihood and effrontery. It is a sort of fashion to express surprise that any notorious criminal, having such crime upon his conscience, can so brave it out. Do you think that if he had it on his conscience at all, or had a conscience to have it upon, he would ever have committed the crime?

Perfectly consistent with himself, as I believe all such monsters to be, this Slinkton recovered himself, and showed a defiance that was sufficiently cold and quiet. He was white, he was haggard, he was changed; but only as a sharper who had played for a great stake and had been outwitted and had lost the game.

'Listen to me, you villain,' said Beckwith, 'and let every word you hear me say be a stab in your wicked heart. When I took these rooms, to throw myself in your way and lead you on to the scheme that I knew my appearance and supposed character and habits would suggest to such a devil, how did I know that? Because you were no stranger to me. I knew you well. And I knew you to be the cruel wretch who, for so much money, had killed one innocent girl while she trusted him implicitly, and who was by inches killing another.'

Slinkton took out a snuff-box, took a pinch of snuff, and laughed.

'But see here,' said Beckwith, never looking away, never raising his voice, never relaxing his face, never unclenching his hand. 'See what a dull wolf you have been, after all! The infatuated drunkard who never drank a fiftieth part of the liquor you plied him with, but poured it away, here, there, everywhere – almost before your eyes; who bought over the fellow you set to watch him and to ply him, by outbidding you in his bribe, before he had been at his work three days – with whom you have observed no caution, yet who was so bent on ridding the earth of you as a wild beast, that he would have defeated you if you had been ever so prudent – that drunkard whom you have, many a time, left on the floor of this room, and who has even let you go out of it, alive and undeceived, when you have turned him over with your foot – has, almost as often, on the same night, within an hour, within a few minutes, watched you awake, had his hand at your pillow when you were asleep, turned over your papers, taken samples from your bottles and packets of powder, changed their contents, rifled every secret of your life!'

He had had another pinch of snuff in his hand, but had gradually let it drop from between his fingers to the floor; where he now smoothed it out with his foot, looking down at it the while.

'That drunkard,' said Beckwith, 'who had free access to your rooms at all times, that he might drink the strong drinks that you left in his way and be the sooner ended, holding no more terms with you than he would hold with a tiger, has had his master-key for all your locks, his test for all your poisons, his clue to your cipher-writing. He can tell you, as well as you can tell him, how long it took to complete that deed, what doses there were, what intervals, what signs of gradual decay upon mind and body; what distempered fancies were produced, what observable changes, what physical pain. He can tell you, as well as you can tell him, that all this was recorded day by day, as a lesson of experience for future service. He can tell you, better than you can tell him, where that journal is at this moment.'

Slinkton stopped the action of his foot, and looked at Beckwith.

'No,' said the latter, as if answering a question from him. 'Not in the drawer of the writing-desk that opens with a spring; it is not there, and it never will be there again.'

'Then you are a thief!' said Slinkton.

Without any change whatever in the inflexible purpose, which it was quite terrific even to me to contemplate, and from the power of which I had always felt convinced it was impossible for this wretch to escape, Beckwith returned,

'And I am your niece's shadow, too.'

With an imprecation Slinkton put his hand to his head, tore out some hair, and flung it to the ground. It was the end of the smooth walk; he destroyed it in the action, and it will soon be seen that his use for it was past.

Beckwith went on: 'Whenever you left here, I left here. Although I understood that you found it necessary to pause in the completion of that purpose, to avert suspicion, still I watched you close, with the poor confiding girl. When I had the diary, and could read it word by word, – it was only about the night before your last visit to Scarborough, – you remember the night? you slept with a small flat vial tied to your wrist, – I sent to Mr Sampson, who was kept out of view. This is Mr Sampson's trusty servant standing by the door. We three saved your niece among us.'

Slinkton looked at us all, took an uncertain step or two from the place where he had stood, returned to it, and glanced about him in a very curious way, – as one of the meaner reptiles might, looking for a hole to hide in. I noticed at the same time, that a singular change took place in the figure of the man, – as if it collapsed within his clothes, and they consequently became ill-shapen and ill-fitting.

'You shall know,' said Beckwith, 'for I hope the knowledge will be bitter and terrible to you, why you have been pursued by one man, and why, when the whole interest that Mr Sampson represents would have expended any money in hunting you down, you have been tracked to death at a single individual's charge. I hear you have had the name of Meltham on your lips sometimes?'

I saw, in addition to those other changes, a sudden stoppage come upon his breathing.

'When you sent the sweet girl whom you murdered (you know with what artfully made-out surroundings and probabilities you sent her) to Meltham's office, before taking her abroad to originate the transaction that doomed her to the grave, it fell to Meltham's lot to see her and to speak with her. It did not fall to his lot to save her, though I know he would freely give his own life to have done it. He admired her; – I would say he loved her deeply, if I thought it possible that you could understand the word. When she was sacrificed, he was thoroughly assured of your guilt. Having lost her, he had but one object left in life, and that was to avenge her and destroy you.'

I saw the villain's nostrils rise and fall convulsively; but I saw no moving at his mouth.

'That man Meltham,' Beckwith steadily pursued, 'was as absolutely certain that you could never elude him in this world, if he devoted himself to your destruction with his utmost fidelity and earnestness, and if he divided the sacred duty with no other duty in life, as he was certain that in achieving it he would be a poor instrument in the hands of Providence, and would do well before Heaven in striking you out from among living men. I am that man, and I thank God that I have done my work!'

If Slinkton had been running for his life from swift-footed savages, a dozen miles, he could not have shown more emphatic signs of being oppressed at heart and labouring for breath, than he showed now, when he looked at the pursuer who had so relentlessly hunted him down.

'You never saw me under my right name before; you see me under my right name now. You shall see me once again in the body, when

'The Murderer Confronted' – an illustration by E. G. Dalziel

you are tried for your life. You shall see me once again in the spirit, when the cord is round your neck, and the crowd are crying against you!'

When Meltham had spoken these last words, the miscreant suddenly turned away his face, and seemed to strike his mouth with his open hand. At the same instant, the room was filled with a new and powerful odour, and, almost at the same instant, he broke into a crooked run, leap, start, – I have no name for the spasm, – and fell, with a dull weight that shook the heavy old doors and windows in their frames.

That was the fitting end of him.

When we saw that he was dead, we drew away from the room, and Meltham, giving me his hand, said, with a weary air,

'I have no more work on earth, my friend. But I shall see her again elsewhere.'

It was in vain that I tried to rally him. He might have saved her, he said; he had not saved her, and he reproached himself; he had lost her, and he was broken-hearted.

'The purpose that sustained me is over, Sampson, and there is nothing now to hold me to life. I am not fit for life; I am weak and spiritless; I have no hope and no object; my day is done.'

In truth, I could hardly have believed that the broken man who then spoke to me was the man who had so strongly and so differently impressed me when his purpose was before him. I used such entreaties with him, as I could; but he still said, and always said, in a patient, undemonstrative way, – nothing could avail him, – he was broken-hearted.

He died early in the next spring. He was buried by the side of the poor young lady for whom he had cherished those tender and unhappy regrets; and he left all he had to her sister. She lived to be a happy wife and mother; she married my sister's son, who succeeded poor Meltham; she is living now, and her children ride about the garden on my walking-stick when I go to see her.

TWELVE

Poor Mercantile Jack

Is the sweet little cherub who sits smiling aloft and keeps watch on the life of poor Jack, commissioned to take charge of Mercantile Jack, as well as Jack of the national navy? If not, who is? What is the cherub about, and what are we all about, when poor Mercantile Jack is having his brains slowly knocked out by penny-weights, aboard the brig Beelzebub, or the barque Bowie-knife – when he looks his last at that infernal craft, with the first officer's iron boot-heel in his remaining eye, or with his dying body towed overboard in the ship's wake, while the cruel wounds in it do 'the multitudinous seas incarnadine'?

Is it unreasonable to entertain a belief that if, aboard the brig Beelzebub or the barque Bowie-knife, the first officer did half the damage to cotton that he does to men, there would presently arise from both sides of the Atlantic so vociferous an invocation of the sweet little cherub who sits calculating aloft, keeping watch on the markets that pay, that such vigilant cherub would, with a winged sword, have that gallant officer's organ of destructiveness out of his head in the space of a flash of lightning?

If it be unreasonable, then am I the most unreasonable of men, for I believe it with all my soul.

This was my thought as I walked the dock-quays at Liverpool, keeping watch on poor Mercantile Jack. Alas for me! I have long outgrown the state of sweet little cherub; but there I was, and there Mercantile

'The Bird of Prey Brought Down' – an illustration by Marcus Stone

Jack was, and very busy he was, and very cold he was: the snow yet lying in the frozen furrows of the land, and the north-east winds snipping off the tops of the little waves in the Mersey, and rolling them into hailstones to pelt him with. Mercantile Jack was hard at it, in the hard weather: as he mostly is in all weathers, poor Jack. He was girded to ships' masts and funnels of steamers, like a forester to a great oak, scraping and painting; he was lying out on yards, furling sails that tried to beat him off; he was dimly discernible up in a world of giant cobwebs, reefing and splicing; he was faintly audible down in holds, stowing and unshipping cargo; he was winding round and round at capstans melodious, monotonous, and drunk; he was of a diabolical aspect, with coaling for the Antipodes; he was washing decks barefoot, with the breast of his red shirt open to the blast, though it was sharper than the knife in his leathern girdle; he was looking over bulwarks, all eyes and hair; he was standing by at the shoot of the Cunard steamer, off tomorrow, as the stocks in trade of several butchers, poulterers, and fishmongers, poured down into the ice-house; he was coming aboard of other vessels, with his kit in a tarpaulin bag, attended by plunderers to the very last moment of his shore-going existence. As though his senses, when released from the uproar of the elements, were under obligation to be confused by other turmoil, there was a rattling of wheels, a clattering of hoofs, a clashing of iron, a jolting of cotton and hides and casks and timber, an incessant deafening disturbance on the quays, that was the very madness of sound. And as, in the midst of it, he stood swaying about, with his hair blown all manner of wild ways, rather crazedly taking leave of his plunderers, all the rigging in the docks was shrill in the wind, and every little steamer coming and going across the Mersey was sharp in its blowing off, and every buoy in the river bobbed spitefully up and down, as if there were a general taunting chorus of 'Come along, Mercantile Jack! Ill-lodged, ill-fed, ill-used, hocussed, entrapped, anticipated, cleaned out. Come along, Poor Mercantile Jack, and be tempest-tossed till you are drowned!'

The uncommercial transaction which had brought me and Jack together, was this: I had entered the Liverpool police force, that I might have a look at the various unlawful traps which are every night set for Jack. As my term of service in that distinguished corps was short, and as my personal bias in the capacity of one of its members has ceased, no suspicion will attach to my evidence that it is an admirable force. Besides that it is composed, without favour, of the best men that can be picked, it is directed by an unusual intelligence. Its organisation against Fires, I take to be much better than the metropolitan system, and in all respects it tempers its remarkable vigilance with a still more remarkable discretion.

Jack had knocked off work in the docks some hours, and I had taken, for purposes of identification, a photograph-likeness of a thief, in the portrait-room at our head police office (on the whole, he seemed rather complimented by the proceeding), and I had been on police parade, and the small hand of the clock was moving on to ten, when I took up my lantern to follow Mr Superintendent to the traps that were set for Jack. In Mr Superintendent I saw, as anybody might, a tall, well-looking, well-set-up man of a soldierly bearing, with a cavalry air, a good chest, and a resolute but not by any means ungentle face. He carried in his hand a plain black walking-stick of hard wood; and whenever and wherever, at any after-time of the night, he struck it on the pavement with a ringing sound, it instantly produced a whistle out of the darkness, and a policeman. To this remarkable stick, I refer an air of mystery and magic which pervaded the whole of my perquisition among the traps that were set for Jack.

We began by diving into the obscurest streets and lanes of the port. Suddenly pausing in a flow of cheerful discourse, before a dead wall, apparently some ten miles long, Mr Superintendent struck upon the ground, and the wall opened and shot out, with military salute of hand to temple, two policemen – not in the least surprised themselves, not in the least surprising Mr Superintendent.

'All right, Sharpeye?'

'All right, sir.'

'All right, Trampfoot?'

'All right, sir.'

'Is Quickear there?'

'Here am I, sir.'

'Come with us.'

'Yes, sir.'

So, Sharpeye went before, and Mr Superintendent and I went next, and Trampfoot and Quickear marched as rear-guard. Sharpeye, I soon had occasion to remark, had a skilful and quite professional way of opening doors – touched latches delicately, as if they were keys of musical instruments – opened every door he touched, as if he were perfectly confident that there was stolen property behind it – instantly insinuated himself, to prevent its being shut.

Sharpeye opened several doors of traps that were set for Jack, but Jack did not happen to be in any of them. They were all such miserable places that really, Jack, if I were you, I would give them a wider berth. In every trap, somebody was sitting over a fire, waiting for Jack. Now, it was a crouching old woman, like the picture of the Norwood Gipsy in the old sixpenny dream-books; now, it was a crimp of the male sex, in a checked shirt and without a coat, reading a newspaper; now, it was a man crimp and a woman crimp, who always introduced themselves as united in holy matrimony; now, it was Jack's delight, his (un)lovely Nan; but they were all waiting for Jack, and were all frightfully disappointed to see us.

'Who have you got up-stairs here?' says Sharpeye, generally. (In the Move-on tone.)

'Nobody, surr; sure not a blessed sowl!' (Irish feminine reply.)

'What do you mean by nobody? Didn't I hear a woman's step go up-stairs when my hand was on the latch?'

'Ah! sure thin you're right, surr, I forgot her! 'Tis on'y Betsy White, surr. Ah! you know Betsy, surr. Come down, Betsy darlin', and say the gintlemin.'

Generally, Betsy looks over the banisters (the steep staircase is in the room) with a forcible expression in her protesting face, of an intention to compensate herself for the present trial by grinding Jack finer than usual when he does come. Generally, Sharpeye turns to Mr Superintendent, and says, as if the subjects of his remarks were wax-work:

'One of the worst, sir, this house is. This woman has been indicted three times. This man's a regular bad one likewise. His real name is Pegg. Gives himself out as Waterhouse.'

'Never had sitch a name as Pegg near me back, thin, since I was in this house, bee the good Lard!' says the woman.

Generally, the man says nothing at all, but becomes exceedingly round-shouldered, and pretends to read his paper with rapt attention. Generally, Sharpeye directs our observation with a look, to the prints and pictures that are invariably numerous on the walls. Always, Trampfoot and Quickear are taking notice on the doorstep. In default of Sharpeye being acquainted with the exact individuality of any gentleman encountered, one of these two is sure to proclaim from the outer air, like a gruff spectre, that Jackson is not Jackson, but knows himself to be Fogle; or that Canlon is Walker's brother, against whom there was not sufficient evidence; or that the man who says he never was at sea since he was a boy, came ashore from a voyage last Thursday, or sails tomorrow morning. 'And that is a bad class of man, you see,' says Mr Superintendent, when he got out into the dark again, 'and very difficult to deal with, who, when he has made this place too hot to hold him, enters himself for a voyage as steward or cook, and is out of knowledge for months, and then turns up again worse than ever.'

When we had gone into many such houses, and had come out (always leaving everybody relapsing into waiting for Jack), we started off to a singing-house where Jack was expected to muster strong.

The vocalisation was taking place in a long low room up-stairs; at one end, an orchestra of two performers, and a small platform; across the room, a series of open pews for Jack, with an aisle down the middle; at the other end a larger pew than the rest, entitled SNUG, and reserved for mates and similar good company. About the room, some amazing coffee-coloured pictures varnished an inch deep, and some stuffed creatures in cases; dotted among the audience, in Snug and out of Snug, the 'Professionals;' among them, the celebrated comic favourite Mr Banjo Bones, looking very hideous with his blackened faced and limp sugar-loaf hat; beside him, sipping rum-and-water, Mrs Banjo Bones, in her natural colours – a little heightened.

It was a Friday night, and Friday night was considered not a good night for Jack. At any rate, Jack did not show in very great force even here, though the house was one to which he much resorts, and where a good deal of money is taken. There was British Jack, a little maudlin and sleepy, lolling over his empty glass, as if he were trying to read his fortune at the bottom; there was Loafing Jack of the Stars and Stripes, rather an unpromising customer, with his long nose, lank cheek, high cheek-bones, and nothing soft about him but his cabbage-leaf hat; there was Spanish Jack, with curls of black hair, rings in his ears, and a knife not far from his hand, if you got into trouble with him; there were Maltese Jack, and Jack of Sweden, and Jack the Finn, looming through the smoke of their pipes, and turning faces that looked as if they were carved out of dark wood, towards the young lady dancing the hornpipe: who found the platform so exceedingly small for it, that I had a nervous expectation of seeing her, in the backward steps, disappear through the window. Still, if all hands had been got together, they would not have more than half-filled the room. Observe, however, said Mr Licensed Victualler, the host, that it was Friday night, and, besides, it was getting on for twelve, and Jack had gone aboard. A sharp and watchful man, Mr Licensed Victualler, the host, with tight lips and a complete edition of Cocker's arithmetic in each eye. Attended to his business himself, he said. Always on the spot. When he heard of talent, trusted nobody's account of it, but went off by rail to see it. If true talent, engaged it. Pounds a week for talent – four pound – five pound. Banjo Bones was undoubted talent. Hear this instrument that was going to play – it was real talent! In truth it was very good; a kind of piano-accordion, played by a young girl of a delicate prettiness of face, figure, and dress, that made the audience look coarser. She sang to the instrument, too; first, a song about village bells, and how they chimed; then a song about how I went to sea; winding up with an imitation of the bagpipes, which Mercantile Jack seemed to understand much the best. A good girl, said Mr Licensed Victualler. Kept herself select. Sat in Snug, not listening to the blandishments of Mates. Lived with mother. Father dead. Once a merchant well to do, but over-speculated himself. On delicate inquiry as to salary paid for item of talent under consideration, Mr Victualler's pounds dropped suddenly to shillings – still it was a very comfortable thing for a young person like that, you know; she only went on six times a night, and was only required to be there from six at night to twelve. What was more conclusive was, Mr Victualler's assurance that he 'never allowed any language, and never suffered any disturbance.' Sharpeye confirmed the statement, and the order that prevailed was the best proof of it that could have been cited. So, I came to the conclusion that poor Mercantile Jack might do (as I am afraid he does) much worse than trust himself to Mr Victualler, and pass his evenings here.

But we had not yet looked, Mr Superintendent – said Trampfoot, receiving us in the street again with military salute – for Dark Jack.

True, Trampfoot. Ring the wonderful stick, rub the wonderful lantern, and cause the spirits of the stick and lantern to convey us to the Darkies.

There was no disappointment in the matter of Dark Jack; *he* was producible. The Genii set us down in the little first floor of a little public-house, and there, in a stiflingly close atmosphere, were Dark Jack, and Dark Jack's delight, his *white* unlovely Nan, sitting against the wall all round the room. More than that: Dark Jack's delight was the least unlovely Nan, both morally and physically, that I saw that night.

As a fiddle and tambourine band were sitting among the company, Quickear suggested why not strike up? 'Ah, la'ads!' said a negro sitting by the door, 'gib the jebblem a darnse. Tak' yah pardlers, jebblem, for 'um QUAD-rill.'

This was the landlord, in a Greek cap, and a dress half Greek and half English. As master of the ceremonies, he called all the figures, and occasionally addressed himself parenthetically – after this manner. When he was very loud, I use capitals.

'Now den! Hoy! ONE. Right and left. (Put a steam on, gib 'um powder.) LA-dies' chail. BAL-loon say. Lemonade! TWO. AD-warnse and go back (gib 'ell a breakdown, shake it out o' yerselbs, keep a movil). SWING-corners, BAL-loon say, and Lemonade! (Hoy!) THREE. GENT come for'ard with a lady and go back, hoppersite come for'ard and do what yer can. (Aeiohoy!) BAL-loon say, and leetle lemonade. (Dat hair nigger by 'um fireplace 'hind a' time, shake it out o' yerselbs, gib 'ell a breakdown.) Now den! Hoy! FOUR! Lemonade. BAL-loon say, and swing. FOUR ladies meet in 'um middle, FOUR gents goes round 'um ladies, FOUR gents passes out under 'um ladies' arms, SWING – and Lemonade till 'a moosic can't play no more! (Hoy, Hoy!)'

The male dancers were all blacks, and one was an unusually powerful man of six feet three or four. The sound of their flat feet on the floor was as unlike the sound of white feet as their faces were unlike white faces. They toed and heeled, shuffled, double-shuffled, double-double-shuffled, covered the buckle, and beat the time out, rarely, dancing with a great show of teeth, and with a childish good-humoured enjoyment that was very prepossessing. They generally kept together, these poor fellows, said Mr Superintendent, because they were at a disadvantage singly, and liable to slights in the neighbouring streets. But, if I were Light Jack, I should be very slow to interfere oppressively with

Dark Jack, for, whenever I have had to do with him I have found him a simple and a gentle fellow. Bearing this is mind, I asked his friendly permission to leave him restoration of beer, in wishing him good night, and thus it fell out that the last words I heard him say as I blundered down the worn stairs, were, 'Jebblem's elth! Ladies drinks fust!'

The night was now well on into the morning, but, for miles and hours we explored a strange world, where nobody ever goes to bed, but everybody is eternally sitting up, waiting for Jack. This exploration was among a labyrinth of dismal courts and blind alleys, called Entrics, kept in wonderful order by the police, and in much better order than by the corporation: the want of gaslight in the most dangerous and infamous of these places being quite unworthy of so spirited a town. I need describe but two or three of the houses in which Jack was waited for as specimens of the rest. Many we attained by noisome passages so profoundly dark that we felt our way with our hands. Not one of the whole number we visited, was without its show of prints and ornamental crockery; the quantity of the latter set forth on little shelves and in little cases, in otherwise wretched rooms, indicating that Mercantile Jack must have an extraordinary fondness for crockery, to necessitate so much of that bait in his traps.

Among such garniture, in one front parlour in the dead of the night, four women were sitting by a fire. One of them had a male child in her arms. On a stool among them was a swarthy youth with a guitar, who had evidently stopped playing when our footsteps were heard.

'Well! how do *you* do?' says Mr Superintendent, looking about him.

'Pretty well, sir, and hope you gentlemen are going to treat us ladies, now you have come to see us.'

'Order there!' says Sharpeye.

'None of that!' says Quickear.

Trampfoot, outside, is heard to confide to himself, 'Meggisson's lot this is. And a bad 'un!'

'Well!' says Mr Superintendent, laying his hand on the shoulder of the swarthy youth, 'and who's this?'

'Antonio, sir.'

'And what does *he* do here?'

'Come to give us a bit of music. No harm in that, I suppose?'

'A young foreign sailor?'

'Yes. He's a Spaniard. You're a Spaniard, ain't you, Antonio?'

'Me Spanish.'

'And he don't know a word you say, not he; not if you was to talk to him till doomsday.' (Triumphantly, as if it redounded to the credit of the house.)

'Will he play something?'

'Oh, yes, if you like. Play something, Antonio. *You* ain't ashamed to play something; are you?'

The cracked guitar raises the feeblest ghost of a tune, and three of the women keep time to it with their heads, and the fourth with the child. If Antonio has brought any money in with him, I am afraid he will never take it out, and it even strikes me that his jacket and guitar may be in a bad way. But, the look of the young man and the tinkling of the instrument so change the place in a moment to a leaf out of Don Quixote, that I wonder where his mule is stabled, until he leaves off.

I am bound to acknowledge (as it tends rather to my uncommercial confusion), that I occasioned a difficulty in this establishment, by having taken the child in my arms. For, on my offering to restore it to a ferocious joker not unstimulated by rum, who claimed to be its mother, that unnatural parent put her hands behind her, and declined to accept it; backing into the fireplace, and very shrilly declaring, regardless of remonstrance from her friends, that she knowed it to be Law, that whoever took a child from its mother of his own will, was bound to stick to it. The uncommercial sense of being in a rather ridiculous position with the poor little child beginning to be frightened, was relieved by my worthy friend and fellow-constable, Trampfoot; who, laying hands on the article as if it were a Bottle, passed it on to the nearest woman, and bade her 'take hold of that.' As we came out the Bottle was passed to the ferocious joker, and they all sat down as before, including Antonio and the guitar. It was clear that there was no such thing as a nightcap to this baby's head, and that even he never went to bed, but was always kept up – and would grow up, kept up – waiting for Jack.

Later still in the night, we came (by the court 'where the man was murdered,' and by the other court across the street, into which his body was dragged) to another parlour in another Entry, where several people were sitting round a fire in just the same way. It was a dirty and offensive place, with some ragged clothes drying in it; but there was a high shelf over the entrance-door (to be out of the reach of marauding hands, possibly) with two large white leaves on it, and a great piece of Cheshire cheese.

'Well!' says Mr Superintendent, with a comprehensive look all round. 'How do *you* do?'

'Not much to boast of, sir.' From the curtseying woman of the house. 'This is my good man, sir.'

'You are not registered as a common Lodging House?'

'No, sir.'

Sharpeye (in the Move-on tone) puts in the pertinent inquiry, 'Then why ain't you?'

'Ain't got no one here, Mr Sharpeye,' rejoin the woman and my good man together, 'but our own family.'

'How many are you in family?'

The woman takes time to count, under pretence of coughing, and adds, as one scant of breath, 'Seven, sir.'

But she has missed one, so Sharpeye, who knows all about it, says: 'Here's a young man here makes eight, who ain't of your family?'

'No, Mr Sharpeye, he's a weekly lodger.'

'What does he do for a living?'

The young man here, takes the reply upon himself, and shortly answers, 'Ain't got nothing to do.'

The young man here, is modestly brooding behind a damp apron pendent from a clothes-line. As I glance at him I become – but I don't know why – vaguely reminded of Woolwich, Chatham, Portsmouth, and Dover. When we get out, my respected fellow-constable Sharpeye, addressing Mr Superintendent, says:

'You noticed that young man, sir, in at Darby's?'

'Yes. What is he?'

'Deserter, sir.'

Mr Sharpeye further intimates that when we have done with his services, he will step back and take that young man. Which in course of time he does: feeling at perfect ease about finding him, and knowing for a moral certainty that nobody in that region will be gone to bed.

Later still in the night, we came to another parlour up a step or two from the street, which was very cleanly, neatly, even tastefully, kept, and in which, set forth on a draped chest of drawers masking the staircase,

was such a profusion of ornamental crockery, that it would have furnished forth a handsome sale-booth at a fair. It backed up a stout old
lady – HOGARTH drew her exact likeness more than once – and a boy
who was carefully writing a copy in a copy-book.

'Well, ma'am, how do *you* do?'

Sweetly, she can assure the dear gentlemen, sweetly. Charmingly,
charmingly. And overjoyed to see us!

'Why, this is a strange time for this boy to be writing his copy. In
the middle of the night!'

'So it is, dear gentlemen, Heaven bless your welcome faces and send
ye prosperous, but he has been to the Play with a young friend for his
diversion, and he combinates his improvement with entertainment, by
doing his school-writing afterwards, God be good to ye!'

The copy admonished human nature to subjugate the fire of every
fierce desire. One might have thought it recommended stirring the fire,
the old lady so approved it. There she sat, rosily beaming at the copy-
book and the boy, and invoking showers of blessings on our heads,
when we left her in the middle of the night, waiting for Jack.

Later still in the night, we came to a nauseous room with an earth
floor, into which the refuse scum of an alley trickled. The stench of
this habitation was abominable; the seeming poverty of it, diseased and
dire. Yet, here again, was visitor or lodger – a man sitting before the
fire, like the rest of them elsewhere, and apparently not distasteful to
the mistress's niece, who was also before the fire. The mistress herself
had the misfortune of being in jail.

Three weird old women of transcendent ghastliness, were at needle-
work at a table in this room. Says Trampfoot to First Witch, 'What are
you making?' Says she, 'Money-bags.'

'*What* are you making?' retorts Trampfoot, a little off his balance.

'Bags to hold your money,' says the witch, shaking her head, and
setting her teeth; 'you as has got it.'

She holds up a common cash-bag, and on the table is a heap of such
bags. Witch Two laughs at us. Witch Three scowls at us. Witch sister-
hood all, stitch, stitch. First Witch has a circle round each eye. I fancy
it like the beginning of the development of a perverted diabolical halo,
and that when it spreads all round her head, she will die in the odour
of devilry.

Trampfoot wishes to be informed what First Witch has got behind the table, down by the side of her, there? Witches Two and Three croak angrily, 'Show him the child!'

She drags out a skinny little arm from a brown dustheap on the ground. Adjured not to disturb the child, she lets it drop again. Thus we find at last that there is one child in the world of Entries who goes to bed – if this be bed.

Mr Superintendent asks how long are they going to work at those bags?

How long? First Witch repeats. Going to have supper presently. See the cups and saucers, and the plates.

'Late? Ay! But we has to 'arn our supper afore we eats it!' Both the other witches repeat this after First Witch, and take the Uncommercial measurement with their eyes, as for a charmed winding-sheet. Some grim discourse ensues, referring to the mistress of the cave, who will be released from jail to-morrow. Witches pronounce Trampfoot 'right there,' when he deems it a trying distance for the old lady to walk; she shall be fetched by niece in a spring-cart.

As I took a parting look at First Witch in turning away, the red marks round her eyes seemed to have already grown larger, and she hungrily and thirstily looked out beyond me into the dark doorway, to see if Jack was there. For, Jack came even here, and the mistress had got into jail through deluding Jack.

When I at last ended this night of travel and got to bed, I failed to keep my mind on comfortable thoughts of Seaman's Homes (not over-done with strictness), and improved dock regulations giving Jack greater benefit of fire and candle aboard ship, through my mind's wandering among the vermin I had seen. Afterwards the same vermin ran all over my sleep. Evermore, when on a breezy day I see Poor Mercantile Jack running into port with a fair wind under all sail, I shall think of the unsleeping host of devourers who never go to bed, and are always in their set traps waiting for him.

M. R. JAMES

The Edwin Drood Syndicate

Several times of late have I been moved to ask members of this University, both old and young, what was their opinion as to the solution of the *Mystery of Edwin Drood*. In a deplorably large number of instances I was met by the counter-question, 'Who is,' or 'Who was,' or 'What is *Edwin Drood*?' In other cases I found that though the question was understood, a palpably wrong solution was offered: while a few, whose names I should like to hold up to public veneration, not only knew Dickens's last work as it should be known, but held the right convictions concerning it.

It is in truth a great pity that the *Mystery of Edwin Drood* should not be familiar to such a public as ours. It is far better constructed than most of Dickens's books: it is free from many of the mannerisms which deter a large number of otherwise respectable people from reading him: and, to a generation with which M. Lecoq and Sherlock Holmes have been popular favourites, it should present very many attractions.

I had written so far when a young boy entered my room and, uttering some unintelligible expressions, placed a number of the *University Reporter* upon my table. No Member of the Senate who has a spark of gentlemanly feeling can allow a fresh issue of that periodical to remain long unopened.

There was something very odd about this particular *Reporter*. The print and paper were the accustomed ones, and as good as ever; but the matter was, I felt sure, unusual. On the second page were, as often, a series of notices with headings in Clarendon type, and of about the ordinary length; only, none of them were dated. Thus, I read:

Notice by the Vice-Chancellor
The Vice-Chancellor gives notice that he feels sure it is going to rain to-morrow, and earnestly begs that Members of the Senate will be careful.

Then:

The Registrary's Notice
The Registrary feels equally sure that it will not, and sincerely hopes that they will do nothing of the kind.

Again:

The Librarian's Notice
The Librarian gives notice that a very interesting book, by Miss M. Corelli, has recently arrived at the Library, and that the Public Orator will be very glad to read it to Members of the Senate, in the Reading Room, between the hours of 2.30 and 4 p.m., on Thursday next.

All this seemed, as I say, unusual. What followed was also out of the common, but, in form at least, a little more familiar. Moreover, it coincided with what had been occupying my mind just before. As I am now quite unable to find the *Reporter* in question, and can learn nothing of it at the University Press, I reprint here the text which interested me so particularly. I have, I may add, a curiously exact verbal memory, and can answer with some confidence for the substantial correctness of my representation of it. It ran thus:

Report of the Edwin Drood Syndicate
The Syndicate appointed to investigate the solution of the *Mystery of Edwin Drood* beg leave to report to the Senate as follows: –
I. They think it well to remind Members of the Senate of the following

points, which are essential to the proper comprehension of their report.

It may be taken as certain (*a*) That John Jasper,* Esq., lay precentor of Cloisterham Cathedral, on Christmas Eve, 186–, made a murderous attack on Edwin Drood, Esq., his nephew, by strangling him with a black silk scarf.

(*b*) That at the time of the attack, Mr Drood had upon him (probably in the breast pocket of his coat) a gold ring set with jewels, which had been the betrothal-ring of Mr and Mrs Bud, the deceased parents of Miss Rosa Bud, the *fiancée* of Mr Drood.

(*c*) That the fact of Mr Drood's being in possession of this ring was unknown to Mr Jasper.

(*d*) That Mr Jasper concealed the body of Mr Drood in the monument or mausoleum of Mrs Sapsea, which was a detached edifice standing in the churchyard of Cloisterham Cathedral: that he removed from the body the watch, chain, and shirt pin, which were, as he believed, the only articles of jewellery on Mr Drood's person: and that his intention was to destroy the body with quick-lime, a quantity of which he had previously conveyed into the interior of the mausoleum.

(*e*) That Mr Datchery, the stranger who made his appearance in Cloisterham (in chapter xviii) was a disguised person.

(*f*) A majority of the Syndics agree in thinking that Mr Datchery is a character who has already appeared in the case. It is on record that Mr Dickens employed the phrase, 'The Datchery assumption.' This, in the opinion of the majority of the Syndics, implies that Mr Datchery is already known in some form to the public.

II. Two main questions have engaged the careful attention of the Syndicate. These are – I. Did Mr Jasper succeed in murdering Mr Drood, or did he not? II. Who was Mr Datchery?

It will be obvious that upon the answers to these questions the solution of the whole mystery very largely depends.

---

*The Syndicate regret that, owing to the defective nature of the materials supplied to them, they have been unable to ascertain the degree and college of any of the gentlemen whose names appear in their report.

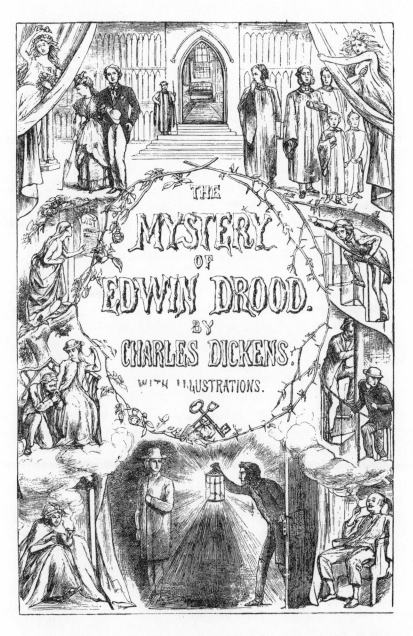

Edwin Drood, Dickens's great unfinished detective story – an illustration
by C. A. Collins for the first monthly part, April 1870

To the first question a large majority of the Syndics return a decided
answer in the negative. Mr Jasper did not succeed, they are convinced,
in killing Mr Drood.

In the first place the method of assault, strangulation, seems to them
to have been designedly selected by Mr Dickens in order to leave open
a loophole for escape. The Syndics have convinced themselves by repeated experiments that it is very easy to be mistaken in regard to this
particular process, if process it may be called. In nearly all cases the
patients (if, again, that be their proper designation) have recovered without
medical aid after several members of the Syndicate had applied the
black silk scarf in the most effective manner at their command. In the
case, however, of a member of the Syndicate who kindly volunteered
his services, and who was consequently manipulated with every precaution, the application, to their great regret, proved to be only too
efficacious.

On the other hand, poison (the use of which might easily have been
foreshadowed by Mr Dickens), the knife, or the bullet (the last of which
was not likely to have been employed), would have been far better and
more certain instruments for ridding Mr Jasper of the presence and of
the imagined rivalry of Mr Drood.

In the second place, the majority of the Syndics are clearly of opinion
that Mr Drood is not intended by Mr Dickens to come to an untimely
end: that he is not, in other words, 'marked for death.' This, they are
well aware, is a consideration of a subjective nature, and will appeal
with unequal force to various members of the Senate. It will, however,
appeal most strongly to those who are most familiar with the works of
Mr Dickens. In this connexion the Syndics would beg the attention of
members of the Senate to two passages descriptive of parallel situations: (*a*) the paragraphs in chapter xiv which treat of Mr Drood's
feelings and surroundings, before he goes up the postern stairs to join
Mr Jasper and Mr Landless at dinner on Christmas Eve, and (*b*) the
passage in *Martin Chuzzlewit*, which describes Mr M. Tigg going down
into the wood in which he is to be murdered by Mr J. Chuzzlewit.

In the third place, the majority of the Syndics above referred to wish
to lay special stress upon the evidence afforded by the vignettes designed by Mr Charles Collins for the cover of the monthly parts in
which the documents relating to this painful case first appeared. In one

of these an individual, evidently intended to represent Mr Jasper, is seen entering a small dark chamber and holding up a lighted lantern. The light of the lantern falls upon the figure of a young man standing erect with one hand in the breast of his coat. The figure must, in the opinion of the majority, represent either (*a*) Mr Drood, (*b*) Mr Drood's ghost, (*c*) a person disguised to resemble Mr Drood. A comparison of the figure with the undoubted picture of Mr Drood in the uppermost vignette shows at once that a resemblance is intended.

The undersigned Syndics feel strongly with reference to the alternatives marked *b* and *c* above, that *b* is entirely out of line with the rest of the documents, and must have been much more plainly foreshadowed by Mr Dickens if it had been contemplated; and the *c*, although supported by Mr J. Cuming Walters in his *Clues to Dickens's Mystery of Edwin Drood*, is totally unworthy to be attributed to Mr Dickens. The remaining possibility, that Mr Dickens had the vignette drawn in order to mislead his readers, the Syndicate unite in dismissing as undeserving of their consideration.

The hypothesis that Mr Drood survived the attack made upon him by Mr Jasper suggests certain other questions and considerations with which the Syndics propose to deal shortly in this place.

(*a*) The majority agree with Mr R. A. Procter and Mr A. Lang (to both of whose writings upon the subject they desire to acknowledge their deep indebtedness) that Mr Grewgious was aware when he interviewed Mr Jasper on December 27th or 28th that Mr Jasper had attempted the life of Mr Drood, and that Mr Drood had survived the attempt.

(*b*) They are divided on the question as to the source of Mr Grewgious's knowledge. They agree in the view that Miss Landless informed him of the true character of Mr Jasper. But while some of them think that Mr Grewgious himself discovered and revived the unconscious Mr Drood, others prefer to believe that the stonemason Durdles and the boy Winks were instrumental in this matter.

(*c*) It is asked how Mr Jasper managed to fail in his great object of killing Mr Drood? And how Mr Drood escaped serious injury from the quicklime? In answer to this, it is pointed out (in agreement with Mr A. Lang), that Mr Jasper had spent the day previous to the murder at the opium den: that after these excesses he was subject to fits: and it is argued that in all probability, such a fit came upon him at the same stage of his attack upon Mr Drood. It is, further, strongly hinted that Mr Drood was drugged on the evening in question. The Syndics think it probable that when he returned to Mr Jasper's house after his walk with Mr Landless to the river to see the effects of the storm, Mr Jasper plied him with a draught of mulled liquor heavily drugged: that on some pretext, he took Mr Drood, when barely conscious, into the Cathedral yard; that he induced him to enter Mrs Sapsea's monument (of which he, Mr Jasper, had a key): that he there attacked him and was in turn attacked himself by an opium fit. Previously to this he must have removed from Mr Drood's person the watch, chain and pin and any coins or keys which he found on the body, but must have left the ring, of the presence of which he was ignorant. Mr Lang has suggested that he should also have removed all Mr Drood's metal buttons. The Syndics see no reason why the buttons should not all have been of horn. Mr Jasper and Mr Drood, then, both lay unconscious within the monument. Mr Drood, reviving first, staggered out into the open air; and neither then, nor for some time afterwards, knew where he had been or what had been done to him. There is thus no necessity to suppose that the quicklime had been applied to Mr Drood's person at all. Mr Jasper, awaking later and finding himself alone, imagined himself to have successfully accomplished what had been so often in his mind, and, with a brain still clouded by the effects of opium, made his way home.

In the meantime, Mr Drood, in a condition which might well be mistaken for intoxication, was met: perhaps by Mr Grewgious wandering late in the precincts (it may be to visit the grave, not of Mr Bud, as suggested by Mr Lang, but of his old friend Mr Drood Senior, as has been pointed out by a member of the Syndicate*): perhaps by Durdles and the boy Winks. In either case it seems clear to the Syndics that Mr Grewgious must have had early communication with Mr Drood. It seems probable that the latter gentleman was totally unable to give an account

---

*The evidence for this is to be found in the words of Durdles, in ch. v, addressed to Mr Jasper, 'your own Brother-in-law.'

of himself, and that the first clue to what had happened was supplied by the black silk scarf, which was known to be Mr Jasper's, and which the latter had left hanging about Mr Drood's neck.

At this point there would be, in the mind of Mr Grewgious, strong suspicion, almost amounting to conviction, against Mr Jasper; in the mind of Miss Landless, complete intuitive conviction; and, in the mind of Mr Drood, complete bewilderment, and only reluctant and dawning suspicion, when he learned that his beloved uncle was his rival in love.

It is clear that Mr Drood would have been secretly conveyed away, to London in all probability, so soon as he could travel. It should be noted that Mr Drood was not very widely known in Cloisterham, and that various persons, such as Mr Crisparkle and Joseph the driver of the city omnibus, who were likely to know him, were employed on Christmas Day in pursuing Mr Landless; also that the pupils at the Nuns' House were no longer in residence.

There is, it seems to the Syndics, an indication, in some words used by Mr Jasper himself, that the attack on Mr Drood had been in some way ineffective. In chapter xxiii, when, in the opium den, he pictures the murder (now over) to himself, he says: 'It has been too short and easy ... this is the poorest of all. No struggle, no consciousness of peril, no entreaty.'

III. The second main question which the Syndicate have had under their consideration is: Who was Mr Datchery?

It has already been pointed out that the phrase 'the Datchery assumption' used by Mr Dickens – apparently in speaking with Miss Georgina Hogarth – seems to imply not only that Mr Datchery is a disguised person, but that he is one already known to the public. This, if correct, excludes the notion that Mr Datchery can be an ordinary detective. It has been pointed out that in the rejected fragment entitled 'How Mr Sapsea ceased to be a member of the Eight Club' (*vide* Forster's *Life of Dickens*, Vol. iii, p. 433), the young man (Mr Poker) who introduced himself to Mr Sapsea, is pretty evidently a first draft or sketch of the character subsequently redrawn as Mr Datchery. Mr Poker, as there presented, might very well be a detective; he could not plausibly be identified with any other character save perhaps one. This possible exception will now be shortly considered.

Mr J. Cuming Walters, in the work already mentioned, has advanced the theory that Mr Datchery is Miss Landless in disguise, and a small minority of the Syndics are inclined to support him. The majority, after carefully weighing the arguments adduced, find that one passage, and one only, appeals to them with some force. It is that in chapter vii, where Mr Landless, speaking of his notes and himself, says 'We ran away four times . . . each time she dressed as a boy, and showed the daring of a man.' They incline, however, to regard this either as a foreshadowing of a plan subsequently changed by Mr Dickens, or else as a deliberate false scent. That the latter is a possibility they think, relying on such parallel passages as that in *Bleak House* (II. ch. xxii), where Mr Bucket on receiving anonymous letters, pointing to Lady Dedlock as the murderess of Mr Tulkinghorn, says, 'Yes, yes. But I could have made the money without this anonymous information,' together with a good deal else in the same episode which is calculated to make the reader believe that Lady Dedlock is indeed the guilty person.

They think it not impossible that Mr Dickens may originally have thought of introducing Miss Landless as a disguised spy. In connection with this, they would refer to the rejected chapter, in which they agree with Mr Walters that Mr Poker might have been Miss Landless in disguise. They are convinced, however, that whether or no Mr Dickens at one time entertained the idea, he certainly rejected it. And here they have been largely influenced by Mr Lang's argument, that Miss Landless, after living in inns and lodgings in male costume for a considerable period, could not without grave scandal marry the Reverend Mr Crisparkle.

Returning to the main question, and dismissing as untenable the suggestion that Mr Datchery is identical either with Mr Bazzard or (as one member of the Syndicate long maintained) with Mr Sherlock Holmes, the Syndicate, materially aided in this portion of their investigation by Birks's Exhaustive Argument (familiar to students of the *Acts*) have come to the conclusion that Mr Datchery can be no other than Mr Drood.

That the situation created by the acceptance of this hypothesis is a difficult one in some respects, they do not deny. It is doubtless hard to believe that Mr Drood's walk and voice could long remain unrecognised by his former acquaintances in Cloisterham. It should, however, be remembered (*a*) that Mr Drood was (as suggested above) not widely known in Cloisterham, (*b*) that Mr Jasper is the one person really likely to recognise him, (*c*) that Mr Datchery is only recorded to have met Mr Jasper on one occasion for a very few moments, (*d*) that Mr Jasper has the best of reasons for believing Mr Drood to be dead, and consequently for not being on the alert to notice chance resemblances to him, presented by casual strangers.

It is also difficult to see at first why Mr Drood does not come forward at once to denouce Mr Jasper. To this it is answered (on lines indicated earlier in the *Report*) (*a*) that at the time of the attack Mr Drood was most likely in a half-conscious state, and after it could give no clear account of anything; (*b*) that he had been fondly attached to Mr Jasper, and was most reluctant to give credence to the accusations made against him; (*c*) that, supposing him to be now really incensed against Mr Jasper and anxious to bring his wrong dealing home to him, he could not supply any clear evidence that the attack had been premeditated or how it had been carried out. In any case, whether his intentions towards Mr Jasper are partly friendly or wholly hostile, it is not unnatural that he should take steps to assure himself of his ground.

The Syndicate also attach considerable weight to the emphatic assertion of Mr Richard A. Proctor (*Watched by the Dead*, p. 64) that the person (Mr Drood) who speaks to the opium lady in chapter xiv, and the person (Mr Datchery) who speaks to the same lady in chapter xxiii *must*, judging from internal evidence, be one and the same.

With regard to the general development of events, the conclusions arrived at by the Syndicate do not materially differ from those set forth by Mr Proctor and Mr Lang. They have, however, a suggestion to offer with reference to the man Durdles. This person, it will be remembered, possessed an extraordinary faculty of detecting, by means of tapping, the presence and even, to some extent, the nature of foreign (or other) bodies lying behind masonry. It has been held that this power enabled him to detect the still living body (or according to others the dead body) of Mr Drood, lying in the quicklime in Mrs Sapsea's monument. The Syndics have already indicated their dissent from these theories. They would point out that in chapter xviii arrangements are made by Mr Datchery for a visit to Durdles. This visit doubtless took place, and in the course of it, Durdles' 'gift,' as it may be termed, was discussed. Questioned upon the point, Durdles, who was then hard by Mrs Sapsea's monument, exemplified his method by tapping that structure, and to his own surprise detected the presence of some foreign body there. He opened the door and entered, and with him Mr Datchery. Durdles was perplexed at finding the heap of quicklime, placed there by Mr Jasper: Mr Datchery, in a flash of recollection, realised that this was a place he had been in before, and, it may be, called to mind something of the circumstances. The evidence thus gained would be highly valuable in the weaving of the plot against Mr Jasper.

To sum up shortly the course of subsequent events, the majority of the Syndics agree that the presence of the jewelled ring (indestructible by quicklime) upon Mr Drood's person at the time of his disappearance was made known to Mr Jasper: that Mr Jasper was compelled on the following Christmas Eve to revisit Mrs Sapsea's monument in order to find the ring: that upon opening the door he was confronted by Mr Drood (previously concealed there): that he fled, pursued by Messrs Crisparkle, Tartar and Landless, and ultimately rushed up the stairs of the Cathedral tower: that a struggle took place, and that Mr Landless was precipitated from the tower with fatal results: that in all probability Mr Landless' faithful hound (like that of Mr Sikes) bore him company, and thus the two visionary cries heard two years before by Durdles found their fulfilment: that Mr Jasper was overpowered, was convicted of the murder of Mr Landless, wrote a confession in the condemned cell, and either committed suicide or was executed: that Miss Bud married Mr (formerly Lieut.) Tartar, Miss Landless the Reverend Mr Crisparkle: and that Mr Drood retired to Egypt, taking with him perhaps the boy Winks, whose part in the *dénouement*, though not unimportant, remains obscure.

Other uncertain points are: (*a*) the extent to which Mr Bazzard was employed. The suggestion that he played false to Mr Grewgious, and was in the pay of Mr Jasper, is plausible; (*b*) the meaning of the vignette on the illustrated cover which shows a young woman with dishevelled hair looking at a placard inscribed LOST; (*c*) the precise reasons for the animosity of the opium woman against Mr Jasper.

The Syndicate accordingly recommended:

That the reward of one thousand pounds offered for the discovery of any evidence throwing light upon the disappearance of Edwin Drood, Esquire, be divided among those members of the Edwin Drood Syndicate who have signed the present Report.

I am not able to give the signatures which followed: there were fifteen of them.

In the same *Reporter*, contrary to all custom (and indeed, as I thought, to all reason) there was actually a report of the discussion which had taken place on the above document. This I cannot give in full: nor would it be seemly to quote such names of speakers as I remember. There was a decided opposition to the recommendation of the Syndicate, led by several Syndics who stated that they had not been allowed by their colleagues to sign the Report.

The following is the substance of some part of the discussion:

Mr A said that he was opposed to the publication of that report. He feared it would cause pain to the surviving relatives of Mr Jasper.

Mr B said that Mr Jasper had no surviving relatives except Mr Drood, who was residing in Egypt.

Mr A said that he had every reason to believe that the *University Reporter* was extensively read in that country.

Mr B said he should be glad to know some of Mr A's reasons for entertaining that belief.

Mr C said that Mr Dickens had described the idea of his works as being 'new' and 'incommunicable.' He would be glad to know whether the Syndicate could in any way explain or justify this expression.

Mr B replied that the Syndicate had considered that point; the signatories of the report agreed in thinking that the 'new' idea was a developed form of one which was evidently a favourite with Mr Dickens (as Mr Proctor had shown), namely, that of a man being watched by a witness whom he did not suspect: the developed idea was that of a man actually murdered (as was supposed) watching and tracking down his murderer. This view implied the identity of Mr Datchery with Mr Drood. Perhaps it should have been mentioned in the report.

Mr D had always understood that the 'new' idea was that of the indestructibility of gold and jewels by quicklime. Certainly Mr Proctor was under that impression.

Mr B pointed out that Mr Forster, on learning of the 'new and incommunicable idea,' pressed Mr Dickens to communicate it to him. It was not likely that Mr Dickens would consent to do this. He probably sought to quiet Mr Forster's importunity by revealing to him a trivial point in the solution.

Mr E said he should like to ask the Syndics one plain question. Had they taken the elementary step, as he might call it, of consulting Mr Dickens himself as to the solution of this so-called mystery? He could not gather from the Report that they had. If they had not, he thought most emphatically that the Report should be referred back to them.

The Vice-Chancellor interposed with a word of explanation. Mr Dickens was dead.

Mr E said that of course that might be taken in some measure as a reply to his question. He was sorry to hear of Mr Dickens's death, but was glad that he had not lived to read the Report of the Syndicate. He had, however, another point to urge. Believing as he did that Miss Landless was identical with Mr Drood – he should perhaps rather have said, with Mr Jasper – he desired to know whether, in the opinion of the Syndics, he was dead or drugged at the time?

Mr B. At what time?

Mr E. If Members of the Syndicate either could not or would not answer a simple question, it was useless to discuss that Report further. He should most certainly *non-placet* the recommendation.

Mr F thought that the Syndicate had failed to notice one or two more or less important matters. In chapter x and elsewhere considerable stress was laid on the extraordinary telepathic sympathy, as he might call it, which existed between Miss Landless and her brother. Would not this have been used in the development of events? Again: it had been suggested by Mr Cuming Walters, that the reason of the 'Princess Puffer's' animosity against Mr Jasper was to be sought in the fact that she had had a daughter whom Mr Jasper had injured – perhaps made away with. Could the lady with dishevelled hair who appeared on the cover, studying a placard on which the word LOST was discernible, be that daughter? Yet again: when Mr Crisparkle suggested to Mr Jasper that Nevile Landless should join the latter's party on Christmas Eve, Mr Jasper at once engaged in mental calculation. Was he, as Mr Proctor thought, calculating whether or no there would be a moon on that fatal night? Lastly, the Syndics had not mentioned, perhaps because they thought it too obvious, the fact that some one (probably Messrs Grewgious and Tartar) must at some time have visited the opium den and listened to Mr Jasper's very damaging admissions while he was under the influence to the drug.

Mr B wished that more Members of the Senate would take as intelligent an interest in the case as did the last speaker. The Syndics were alive to the importance of the sympathy between the two Landlesses: but this was one of the threads whose course they could not follow up. They had considered, and finally rejected, the idea of the daughter of the 'Princess Puffer.' It was their belief that all the characters of prime importance connected with the case had already made their appearance in the extant documents. The illustration on the cover remained a puzzle.

As to Mr Jasper's calculations, Mr Proctor's opinion seemed fanciful. More probably Mr Jasper was reflecting whether the addition of a third person, Mr Landless, to his party, would frustrate his designs upon Mr Drood; and finally concluded that the addition would be rather convenient, as enabling him more easily to throw suspicion upon Mr Landless. The last point, he acknowledged, was an omission. The visit of Mr Grewgious and Mr Tartar, or of some members of that party, to the opium den must of course have taken place. Mr Datchery's acquaintance with the 'Princess Puffer' naturally led up to that. Most likely Mr Datchery went there himself; and what he heard from Mr Jasper's lips would go further than anything else to convince him that the latter's attack had been long premeditated. This the Syndics had fully realized, and it should have been mentioned in the report.

This is all of the discussion that I can reproduce. What I now wish to know is whether anyone besides myself has seen the copy of the *Reporter* which contains it, and whether the recommendation of the Syndicate was carried. Perhaps we had better appoint a Syndicate to inquire into *that*.

Charles Dickens

When Dickens was a
10 years old his father
In order for the fam
stay out of debtors pre
young Dickens was
work. His father died

Later in his life
wrote of the things
seen and situation
had known.

His Detective s
are not as well k
as his books

Oliver Twis
David Cop
a Tale of T
Great Expe
Nicholas
a Christ
and many